Percy H. Fitzgerald

A Critical Examination of Dr. G. Birkbeck Hill's Johnsonian Editions

Percy H. Fitzgerald

A Critical Examination of Dr. G. Birkbeck Hill's Johnsonian Editions

ISBN/EAN: 9783337325961

Printed in Europe, USA, Canada, Australia, Japan

Cover: Foto ©Andreas Hilbeck / pixelio.de

More available books at **www.hansebooks.com**

DR JOHNSON

HIS FRIENDS AND HIS CRITICS

BY

GEORGE BIRKBECK HILL, D.C.L.

PEMBROKE COLLEGE, OXFORD

LONDON

SMITH, ELDER, & CO., 15 WATERLOO PLACE

1878

TO

SIR ROWLAND HILL, K.C.B. D.C.L. F.R.S.

ETC.

This Volume is Dedicated

WITH MUCH RESPECT AND AFFECTION

BY HIS NEPHEW

THE AUTHOR

PREFACE.

THOUGH I cannot say with Lord Macaulay that I was never better pleased than when at fourteen I was master of Boswell's 'Life of Johnson,' yet I was still a schoolboy when I first read the book. When later on I entered the University of Oxford I was proud as a member of Pembroke College to boast of the great man who is the glory of that society. I little thought, however, in those days that the study of his life was to fill up much of the leisure time of not a few of my busiest years, and that, on my retirement from a laborious occupation, and my recovery from a tedious illness, I should attempt to describe Oxford as it was known to him.

It might at first sight seem that he who should at the present day venture to write about Johnson would justly incur the same kind of criticism as that which Johnson himself passed on one of the writers of his time. 'How,' he says 'must the

unlearned reader be surprised when he shall be told
that Mr. Blackwell has neither digged in the ruins
of any demolished city, nor found out the way
to the library of Fez, nor had a single book in
his hands that has not been in the possession of
every man that was inclined to read it, for years
and ages ; and that his book relates to a people
who above all others have furnished employment
to the studious, and amusements to the idle.'

My justification is twofold. In the first place
I have 'found out the way' in Oxford to rooms in
Christ Church and Pembroke College in which are
stored up the documents which have enabled me to
set a matter at rest which has been the puzzle of
Johnsonian critics for more than forty years. Only
the other day I discovered an entry in the battel-
books of Christ Church, which, combined with what
I had previously found out, has, in my opinion,
settled beyond doubt the question of the duration
of Johnson's residence at the University. I have,
moreover, in the hours that I have spent in the
Bodleian Library, turned over many an interesting
record of Oxford as it was in the early part of last
century. But the chief part of my labour has certainly lain among books that have been for years

in the possession of every man that was inclined to read them. When I first began to study these works I read with the eager interest of one who was merely anxious to learn, and not as one who had any thoughts of setting up for a teacher himself. I was as yet but half of Chaucer's Oxford scholar of whom it was said ' Gladly wolde he lerne and gladly teche.' I was, to use Johnson's words, merely ' filling the hunger of ignorance and quenching the thirst of curiosity.' I had all the pleasure of a reader while I was altogether free from the necessity of exerting that almost painful degree of attention which is too often the lot of one who intends to write. But as I continued to read and passed from Boswell to the works of Hawkins, Murphy, Madame Piozzi, Madame D'Arblay, and other writers, who had themselves known Johnson, I began to feel that in every separate portrait that had been drawn of that great man there were great imperfections. Boswell's indeed was worth all the rest taken together, but even Boswell had not seen Johnson in every light. The sketch that Lord Macaulay has given in his celebrated Review, which I had once accepted without misgiving, now seemed to me singularly unjust and distorted. Even the Life of Johnson that he contributed to the ' Encyclopædia Britannica,' finely though it is written, I yet found to be greatly wanting in truthfulness. Mr. Carlyle's noble portrait of my hero, while it delighted me, did not fully satisfy me. It was too much like a portrait drawn by Rembrandt, in which the light that the artist lets in on his picture but too often serves to give the spectator a greater impression of gloom.

If Johnson had had but scant justice done to him, the greatest injustice, I felt, had been done to Boswell. Mr. Carlyle had, indeed, defended him, as he had defended Johnson, from the violent attacks of Macaulay, but he had not gone into the whole case. In some points also even he, I held, had not formed a right estimate of Boswell's character. As these convictions grew upon me I began to set forth the views that I had formed in articles that I contributed from time to time to some among the leading newspapers. I also formed the plan of writing sketches of the lives of some of Johnson's friends. Two of these sketches I had finished and published, when the continuance of my task was hindered by the serious illness, of which I have spoken. On my partial recovery, when I took up the pen that had lain idle for two long years, I resolved to recast much of what I had already written, and to combine that which lay scattered in a variety of papers. At the same time I began to use the fresh materials which I had gathered together, and to add to the essays that I had already written. The contents of this book therefore may be divided into three parts. The largest of these divisions consists of matter that is here published for the first time. The second division consists of articles which I have so recast and so enlarged that, so far as form at least is concerned, they may fairly claim to be original. The third portion is composed of essays that are republished in the same form in which they at first appeared. But even to many of these I have made considerable additions.

I trust that I have done something to give a juster view of Johnson and his biographer, and that I have, in the chapters which do not concern them so directly, helped some little towards a better understanding of one or two among the men whom they reckoned as their friends. Should my book be received with any degree of favour, I shall hope in another volume to write of others among Johnson's friends and, perhaps, of others among his critics.

I must not forget to express my grateful acknowledgments to the Editors and Proprietors of 'The Cornhill Magazine,' 'The Pall Mall Gazette,' 'The Saturday Review,' and 'The Times,' for the permission they have kindly given me to use in this volume my various contributions to their papers.

GEORGE BIRKBECK HILL.

THE POPLARS, BURGHFIELD:
May 28, 1878.

CONTENTS.

CHAPTER	PAGE
I. Oxford in Johnson's Time	1
II. Lord Macaulay on Johnson	97
III. Mr. Carlyle on Boswell	146
IV. Lord Macaulay on Boswell	160
V. The Melancholy of Johnson and Cowper	200
VI. Lord Chesterfield and Johnson	214
VII. Lord Chesterfield's Letters	230
VIII. Bennet Langton	248
IX. Topham Beauclerk	280
X. Oliver Goldsmith	319

APPENDIX.

The Duration of Johnson's Residence at Oxford	329

DR. JOHNSON:

HIS FRIENDS AND HIS CRITICS.

CHAPTER I.

OXFORD IN JOHNSON'S TIME.

THE Oxford of last century is with most readers the Oxford not of Johnson, but of Gibbon. They call to mind the just indignation which the great historian felt in his riper years against that University where he spent the most idle and unprofitable fourteen months of his whole life. 'To the University of Oxford I acknowledge no obligation,' he wrote, 'and she will as cheerfully renounce me for a son as I am willing to disclaim her for a mother.' It is but a few pages that he gives to this mother whom he thus renounces, but his description is so lively, his satire so pointed, and his scorn so marked, that it is the sketch that he thus paints that remains fixed in our minds as the very picture of Oxford herself.

We call to mind the lad in his fifteenth year suddenly raised from a boy to a man; his decent allowance of money; the indefinite and dangerous latitude of credit that he could command; his velvet cap and silk gown which distinguished him as a gentleman-commoner from an ordinary student; the key which was delivered into his hands, which gave him the free use of a numerous and learned library; his three elegant and well-furnished rooms in the new building—a stately pile, as he calls it —of Magdalen College; his first tutor—one of the best of the tribe—who proposed to read with him one hour every day, and who, with a smile, accepted his first apology for his omission to attend, and encouraged him to repeat the offence with less ceremony; his second tutor, who well remembered that he had a salary to receive, and only forgot that he had a duty to perform, who never summoned him to attend even the ceremony of a lecture; his growing debts; the tour he made to Bath, the visit to Buckinghamshire, and the four excursions to London, as if he had been an independent stranger in a hired lodging, without once hearing the voice of admonition, without once feeling the hand of control; his first appearance before the Vice-Chancellor, who said that he was not old enough as yet to sign the Thirty-nine Articles, but, directing him to return when he

was sixteen, recommended him in the meantime to the
instruction of his college ; the forgetfulness of his college
to instruct, his own forgetfulness to return, and the forgetfulness of the Vice-Chancellor to send for him ; his
groping his way, unaided and untaught, into the dangerous
mazes of controversy, and his bewilderment into the
errors of the Church of Rome.

We call to mind the Fellows of Magdalen—those
decent, easy men—into whose common-room he was,
as a gentleman-commoner, of right admitted ; their days
filled by a series of uniform employments—the chapel
and the hall, the coffee-house and the common-room—
till they retired, weary and well satisfied, to a long slum-
ber ; their conversation that stagnated in a round of
college business, Tory politics, personal anecdotes, and
private scandal ; their dull and deep potations, and their
toasts that were not expressive of the most lively loyalty
for the House of Hanover. We call to mind the tradi-
tion that prevailed that some of his predecessors had
spoken Latin declamations in the hall, and the total
absence in his time of public exercises and examinations.
We remember, too, that in the University itself he could
find nothing to make up for the shameless neglect of his
college ; for in the University the greater part of the

public professors had for these many years given up altogether even the pretence of teaching.[1]

But just as may be the picture that we shall thus raise before ourselves of Magdalen College, just as may be the picture that we shall raise of the University of Oxford as a whole, we shall wander very far from the truth if we go on to infer that every one of the numerous colleges and halls was a second Magdalen. Had Gibbon been entered.at some other college, the University of Oxford would not, to her great and lasting disgrace, have been disclaimed by one of the greatest of her sons. There were bad colleges and indolent tutors in his time as there are bad colleges and indolent tutors now. Though doubtless there were many more bad colleges and many more indolent tutors in those days, when the University, neither by examination nor by any other way, exercised the slightest control over the studies of the

---

[1] 'What do you think of being Greek Professor at one of our Universities? It is a very pretty sinecure, and requires very little knowledge (much less than I hope you have already) of that language.'—*Lord Chesterfield's Letters to his Son* (January 15, 1748). Cumberland, who entered Trinity College, Cambridge, in 1746, had the same kind of tutors as Gibbon. His first tutor left him to choose and pursue his studies as he liked. From his second, whose zeal or whose piety was afterwards rewarded with a bishopric, he never received a single lecture.—*Memoirs of Richard Cumberland*, vol. i. p. 91.

students. Richard Lovell Edgeworth, who entered Corpus Christi College eight years after Gibbon left Magdalen, and who was not likely to have loved a place merely because it was venerable, bears high testimony to the merits of his college. 'I applied assiduously not only to my studies,' he writes, 'under my excellent tutor, but also to the perusal of the best English writers. Scarcely a day passed without my having added to my stock of knowledge some new fact or idea ; and I remember with satisfaction the pleasure I then felt from the consciousness of intellectual improvement.'

More than one hundred years have passed since these men left Oxford. Magdalen can still boast of its graceful tower, its venerable cloisters, its noble hall, and Addison's Walk. Corpus, if you ask what it can show that is beautiful or venerable, must still borrow its prospect from its neighbours, and point to Merton Tower on its left and the Cathedral Tower on its right. But a second Edgeworth, perhaps, if fate were to place him there, would not boast of Magdalen, nor would a second Gibbon, if a second could arise, disclaim Corpus.

It is difficult, we must remember, at any time to arrive at a fair estimate of an ancient seat of learning. Some men are more touched with resentment when they come to learn by experience where their education was faulty than moved by gratitude for the training they received, however judicious, considered as a whole, it may have been. Their deficiencies they attribute to their teachers, and to the system under which they were brought up. Their merits they derive from themselves alone. Some men, on the other hand, look upon their *Alma Mater* as a mother indeed. Her failings they will not see, much less will they avow. They are proud of being her sons, and they increase their pride by magnifying her merits. But much more difficult is it to form this estimate when we are considering an age in which party spirit ran high, and the Church brought anything but peace into the world. Johnson, in writing his 'Debates of Parliament,' always took care, as he says, that the Whig dogs came off worse. Consciously or unconsciously judgments were formed and evidence was given in much the same way as the composition of these 'Debates' was managed. Thus, if we may trust Prideaux, Dean of Norwich, Christ Church under Dean Aldrich was, though not the worst, yet one of the worst colleges in Oxford. 'It is totally spoilt,' he wrote in one letter, 'and for that reason when chosen a Canon and Professor of Oriental Literature I refused to go.' In another letter he admitted that bad though it was, there was at least one other college worse. 'Who-ever advised you there [to Exeter College] was no friend.

'That is worse than Christ Church, for at the latter there
is something of ingenuity and genteel carriage in the genius
of the place, but in the other I never knew anything
all the while I was at Oxford but drinking and duncery.'

If Prideaux spoke ill of Aldrich's college, Aldrich in
return used to speak slightingly of Prideaux as 'an inaccurate, muddy-headed man.' If we turn from Prideaux to
Hearne, we should be inclined to consider Christ Church
as looked after, under Aldrich, if anything, too carefully.
'The Dean used to rise to five o'clock prayers, summer
and winter. He visited the chambers of the young
gentlemen on purpose to see that they employed their
time in useful and commendable studies. . . . He was
always for encouraging industry, learning, integrity, and
whatever deserves commendation.' It is no wonder,
therefore, putting aside all differences in their colleges,
that not only men like Gibbon and Edgeworth who had
but little in common, but also that men like Gibbon and
Johnson who, widely as they differed in many things, yet
were both scholars, felt so differently towards Oxford.

It is, indeed, interesting to compare the feelings of
scornful indignation with which the younger of the two
looked upon Oxford, with the love that the elder, through
his long life, bore to his old college and his old university.
In the last summer of his life, when his strength that was

rapidly ebbing away had returned with the warm weather, it was to Oxford that Johnson longed to go as his first jaunt after his illness.   Boswell, who travelled with him, tells us that the old man 'seemed to feel himself elevated as he approached Oxford, that magnificent and venerable seat of learning, orthodoxy, and Toryism.'   The regard which he bore to his old college had always been strong, and remained with him to the last.   A short time before his death he presented its library with his books, and had he not been reminded of the necessities of his relations he would have left it his house at Lichfield.   He always took pleasure 'in mentioning how many of the sons of Pembroke were poets ; adding with a smile of sportive triumph, "Sir, we are a nest of singing-birds."'   And yet his obligations to Oxford would not seem, at first sight, to have been very great.   He had come up like the young enthusiast of his own noble poem, though it most certainly was not ease that he had quitted for fame.   We may feel certain that he was recalling his own feelings when, nearly twenty years after he left college, he wrote those fine lines :

> When first the college rolls receive his name,
> The young enthusiast quits his ease for fame ;
> Through all his veins the fever of renown
> Burns from the strong contagion of the gown ;
> O'er Bodley's dome his future labours spread,
> And Bacon's mansion trembles o'er his head.

We know that the lines that follow, in which he bids us 'mark what ills the scholar's life assail,' so truly told of his own sufferings, that when in his old age he tried to read them aloud he burst into a passion of tears.

The eagerness, the ambition, the enthusiasm with which he entered Oxford were soon deadened. He came to a place rich in endowments, though his own college indeed was poor. He soon gave proof of his power and his knowledge. His translation into Latin verse of Pope's 'Messiah' 'kept him high in the estimation of his college, and, indeed, of all the university.' Pope, when he read it, with much kindness said, 'the writer of this poem will leave it a question for posterity whether his or mine be the original.' And yet, with all the proofs Johnson gave of his great powers, he was forced by poverty to leave Oxford without even taking his degree. Nay even, there is good reason to believe that, like Gibbon, he stayed there but fourteen short months.[1] His college bills came to only some eight shillings a week. Fifty pounds, no doubt, would have covered, and much more than covered, his whole yearly expenses. Whitfield, who was, however, a servitor, only cost his relations about eight pounds a year. One of the colleges forty years before Johnson's

---

[1] See Appendix.

time 'was popularly said to be wealthier than the wealthiest abbeys of the Continent.' But Johnson, in the midst of all this wealth which the piety of past ages had left for the encouragement of learning, had to leave Oxford because he was poor. A few years later on, when he had published his poem of 'London' and had become famous, when he found that the want of a degree stood in the way of his advancement in life, when without it he could neither, as he at one time wished, get the mastership of a grammar-school, nor, as he at another time wished, practise in Doctor's Commons, he learnt that 'it was thought too great a favour even to be asked' of the University that it should confer on him its degree.

Johnson might not unreasonably have borne towards Oxford an ill-will that would have lasted through life. No doubt he was a high Tory and a high Churchman, and as such would be the less inclined to find anything wrong in the seat of Toryism and orthodoxy. But it was not to his prejudices alone that his affections were due. Whatever the length of his residence was— whether three years, as his biographers say, or only fourteen months, as seems more probable—he never regretted the time that he spent at the University. He delighted to expatiate on the advantages of Oxford for learning, and on the excellent rules of discipline in every college. 'That the rules are sometimes ill observed may be true, but is nothing against the system.' When the University at length did honour to itself by giving him his Master's Degree, he took as much pleasure in his gown as if he had been five and twenty years younger. 'I have been in my gown ever since I came here' he writes. 'It was at my first-coming quite new and handsome.' He made frequent visits to Oxford, and 'he prided himself,' as we learn from Lord Stowell, 'in being accurately academic in all points ; and he wore his gown almost ostentatiously.' The Christ Church men had mocked at his worn-out shoes when he was an undergraduate. Nearly fifty years later he must have felt that an ample apology was offered for the insult, for a Canon of Christ Church invited him to dinner. 'Sir,' he said to Boswell, 'it is a great thing to dine with the Canons of Christ Church.'

He delighted, as Madame Piozzi tells us, in his partiality for Oxford. He one day in her presence entertained five Cambridge men with various instances of the superiority of his own university. She reminded him that there were no less than five Cambridge men in the room. 'I did not,' said he, 'think of that till you told me, but the wolf does not count the sheep.' In speaking of a Cambridge friend for whom he had a high regard, he said, ' a fellow deserves to be of Oxford that talks so.' Hannah More met him at dinner at his old college two years before his death. He looked very ill—spiritless and wan, but after dinner he took her over the College and would let no one show it but himself. ' This was my room, this Shenstone's.' Then after pointing out all the rooms of the poets who had been of his college, ' In short,' said he, ' We were a nest of singing birds. Here we walked, there we played at cricket.' We very much doubt, by the way, Johnson's playing at cricket. His sight, as we know, debarred him from almost all the games of boyhood. ' He ran over with pleasure the history of the juvenile days he passed there. When we came into the common-room we spied a fine large print of Johnson, framed and hung up that very morning, with this motto, "And is not Johnson ours, himself a host?" Under which stared you in the face, " From Miss More's Sensibility."'

In his Life of Sir Thomas Browne, who was a Pembroke man, he tells us that Browne was the first man of eminence graduated from the new college, and adds, ' to which the zeal or gratitude of those that love it most can wish little better than that it may long proceed as it began.'

Johnson was, it is true, by nature easily contented.

'Sir,' he once said, 'I have never complained of the world, nor do I think that I have reason to complain. It is rather to be wondered at that I have so much.' But it was not only the habit of easy contentment that made him bear no ill-will against his college. There had been no shameful neglect of duty on the part of his tutors, no unworthy example set by the Fellows to excite his indignation as it excited Gibbon's. Gibbon complained that though the government of his college and, indeed, of the University, was in the hands of the clergy, yet he received no instruction in religion. Johnson, on the other hand, said that it was to Oxford that was due the first occasion of his thinking in earnest of religion, after he became capable of rational enquiry. The tutors of Pembroke were not, indeed, so far as ability went, worthy of their illustrious pupil. Each of them might have said with Dr. Adams, ' I was his nominal tutor ; but he was above my mark.' Yet Johnson revered Adams' learning, and felt that he had received a high compliment. ' His eyes flashed with grateful satisfaction ' when Boswell told him what Adams had said, and he exclaimed, ' That was liberal and noble.' But the tutors of Pembroke, if they were not very able, were at least honest men, and did their duty. Of one of them, Jorden, he said, 'Whenever a young man becomes Jorden's pupil he becomes his son.'

He retained for him a great regard, and when he visited Oxford twenty-five years after he had left he learnt with regret that he was dead.

Every reader of Boswell will remember how Johnson, like Gibbon, was one day absent from a lecture, and how his tutor after dinner sent for him to his room. 'I expected a sharp rebuke for my idleness, and went with a beating heart. When we were seated he told me he had sent for me to drink a glass of wine with him, and to tell me he was *not* angry with me for missing his lecture. This was indeed a most severe reprimand.' If we may trust Hawkins' statement, he once, on being fined for not attending a lecture, said to his tutor, 'Sir, you have sconced me two-pence for non-attendance at a lecture not worth a penny.' If he really made this rude speech, it is not impossible that a second most severe reprimand followed in a second glass of wine in the kindly tutor's room.

What it was that led old Michael Johnson to select Pembroke College for his son we can only conjecture. Hawkins says that he was placed there in the position of a commoner by a neighbouring gentleman in quality of assistant to his son in his studies, who entered as a gentleman-commoner. This statement is confirmed by Johnson's old friend, Dr. Taylor. But Pembroke was the college of his god-father, Dr. Samuel Swinfen, of Lichfield, from whom, no doubt, he took his name, and who may have borne part of the expenses of his education. Even if Johnson went as a kind of tutor to another student, it was likely enough on Dr. Swinfen's advice that Pembroke College was chosen for the two young men. It had borne a high name even at the end of the previous century. In February 1695–6, a Mr. Lapthorne wrote to a Mr. Coffin : 'I have placed my son in Pembrook Colledge, the Society being under the care of the Bishop of Bristol, Dr. Hall, who is Master and constantly resident. The house, tho' it bee but a little one, yet is reputed to be one of the best for sobriety and order.'[1]   Bishop Hall was master for forty-five years, so that he had time to work a thorough reform, if a reform had been needed. He had died the year Johnson was born. The master in Johnson's time was that 'fine Jacobite fellow,' Dr. Matthew Panting. Hearne calls him 'an honest gent,' and tells how 'he had to preach the sermon at St. Mary's on the day on which George, Duke and Elector of Brunswick, usurped the English throne, but his sermon took no notice, at most very little, of the Duke of Brunswick.'

---

[1] Historical Manuscripts Commission, 'Appendix to Fifth Report,' p. 385.

The buildings have been not a little altered since Johnson's day ; yet we can still bring back before ourselves the little college as it was when his father, proud of his son, brought him up to Oxford on the last day of October in the year 1728. The tower has undergone considerable changes, but we can still look up with reverence to the second floor above the gateway, where Johnson lived and whence he was overheard by the Master from his house hard by uttering, in his strong emphatic voice, 'Well, I have a mind to see what is done in other places of learning. I'll go and visit the Universities abroad. I'll go to France and Italy. I'll go to Padua. And I'll mind my business. For an Athenian blockhead is the worst of all blockheads.' We can think how it was in that room no doubt that, at the end of his first year's residence, he recorded in his diary, *Desidiæ valedixi; syrenis istius cantibus surdam posthac aurem obversurus.* ' I bid farewell to Sloth, being resolved henceforth not to listen to her syren strains.' We can stand in the gateway and remember how he used to lounge there with a circle of young students whom he was entertaining with his wit and keeping from their studies. To those around him he seemed 'a gay and frolicsome fellow ; but ' it was bitterness,' he said, ' that they mistook for frolic. I was miserably poor, and I

thought to fight my way by my literature and my wit.'
' They all feared him, however,' as one of them nearly
fifty years afterwards admitted. He used to criticise the
words they used, ' for even then he was delicate in
language. Sir, I remember you would not let us say
prodigious at college.'

The quadrangle is much as he knew it. The present library was in his time the hall. The raised dais at
the western end, where the high table stood, was an
addition made by Clayton, the first Master, to a more
ancient building which had formed part of an earlier
foundation called Broadgate Hall. The eastern end is,
I believe, all that is left of this ancient foundation.
Bishop Bonner belonged to this society, and must have
dined many a day within these walls while he was still a
young student unstained by blood, little thinking how
hateful a name he was destined to bear through all time.
It was in the hall that at the classical lecture Johnson
sat as far away from Meeke as he could, that he might
not hear him construe, for he could not bear his superiority. In this venerable building is treasured up Johnson's writing-desk. What memorial is preserved of Meeke?

It was here, too, that he made his first declamation. He wrote but one copy, and that coarsely,
and he had given it into the hands of his tutor. He had

got but little of it by heart, and he trusted to his present powers to supply what he forgot. ' A prodigious risk,' said some one. ' Not at all,' exclaimed Johnson. ' No man, I suppose, leaps at once into deep water who does not know how to swim.'

It was here that would have been recited his exercise on Gunpowder Plot Day, had he not been too indolent to write it, to Boswell's great regret, who thinks that he would probably have produced something sublime. November was kept with great solemnity at Pembroke College. Seven years before Johnson's time ' Mr. Peyne, Bachelor of Arts, made,' as an old diary tells us, ' an oration in the hall suitable to the day.' Here, early in every November, was kept ' a great Gaudy in the college, when the Master dined in public, and the Juniors (by an ancient custom they were obliged to observe) went round the fire in the hall.' We can picture to ourselves among the Juniors in November, 1728, Samuel Johnson, who had but just entered the college, going round the fire with the others. Warton records how Johnson, in one of his visits to Oxford, when, talking of the form of old halls, said, ' In these halls the fire-place was anciently always in the middle of the room till the Whigs removed it on one side.' If in his time the fire in Pembroke hall was still in the middle of the room, the ancient custom did not press very heavily. Here day after day he heard the Latin Grace which the learned Camden had written for the society, and no doubt the signal for Grace was given, as it was for many a year after, by three blows with a piece of wood, in honour of the Trinity. The ordinary dinner-hour was early, as is shown by Hearne in one of those delightfully foolish passages in which the foolish old Jacobite antiquarian abounds. On February 27, 1722-3, he solemnly records, 'It hath been an old custom in Oxford for the scholars of all houses, on Shrove-Tuesday, to go to dinner at ten o'clock (at which time the little bell called *pan-cake bell* rings, or at least should ring, at St. Maries), and at four in the afternoon ; and it was always followed in Edmund Hall as long as I have been in Oxford till yesterday, when they went to dinner at twelve and to supper at six. Nor were there any fritters at dinner as there used always to be. When laudable old customs alter, 'tis a sign learning dwindles.'

The library in Johnson's days, where he read in the French Lobo's 'Voyage to Abyssinia,' was in a large room over the hall. It had been removed there a few years earlier from a room above a side chapel in the church of St. Aldate's, which stands just outside the college gates. He borrowed the book a few years after he left and translated it for a Birmingham bookseller, receiving as his payment for his first literary venture five guineas. Whether he forgot to return the book, or whether he returned it and it has been since carried off as a curiosity by some one who had a greater regard for the great moralist than for morality, I know not. At all events, the book is no longer in the library. So far as it goes, it would seem to show that the Fellows of Pembroke took a lively interest in modern literature, when we find that a foreign book of travels was to be found on their shelves three or four years at most after it was published.

The side chapel beneath the old library was the college chapel. Six months before he came into residence the foundations of the present chapel were laid. During the whole of his stay at Oxford he had rising before his eyes a building which for ugliness has, perhaps, but one rival in Oxford. Johnson, however, cared nothing for architecture. 'A building,' he said, 'is not at all more convenient for being decorated with superfluous carved work.' Perhaps it is fortunate for his reputation that in architecture he lay claim to neither taste nor knowledge. Otherwise he might have described Pembroke chapel as a stately pile, as Gibbon described the new building at Magdalen. In Logan's print of the college we see a pleasant row of trees where now this chapel stands. As it is not easy to see that either piety or convenience was increased when the members of a society who, in going to service, had hitherto taken a few paces to the north, now began to take the same number of paces to the south, we may be allowed to regret the loss of the trees. On the Fellows' garden the present hall is built ; but to this garden it is probable that Johnson had no right of admission, as he was not a fellow-commoner. The common-room, where he used to play at draughts with Phil. Jones, who loved beer and did not get very forward in the Church, and with Fludyer, who turned out a scoundrel and a Whig, stood where now the kitchen stands. It was a detached building, with a sanded floor and wooden chairs. Carpets were not generally seen in Oxford common-rooms till well on in the present century. In an out-house the grate of the old fire-place is stowed away. Johnson must have warmed his feet at it many a time. Perhaps Whitfield, who was a servitor of the college, more than once cleaned it. Less interesting relics have received more honourable treatment.

In every Oxford common-room at this date all the members of the college—tutors, fellows, and commoners, with the exception, no doubt, of the servitors—met on an equal footing. More than forty years later Johnson learned that in some of the colleges the Fellows had excluded the students from the common-room. 'They are in the right, Sir,' he said ; 'there can be no real conversation, no fair exertion of mind amongst them, if the young men are by; for a man who has a character does not choose to stake it in their presence.' According to Gibbon, it was rather the younger men who lost their character by this association, than the older men who staked theirs. 'The dull and deep potations of the Fellows,' he said, 'excused the brisk intemperance of youth.'

The Master's house has been greatly altered. It is no longer as it was when Johnson was at college, nor as it was when, more than twenty years later, he visited the Master of that day, and was not asked to dinner. With the old college servants, whom he found all still there, he was highly pleased. The Fellows in residence pressed him very much to have a room in college. But the Master showed him no civility, nor did he even order a copy of his Dictionary. As he left his house he said, ' *There* lives a man who lives by the revenues of literature, and will not move a finger to support it.'

Close to the college stands an old inn, which must have been old in Johnson's time. As we pass it we think of the day when he and Edwards 'were drinking together at an ale-house near Pembroke Gate,' and giving instances of fine lines in modern Latin verse. Edwards must have altogether lost his interest in literature, for when he met Johnson forty-nine years after he said to him, ' I am told you have written a very pretty book called 'The Rambler.' Johnson was unwilling that he should leave the world in total darkness, and sent him a set.

The college accounts—the buttery-books, as they are called—are still preserved. The offices of the servants are given in Latin, and we find the *Promus* against whom Johnson wrote his epigram :

Limosum nobis Promus dat callidus haustum.

He must have forgotten, or at least forgiven, his muddy beer, for at the time when he was so pleased to find the old college servants, he was particularly pleased to find ' the very old butler.' Among the scribbling at the end of the books I eagerly searched for Johnson's name, but I could not find it. Shenstone and Sheny occur many times. There is even some kind of evidence of Phil. Jones' love of beer ; for we find entered, ' O yes, O yes, come forth, Phil Jones, and answer to your charge for exceeding the batells.' His excess, perhaps, was in liquor.

Mr. Meeke is entered as ' Honest Jack Meek of Pemb.

Coll.' The young servitor who kept the buttery-book must have had an admiration for the Master's daughter, for he has written down, ' Pretty Miss Pan., dear Miss Panting.' He confided, too, to the same record the indignation that he felt at some harsh treatment that he had received.   ' Nothing is so imperious as a Fellow of a college upon his own dunghill, nothing so contemptible abroad.'

By the help of these old books the curious can still follow Johnson's expenditure from week to week. Mr. Carlyle, in his article on Boswell's ' Life of Johnson,' says, ' Meat he has probably little. . . . The Rev. Dr. Hall (the Master of Pembroke forty years ago) remarks, "As far as we can judge from a cursory view of the weekly account in the buttery-books, Johnson appears to have lived as well as other commoners and scholars." Alas ! such " cursory view of the buttery-books " now, from the safe distance of a century, in the safe chair of a college Mastership, is one thing ; the continual view of the empty or locked buttery itself was quite a different thing.'

This is nonsense so far as I can see. Whatever was Johnson's want of proper clothing and of ready cash, he lived, so far as food went, as the accounts show, in the same way as his fellow-students. They all dined in common, and for his other meals, so long as he was in residence there was no empty or locked buttery for him. If a student could not pay for his food, he would have been sent away and not allowed to stay and starve. No doubt Johnson left because he could not afford to stay any longer, but while he was at college he had, we may be sure, abundant food. Whitfield, who, as we have said, was a servitor, and waited on the others when they dined, and dined himself with the other servitors on what was left, says that when 'I thought to get peace and purity by outward austerities, I always chose the worst sort of food, though my place furnished me with variety.'

Mr. Carlyle, in his 'Heroes and Hero Worship,' makes another error about Johnson. He writes, 'One always remembers that story of the shoes at Oxford : the rough, seamy-faced, raw-boned college servitor stalking about in winter season with his shoes worn out ; how the charitable gentleman-commoner secretly places a new pair at his door ; and the raw-boned servitor lifting them, looking at them near, with his dim eyes, with what thoughts —pitches them out of window !'

Johnson was most assuredly not a servitor, nor is there anything to show that it was a gentleman-commoner who placed the shoes. Hawkins, from whom the story comes, says it was a gentleman of his college.

Furthermore, it is not on evidence where the shoes were thrown. It is more likely that they were thrown down the stairs than out of the window. Johnson was so far from being a servitor that, if we can trust Hawkins, he for a time joined with the other students in persecuting them. 'It was the practice for a servitor,' Hawkins writes, 'by order of the Master, to go round to the rooms of the young men, and knocking at the door to enquire if they were within : and if no answer was returned to report them absent. Johnson could not endure this intrusion, and would frequently be silent, when the utterance of a word would have ensured him from censure, and . . . . would join with others of the young men in college in hunting, as they called it, the servitor who was thus diligent in his duty, and this they did with the noise of pots and candlesticks, singing to the tune of " Chevy Chase " the words in that old ballad—

To drive the deer with hound and horn.'

We cannot tell how far this account is true ; Hawkins knew Johnson well, and knew him rather early in life, but he is by no means trustworthy. He certainly too often 'lies,'—we use the word as Johnson used it— though we will not go on to add 'he knows that he lies.' If Johnson had gone to college three years later, or

Whitfield three years earlier, the great champion of the High Church party might, in after life, have had it to boast, if it were a boast, that he had in his youth hunted the great leader of the Methodists.

In the attempt to bring before ourselves college life as it was in these days, we must not overlook this class of servitors—these scholars among servants and servants among scholars. To many of them the position must have been most galling. No commoner could appear in public with a servitor without loss of position ; and as each order in the University constantly wore its appropriate gown, a servitor was at once distinguished. If a commoner visited a servitor he had to visit him privately. To whatever post a servitor might rise in after-life—and some rose very high—' it was always in the power of a purse-proud collegian to point out that he had waited on him, though, perhaps, all the obligation he had lain under to such a patron was the receiving six-pence a week, not as an act of generosity, but as a tribute imposed on him by the standing rules of the society.'

Whitfield's narrative shows that the servitor's life, even at a well-ordered college like Pembroke, was not an easy one, though he did not seem to have felt anything painful in the position so long as he was left alone. He had been used to waiting in his mother's inn at Gloucester, and must therefore have looked upon a servitorship as a rise in life. The account that he gives of the circumstances that brought him to Oxford is curious. An old school-fellow who was himself a servitor at Pembroke came to pay his mother a visit, and told her how he had not only discharged his college expenses for the term, but had received a penny. She cried out, 'This will do for my son.' Then turning to Whitfield she said, 'Will you go to Oxford, George?' I replied, 'With all my heart!' He found that his having been used to a public-house was of service to him at Pembroke. 'For many of the servitors being sick at my first coming up, by my diligent and steady attendance I ingratiated myself into the gentlemen's favours so far, that many who had it in their power chose me to be their servitor.'

The servitors slept several together in the same room; though this could not have been looked upon in those days as any very great hardship, for only fifty years before Whitfield's time we read of three gentlemen-commoners chumming[1] together. No doubt the great size of some of the rooms in college is explained by the fact that they were intended to be shared by three or four students. The sitting-room of the present day must

[1] They call chamber-fellows by the name of chums.—*Hearne.*

have been the common bed-room, while the bed-room and, perhaps, the pantry were used as studies.

Whitfield says that he was solicited to join in excess of riot with several who lay in the same room. 'But God gave me grace to withstand them; and once in particular it being cold, my limbs were so benumbed by sitting alone in my study because I would not go out amongst them, that I could scarce sleep all night.'

He speaks of the kindness of his tutor, but when he joined Wesley's small set he met with harsh treatment from the Master who frequently chid him, and once threatened to expel him if ever he visited the poor again. By the collegians—by some only we would hope— he was most grossly treated. 'I had no sooner,' he writes, 'received the Sacrament publicly on a week-day at St. Mary's, but I was set up as a mark for all the polite students that knew me to shoot at . . . . I daily underwent some contempt from the collegians. Some have thrown dirt at me, and others took away their pay from me.'

Johnson, Hawkins tells us, would have done away with the whole system of servitors, as indeed it has been long done away with. 'He thought that the scholar's like the Christian life levelled all distinctions of rank and worldly pre-eminence.' But years later on when he was passing the night in the house of Lord Macaulay's great-uncle, the minister of Calder, 'he gave such an account of the education at Oxford in all its gradations, that the advantage of being a servitor to a youth of little fortune struck Mrs. Macaulay much.' Johnson undertook to get her son made a servitor if they sent the boy to him. He did in fact obtain a servitorship for him, though the lad did not accept it, as he had other views.

Could Johnson have looked nearly sixty years forward and seen how another Macaulay would misunderstand him and abuse him, and yet spread his fame far more widely than ever, he might have hesitated about the benefit he proposed to confer. And yet had his offer been accepted who can tell what the result might have been? The members of a family commonly go to the same university, and many a man has gone to Oxford or to Cambridge merely because his uncle went before him. It is as pleasant to picture to ourselves Thomas-Babington Macaulay at Oxford as it is impossible to guess what sort of a man an Oxford Macaulay would have been.

Servitorships, as we have said, have been abolished. We must not forget, however, that they were not an unmixed evil. As many a poor man has worked his passage over the sea to some settlement where a freer and a larger life awaited him, so by a servitorship has many a man worked his way from a life of low drudgery to some high and honourable calling. The student-servant is no longer to be found at Oxford. But the poor student who, in his eagerness to fight his way by his learning, is ready for any duty, however humble it may be, finds one way barred to him that was open to the men of former generations.

While from Whitfield we learn what was the position of a servitor in Pembroke College in Johnson's time, we get a curious and pleasant insight into the life of a gentleman-commoner by means of the diary[1] kept by Mr. Erasmus Philipps (afterwards the fifth baronet of that name), of Picton Castle. He entered into residence on August 1, 1720, only eight years before Johnson. He was fond of sports. He more than once was present at the races on Poit Mead ; he saw Lord Tracey's mare 'Whimsey' run, the swiftest galloper in England, and yet he does not note down in his diary either how much he had betted on her or against her, or how much he had lost or won, as we should expect a young heir to a baronetcy of the present day to note down. 'I could not help thinking,' he records, ' of Job's description of

---

[1] Published in *Notes and Queries*, 2nd series, vol. x. p. 366. My attention was drawn to this diary by Mr. Wordsworth's *Social Life at the English Universities*.

the horse, and particularly of that description in it, *he swalloweth the ground*, which is an expression for prodigious swiftness, in use among the Arabians, Job's countrymen, at this day.' He went to see a foot-race between tailors for geese, and another day he went to a great cock-match in Holywell, fought between the Earl of Plymouth and the town cocks, which beat his lordship. One night he went 'to the Ball at the " Angel," a guinea touch.' Another night he and some gentlemen-commoners of Balliol 'made a private ball for Miss Brigandine, my partner, Miss Hume, &c.' Curiously enough, on an old pane of glass in University College, in the hand-writing of the early part of last century, I have found a name written which we can please ourselves with thinking is that of young Mr. Philipps' partner. There is the difference of one letter in the spelling, but this may be due to the mistake of the printer of ' Notes and Queries.' The inscription is as follows :

Charming Pen Stonehouse,
Loveliest of women, Heaven is in thy soul ;
Beauty and virtue shine for ever round you,
Brightening each, thou art all divine,
Nanny Brigantine.

I have already pointed out the much greater intimacy that existed between the Fellows and the commoners in those days. A gentleman-commoner, no doubt, was on still closer terms. One day Mr. Philipps went out riding with the Rev. Mr. Wilder, the Vice-gerent of his college, and another gentleman, to Newnham, where they dined. The Vice-gerent, as his name implies, is in authority second only to the Master, and is specially answerable for the discipline of the college. Yet Mr. Philipps notes down : 'Coming home a dispute arose between these two gentlemen, whom with great difficulty I kept from blows.'

The Rev. Mr. Wilder had left before Johnson's time. This reverend Vice-gerent must have enjoyed what Johnson would have called ' a frisk with the lads,' for one fine day in summer, he, the author of the diary, and four other Pembrokians, went fishing up the river as far as Burnt Island, where they landed and dressed a leg of mutton, which they despatched in the wherry. Mr. Philipps' tutor, Mr. Horn, shared in these amusements. One day he gave him an Essay on Friendship, and in the evening, I suppose as a practical commentary on his essay, the two went together to Godstow by water, with some others, taking music and wine.

Another of the Fellows, Mr. Tristram, took him to a poetical club at ' The Tuns,' where he drank Gallicia wine, and was entertained with two fables of Dr. Evans' composition, ' which were, indeed, masterly in their kind,

but the doctor is allowed to have a peculiar knack and
excellence at a fable.'

This Mr. Tristram seems to have been somewhat of a
humourist.   He once greatly offended poor Hearne, who,
in his diary, records, 'Beyond High Bridge is a little
house called "Antiquity Hall," which one Wise of Trinity
College, and one Tristram of Pembroke College (both of
them very conceited fellows and of little understanding,
though both are Masters of Arts), have had a draught
taken of, and printed with very silly, ridiculous things
and words in it, for which they are much laughed at by
all people, who cannot but look upon it as one of the
weakest things ever done.'

Dr. Bliss, in a note, tells us where the point of the
jest lay.   'The silly things and words which gave Hearne
so much offence were inserted in order to ridicule some
of his own plates, in which he has given explanations of
the objects, or what they were intended to represent.
Wise and Tristram have done the same, and have introduced Hearne himself as entering at the court-yard
holding up his gown behind, according to his usual manner of walking.'   Johnson must have known Tristram,
and, perhaps, enjoyed his humour.

But to return to Mr. Philipps.   He, a second time,
went to 'The Tuns,' with three other Pembrokians,

'where they motto'd, epigrammatiz'd,' &c. He evidently had a liking for literary pursuits. He was present in the Sheldonian Theatre on a speech-day, and present as one competent to criticise, and not, as young men attend now, merely to make a noise. 'The Proctor's speech,' he notes down, was a delicate and masterly piece of oratory.' With an honest pride in his college, he adds, 'Mr. Church, the Junior Collector, a Pembrokian, came off very handsomely.' He wrote an essay on Pride, and took it to the Master, who then desired him to declaim in the Hall on the following thesis, ' *Virtutem amplectimur ipsam, præmia si tollas.*' He presented to the Bodleian Library a Malabar Grammar, a very great curiosity, and received the thanks of the Keeper. The same day he presented to the library of his own college Mr. Prior's Works in folio, neatly bound, ' which cost me £1 3*s.*' He was entered, as he records, a benefactor to the library. He fell acquainted with Mr. Solomon Negri, a native of Damascus, a great critic in the Arabic language, who had come to Oxford to transcribe Arabic manuscripts, and he enjoyed abundance of satisfaction in his conversation. He met another day in Mr. Tristram's room Mr. Wanley, the famous antiquarian, and Mr. Hunt, who is skilled in the Arabic. On leaving Pembroke, he presented one of the scholars with his key of the garden, for which he had on entrance paid ten shillings, treated the whole college in the 'common-room, and then took up his caution money (£10) from the Bursar, and lodged it with the Master for the use of Pembroke College.   Altogether, if we put aside the ride to Newnham, young Mr. Philipps gives us a very pleasant picture of life in his little college.

In the two years in which he was in residence he left Oxford but twice.   He went to London for a few weeks each Christmas.   He travelled in Bartlett's stage, paying ten shillings for his 'passage,' and taking two days on the road.   In Gibbon's time (1752) the Long Vacation, as he tells us, emptied the Colleges of Oxford as well as the Courts of Westminster.   But both Johnson and Philipps stayed up the Long Vacation.   Johnson was, perhaps, absent one week, but certainly not more.   The following table which I have compiled from the batell-books shows the number of men (graduates and undergraduates) in residence at Pembroke at the end of each fourth week from June to December, 1729 :—

	Members in residence
June 20, 1729	54
July 18, „	34
Aug. 13, „	25
Sept. 12, „	16
Oct. 10, „	30
Nov. 7, „	52
Dec. 5, „	49

At Christmas there were still sixteen men left in the college. How little those who did leave Oxford in the Vacation were given to roving after the manner of the modern undergraduate is shown by a curious letter published among the Historical Manuscripts. 'He hath,' says the writer, speaking of a young Oxonian, 'a fancy to pass over into the Isle of Wight. But this I dissuade him from, because he can see nothing worth the hazard of passing the sea to it ; and he has agreed to let it alone.'

Shortly after Johnson left Pembroke College, Shenstone the poet entered. In the same year entered also Richard Graves, the author of the 'Spiritual Quixote.'[1] In a series of letters that were published more than fifty years later Mr. Graves gives an interesting account of the 'sets' into which the college was at that time divided. As Johnson certainly did not leave three years, and, perhaps, not one year, before Graves entered, we may assume that no great change had come over the college in this short time.

Graves' account, which I slightly abridge, is as follows :—'The young people of the college at that time

---

[1] It is curious that his name is not given in any edition of Boswell that I have seen, among the men of note who were educated at Pembroke.

(as I believe is the case in most colleges) were divided into different small associations according to their different tastes and pursuits. Having been elected from a public school and brought with me the character of a tolerably good Grecian, I was invited by a very worthy person, now living, to a very sober little party who amused themselves in the evening with reading Greek and drinking water. (Dr Cheyne had then brought water-drinking into great vogue.) Here I continued six months, and we read over Theophrastus, Epictetus, Phalaris's Epistles, and such other Greek authors as are seldom read at school. But I was at length seduced from this mortified symposium to a very different party, a set of jolly, sprightly young fellows, most of them West-country lads, who drank ale, smoked tobacco, punned, and sung bacchanalian catches the whole evening : our " pious orgies " generally began with—

> Let's be jovial, fill our glasses,
> Madness 'tis for us to think,
> How the world is ruled by asses,
> And the wisest sway'd by chink.'

To this set belonged, we may readily believe, Phil Jones, who loved beer, and Edwards, who considered supper as a turnpike through which one must pass in order to go to bed.

'I own with shame,' continues Mr. Graves, 'that being then not seventeen, I was so far captivated with the social disposition of these young people (many of whom were ingenious lads and good scholars) that I began to think *them* the only wise men, and to have a contempt for every degree of temperance and sobriety. Some gentlemen-commoners, however, who considered the above-mentioned as very *low* company (chiefly on account of the liquor they drank), good-naturedly invited me to their party ; they treated me with port wine and arrack-punch ; and now and then when they had drunk so much as hardly to distinguish wine from water. they would conclude with a bottle or two of claret. They kept late hours, drank their favourite toasts on their knees, and in short were what were then called " bucks of the first head." This was deemed good company and high life ; but it neither suited my taste, my fortune, or my constitution.

'There was besides a sort of flying squadron of plain sensible, matter-of-fact men, confined to no club, but associating with each party. They anxiously enquired after the news of the day, and the politics of the times. They had come to the University on their way to the Temple, or to get a slight smattering of the sciences before they settled in the country.'

At length he became acquainted with Shenstone, and was invited by him to breakfast, together with a Mr. Whistler. This latter gentleman was 'a young man of great delicacy of sentiment, and though with every assistance at Eton, he had such a dislike to learning languages that he could not read the classics in the original. Yet no one formed a better judgment of them. He wrote, moreover, great part of a tragedy on the story of Dido.' The three young men dragged out the breakfast in literary talk. Each one quoted his favourite humourist. 'Mr. Whistler, who was a year or two older than either of us, and had finished his school education at Eton, preferred Pope's "Rape of the Lock," as a higher species of humour than anything we had produced.' They constantly met afterwards in each other's rooms, and 'read plays and poetry, "Spectators" or "Tatlers," and sipped Florence wine.' Graves says that he at least did not neglect his more serious studies. He was a scholar of the house, and had some dry studies prescribed to him, which he had to pursue with regularity and strict attention the whole morning.

We may amuse ourselves with guessing to which set Johnson belonged. Among the gentlemen-commoners, we may be sure he never spent a single evening. We can picture him to ourselves equally well reading Greek with the water-drinkers, or drinking ale and singing catches with the West-country lads, or talking politics with the matter-of-fact men.

'At this time,' says Mr. Graves, 'every schoolboy so soon as he was entered at the University, cut off his hair, and without any regard to his complexion, put on a wig, black, white, brown, or grizzle, as "lawless fancy" suggested.' Shenstone had the courage to wear his own hair, though 'it often exposed him to the ill-natured remarks of people who had not half his sense.' 'After I was elected,' Mr. Graves writes, 'at All Souls, where, though there were very many studious young men,[1] yet there was often a party of loungers in the gateway, on my expostulating with Mr. Shenstone for not visiting me so often as usual, he said, "he was ashamed to face his enemies in the gate."'

In a satire published four years before Johnson matriculated, we have a lively description of the Oxford fop. 'A college smart is a character few are unacquainted with. He is one that spends his time in a constant circle of engagements and assignations; he rises at ten, tattles over his tea-table till twelve, dines, dresses, waits upon his mistress,

---

[1] The Oxonian of the present day will learn with not a little satisfaction that there once were studious young men in All Souls' College.

drinks tea again, flutters about in public till it is dark, then to the tavern, knocks into college at two in the morning, sleeps till ten again, and disposes of the following day just as he did of the last. He affects great company, and scrapes acquaintance with " golden tuffs " (*sic*) and brocaded gowns ; and, after a course of studies of this nature for three or four years, he huddles over the public exercises, disputes, and passes examination in the sciences after the modern fashion, without understanding a word of what, like a parrot, he is taught memorially to utter.' Such a gentleman as this could not be content with a stuff gown. 'Silk gowns, tye-wigs, and ruffles are become necessary accomplishments for a man of sense.' He had no need to fear crosses in love. 'Anything in a cap and gown that has the appearance of a man, a little money, and tolerable assurance, never fails in his addresses.'

These 'university gallants' had their troubles. They made a brave show for a time, but paid dearly for it. In a mock ballad opera published after the Oxford Act—the Commemoration, as it is now called—of 1733, we have three of them represented under the names of Spendthrift, Sprightly, and Thoughtless. Thoughtless is discovered wandering up and down Merton Walks and lamenting his folly in having spent all his Midsummer quarteridge (*sic*) of 50*l.*, only to make a gaudy appearance for a few days this Public Act. He had sold his books, his furniture, and even his bed, and so he thinks he may as well 'walk the parade' all night as sneak into college. He ends by wishing that he 'had been help building the new town at Georgia, rather than in this cursed place.' That colony had been founded by Oglethorpe only the year before.

Thoughtless' companions are in just as bad a way, and even some of the Fellows are no better off. 'There is a universal complaint,' says the Proctor, 'from all our members, masters, bachelors, as undergraduates, that this Act has exhausted their pockets. Most of our colleges are beset with bailiffs.' The play ends in an ale-house, where the three luckless undergraduates, and Haughty and Pedant, the two Fellows, resolve to go in a body to seek their fortunes in Georgia.

Sprightly, Thoughtless, and Spendthrift are not un-common in Oxford even in these latter days. They go eastward to Australia instead of westward to Georgia, and they have not Fellows for their comrades; in most other respects, however, they are very like 'the college smarts' of many generations back. Extravagance was largely caused by that 'mischievous and unstatutable practice of scholars having private entertainments and company at

their chambers.' Convocation protested against it, as a
practice which is 'generally attended with great intemperance and excess, and always with expenses that are both
needless and hurtful.' All bursars, deans, and censors
were earnestly recommended to prevent it, as much as
in their power, and to oblige all persons to attend
in the common hall at the usual hours of dinner and
supper.

A Fellow of Pembroke, of Johnson's time, published
a letter to his brother Fellows of the University, entitled
'The Expense of University Education Reduced.' In
fourteen years it went through four editions. Haughty
and Pedant of the 'Mock Comic Opera' were no doubt
exaggerations ; yet this letter shows that there was some
truth in the satire. Even the best endowed fellowships,
we are told, were but barely sufficient for maintenance,
for decent apparel, and for a few useful books. Yet
every Fellow thought himself bound to spend his money
in absurd and conceited entertainments for every trifling
acquaintance who has a mind to visit Oxford on his way
'to the Bath.' Yet one such entertainment in a Fellow's
private chamber exceeded a month's allowance from his
founder.

The ale in the common cellar was a great source of
extravagance. Ale in itself was a liquor innocent, cheer-

ful, and useful. It wanted its situation changed. At present it was too near. It was drunk even in the morning, a time that was friendly to the Muses without its pretended aid. If the ale is excellent, its fame reaches to distant parts. 'My friends will oblige me so far as to come and taste it. They will be so just as to speak very well of it to others, who likewise may want to give their opinion whether it doth indeed answer the high character that is given of it. Nay, I am not sure that my intimate acquaintances will not sometimes carry their complaisance so far as to send for it to their own colleges.'

To the college servants, too, another large stream will run at their master's expense. 'Their state of servitude, the most miserable that can be conceived amongst so many masters, requires frequent consolation and relief. The kicks and cuffs and bruises they submit to entitle them, when those who were displeased relent, to this sort of compensation. They likewise, at other times, can insinuate their little merits towards me, and being always about me know the *mollia tempora*, as well as persons of the best education and address. There is not a college servant, but if he have learnt to suffer, and to be officious, and be inclined to tipple, may forget his cares in a gallon or two of ale every day of his life.'

The state of life thus described seems strange enough.

It is well to remember that when we try to study the manners of a past age, it is to the satirist and the moralist that we have chiefly to go. They both alike, though from different reasons and in different ways, exaggerate whatever is vicious, extravagant, or absurd. There is one little trait of bygone life that comes out in this letter that will amuse the bursar of the present time. When he suffers under the ever-repeated complaints of the badness of the college ale, he will smile when he finds that one hundred and forty years ago a Fellow, in remarking that the undergraduates sent out into the town for ale, noted down 'There is that humour in young men as to despise what is before them, and is cheaper, and to covet what is at a distance, and of greater price, though not more excellent.'

The abstemious Pembroke Fellow did not escape attack. At that time, at the Commemoration, a licensed buffoon, under the name of 'Terræ Filius,' used 'to sport and play with the reputation of others.' At the Grand Commemoration of 1733 he was not allowed to speak. The 'Terræ Filius Speech,' as it was to have been spoken, was nevertheless published. Its scurrility is extraordinary. In fact, the gross licentiousness of the satires commonly written on the University authorities is very striking. . The author of 'University Education' comes off very easily, when compared with many others. 'Say, abstemious Don, have you never transgressed your own rules? never exceeded a twopenny commons and a halfpenny small for dinner or supper? How came the cook, then, to convey privately into your own apartment a cold fowl or neat's tongue, with a bottle or two of good wine, to stuff your maw with in secret?' All Souls' College, if we may trust Terræ Filius, was most given to drinking. He had been to look for it, but he could not find it. It used to stand above Queen's, but it would seem to have been translated over the way to the Three Tuns Tavern. So deserted was it as a place of learning that a cat had lately been starved to death in its library. Terræ Filius can be proved to have libelled the Fellows of All Souls' College, for at least on one night in every year, if they did drink, at all events they drank at home. 'On the 14th January in every year,' as Hearne tells us, 'being All Souls' College Mallard, 'tis usual with the Fellows and their friends to have a supper, and to sit up all night drinking and singing.'

In the year 1716, it was said that there were ' 300 ale-houses in Oxford of the worst fame and reputation, without even the least offer of discommuning them.' Only five years before Johnson entered, the senior Proctor and his pro-proctor were found by the Vice-

Chancellor at a tavern, at an unreasonable hour, and 'to their great reluctance' were forthwith sent to their colleges. I suspect that the Vice-Chancellor was inspired quite as much with zeal against the Hanoverians as with any love of temperance and early hours. It was 'on the Coronation-day of the Duke of Brunswick, commonly called King George,' that these gentlemen had thus met together. The proctor and the pro-proctor both belonged to Merton, the stronghold of the Hanoverian party, and they had, no doubt, assembled to drink loyal toasts. On the tenth of June late drinking would have been quite another matter. A few honest lads who had come together to drink to 'the King over the water,' on his birthday, would have had no fear of being troubled by the Vice-Chancellor.

Story, the Quaker, visiting Oxford in the year 1731, records in his journal, 'Of all places wherever I have been, the scholars of Oxford were the rudest, most giddy and unruly rabble, and most mischievous. They used to come to the Meeting House to make fun. Some of them looked wild and airy, but others more solid ; some sat down and were quiet, others restless and floating, full of tricks, whisperings, smirkings, and sometimes fleerings.' He adds, however, that when he addressed them 'several were affected and chained.'

Some sixteen years earlier, as I shall presently show, the Quakers had had far worse treatment to undergo in Oxford, but the head of the Quaker family in the town had, as Story says, ' borne a faithful testimony in that old seat of the power of darkness against all the envy, scoffs, flouts, and jeers, and other immoralities of the young brood hatched in this place, till by patience in well-doing he is now treated with general respect.' Johnson in his old age said to Boswell, that he liked individuals among the Quakers, but not the sect. At Oxford he would have found it hard to distinguish between the individuals and the sect.

It was at the very time that Johnson entered Oxford that the two Wesleys were laying the foundations of their sect. Three or four years later, Whitfield saw them 'go through a ridiculing crowd to receive the holy sacrament at St. Mary's.' They went by the name of the Sacramentarians, Bible-bigots, Bible-moths, the Holy Club, and the Godly Club. There were three points to which, they said, they would adhere, though their practice of them had brought upon them reproaches. The three points were as follows :—

1. Visiting and relieving the prisoners and the sick, and giving away copies of the Bible, the Prayer Book, and the ' Whole Duty of Man.'

2. Weekly Communion.

3. Strict observance of the Fasts of the Church.

They had been attacked by even 'forcible arguments and menaces.' One 'worthy gentleman' wrote to his son: 'You can't conceive what a noise this ridiculous society you have engaged in has made here. . . . Besides follies at Oxford, to hear that you were noted for going into the villages about Holt, entering into poor people's houses, calling their children together, teaching them their prayers and catechism, and giving them a shilling at your departure.'

The Vice-Chancellor and the Heads of Houses, strongly as they were against the Methodists, had themselves become alarmed at the progress of what is called infidelity. They had, when Johnson had been in residence barely three months, put forth 'a *Programma* in which they exhorted the tutors to discharge their duty by double diligence; and forbade the undergraduates to read such books as might tend to the weakening of their faith.'

It is not at all likely that Johnson ever met Wesley in these early days, though he knew him in after life, and enjoyed his society—so much of it, that is to say, as he could get. 'John Wesley's conversation is good,' he said, 'but he is never at leisure. He is always obliged to go at a certain hour. This is very disagreeable to a man who loves to fold his legs and have out his talk, as I do.'

For Methodistical students Johnson had no liking. Years later he defended the expulsion of six of them from the University. 'Sir, that expulsion was extremely just and proper. What have they to do at an University, who are not willing to be taught, but will presume to teach? Sir, they were examined and found to be mighty ignorant fellows.' *Boswell*: 'But was it not hard, Sir, to expel them, for I am told they were good beings. *Johnson*: 'I believe they might be good beings, but they were not fit to be in the University of Oxford. A cow is a very good animal in the field, but we turn her out of a garden.'

The case of these six Methodists throws so much light on the state of Oxford last century, that though they were nearly forty years later than Johnson's days as an undergraduate, I shall not hesitate to give a brief account of it. All the six were members of St. Edmund Hall. The Principal was satisfied with their conduct, and had no wish to trouble them. But the Vice-Principal, who was their tutor, appealed to the Vice-Chancellor as the Visitor of the society to expel them. He thereupon, acting, it must be remembered, in his capacity of Visitor and not of Vice-Chancellor, held an enquiry. The chief charges made against them by the Vice-Principal were as follow :—

' 1. Three of the six had been bred to trades, while all the six were at their entrance and still continued to be destitute of such a knowledge of the learned languages as is necessary for performing the usual exercises of the Hall and the University.

' 2. They were all enemies to the doctrine and discipline of the Church of England, which appeared either by their preaching or expounding in, or frequenting illicit conventicles, and by several other actions and expressions.

' 3. They neglected to attend lectures, or misbehaved themselves when they did attend.'

In a pamphlet published by Dr. Nowell, the Principal of St. Mary Hall, in defence of the Vice-Chancellor, a full report is given of the proceedings. Considerably abridged, it is as follows :—

' J. Matthews, thirty years of age, accused that he was brought up to the trade of a weaver, and had kept a tap-house.—Confessed. Accused that he is totally ignorant of Greek and Latin, which appeared by his declining all examination. Accused of being a reported Methodist, that he entered himself at Edmund Hall with a design to get into holy orders, that he still continues to be wholly illiterate and incapable of doing the exercises of the Hall.—Proved. That he had frequented illicit conventicles held in a private house in Oxford.—Confessed.

'T. Jones, accused to have been brought up to the trade of a barber, which he had followed very lately.—Confessed.

'J. Shipman, accused that he had been brought up to the trade of a draper, and that he was totally illiterate, which appeared in his examination.

'B. Kay confesses that he has been present at meetings held in Mrs. Durbridge's house, where he heard extempore prayers offered up by a stay-maker. Had endeavoured to persuade a young man of Magdalen College to attend also. Holds that the Spirit of God works irresistibly.

'T. Grove confessed that he had lately preached to an assembly of people called Methodists in a barn, and had offered up extempore prayers.'

These four and two others were expelled. One Benjamin Blatch had also been accused. He confessed his ignorance, and declined all examination. 'But'—we quote Dr. Nowell's own words—'as he was represented to be a man of fortune, and declared that he was not designed for holy orders, the Vice-Chancellor did not think fit to remove him for this reason only, though he was supposed to be one of "the righteous overmuch."' The Vice-Chancellor had been reproached with his cruelty in thus depriving these men of their living. 'There is no fear of their starving,' replied Dr. Nowell. 'Mr. J——s makes a good periwig; he need not starve. Mr. M——s and Mr. S——n may maintain themselves ·and serve their country better at the loom, or at the tap, or behind the counter, than they were likely to do in the pulpit. *Tractant fabrilia fabri.*' There was, he main·-tained, no need of excuse, for the Vice-Chancellor's whole proceeding 'was an act of discipline commendable in itself and pleasing to the true friends of learning and religion.'

Commendable and pleasing though this act was, yet it led to hot controversy. The Apostles themselves, it was objected, were not men of learning. These six students were not so ignorant as had been asserted. They had been confused and frightened when they had been called upon to give a proof of their learning in a public court. There were much more ignorant men— men who were abandoned as well as ignorant—who were not expelled. They had been called upon as a proof of their knowledge of Latin to construe the Statutes of the University; and it was not reasonable, it was maintained, to expect that they should be familiar with the barbarous Latin in which these statutes are written.

Perhaps the Vice-Chancellor required them to translate the section *De Conventiculis illicitis reprimendis*, where it is written, ' Ne quis confœderationes sive conspirationes ineat unde Cancellarius, Procuratores, seu alii Ministri Universitatis in executione Officiorum suorum secundum Statuta et Ordinationes ejusdem impediri vel perturbari possint, sub pœna bannitionis ab Universitate.' Cicero might certainly have been puzzled with such Latin ; but to a Methodistical student it would have appeared, I should have thought, a good deal like the Latin that he himself was wont to write. In Greek they had been asked to translate a passage from the New Testament in the original.

If, it was objected, all academics were expelled who could not construe the Greek Testament and the University Statutes, the colleges would be much more empty. ' At the great examination,' as the advocate for the six students asserted, ' all the classical learning required is to be able to construe one Greek and two Latin books ; and the custom of the place while I resided there allowed the candidate himself to fix on the three books—Epictetus, for instance, Eutropius and Cornelius Nepos.' Why were not the vicious expelled ? Why was not Mr.

Welling expelled, who also belonged to Edmund Hall, and who had said that whoever believed the miracles of Moses must be a knave. What was the history of this drunken infidel? He was a poor foundling beggar-boy, bred in a workhouse, and thence received into the house of a hatter to run errands. Next he had been the scout of an apothecary. Then he had been taken into the house of a pious clergyman and schoolmaster, where he got a smattering of learning. Next he had been assistant in a school. Here he maintained his Deistical principles, till the maid-servant being found with child, both he and she were dismissed. He married her, and she getting a place in a Jew's family, could now contribute to his support.

The charge brought against Mr. Welling about Moses' miracles was too serious for the Vice-Chancellor to overlook, and he at once instituted an enquiry. Mr. W. Wrighte, a gentleman-commoner of Edmund Hall, gave evidence as follows. When walking in St. John's Garden, he saw the said Welling to be concerned in liquor. (It was St. John the Baptist's day, and Welling had been helping to celebrate the patron saint of the college at the college dinner.) He took occasion to expostulate with him thereon. A dispute then arose concerning some points in religion. Welling said, 'What, fool, do you believe in the miracles of Moses?' Upon which informant threatened him very severely. Next day Welling came to ask pardon, and since then informant has taken occasion to examine into his real sentiments in regard to the miracles of Moses. Before the Vice-Chancellor Welling declared his unfeigned assent to Divine revelation in general, and the miracles of Moses in particular. But the Vice-Chancellor was not satisfied till he had read a declaration of orthodoxy and regret of drunkenness before congregation. He had since obtained a cure of souls, and, as it was asserted, when asked why he had been ordained, had replied, 'Why should I not read the Bible for money as well as any other book?'

A yet worse instance was brought forward by the advocate of the six Methodists than even Mr. Welling's. Not many years before this the sacrament had been administered to an ass in the chapel or the ante-chapel of one of the colleges ; and yet the man who had administered it was not expelled, but had merely lost his fellowship.

All these arguments availed nought. The six Methodists were not allowed to return. There is little doubt that in an University they were, to use Johnson's comparison, like a cow in a garden. It is equally clear that they were expelled, not for their ignorance, but their Methodism. The gentleman of fortune who, as Dr. Nowell admitted, 'had not had any school learning,' was allowed to stay, partly because he was a gentleman of fortune, and partly because he was not designed for holy orders. Had Johnson been brought before the Vice-Chancellor of his day, and had he been accused of having been brought up to the trade of a bookbinder, we should have found entered against the charge 'confessed.'[1] It is worth noticing, moreover, that not many years before Dr. Nowell's time, one among the Heads of Halls, as soon as he was appointed Principal, refused to admit any students, but shut up the gate altogether, and wholly lived in the country. 'Whereas,' as Hearne says, ''twas expected that he, being a disciplinarian, and a sober, studious, regular, and learned man, would have made it flourish in a most remarkable manner.' While the head of a Hall could thus shamefully shirk his duty; while the tutor of Magdalen could well remember that he had a salary to receive and only forgot that he had a duty to perform; while the Fellows of that society, by their dull and deep potations, could excuse the brisk intemperance of youth; these six Methodist students might have been borne with by the Vice-

---

[1] He had, at all events, learnt how to bind a book.

Principal of St. Edmund Hall and its Visitor, the Vice-Chancellor.

Mighty though Methodism was to be, yet the Oxford of Johnson's time saw nothing of its destined greatness. The young giant was one of her own children, yet she mocked it from its very birth and cast it out of her house with scorn. Oxford was looking backwards to a time that had happily passed by, never to return. Her golden age was the age of the Stuarts. The Wesleys and Whitfield bade men look across this world to some far happier and far better world beyond. Oxford also had her hopes for the future as well as her longings for what was past. The golden age was, indeed, no more, but Astræa might once more return. The poet might again sing,

> And now Time's whiter series is begun,
> Which in soft centuries shall smoothly run.

For Oxford there was no need to cross the River of Death ; it would be enough for her that the king who was over the water should come back to his own again. She had suffered grievously under the tyrant James. Yet her wrongs were forgotten, and she was ready once more to put the generosity of the Stuarts to the proof. The town, widely though it had always differed from the University, was at one with it in this. Gownsmen and townsmen alike were Jacobite to the backbone. Old Michael Johnson, staunch Jacobite as he was, though 'he had reconciled himself by casuistical arguments of expediency and necessity to take the oaths' as a magistrate of Lichfield, must have felt, as he placed his son at Oxford, that there was little chance that the young student's loyalty would ever be shaken. Was not the whole University loyal, and was not the Master of Pembroke 'a fine Jacobite fellow'?

George I. had not been many months on the throne before town and gown, joining together in a mad riot, showed their hatred of him and the Whigs who supported him. On the king's birthday, May 28, in the year 1715, the Quaker Story chanced to visit Oxford He went to view the college buildings and gardens, and found them, in their kinds, pleasant and commodious. But the great load of the power of darkness which he felt was an over-balance to any satisfaction he had therein. At the Friends' afternoon meeting some scholars were present, but he found them fluctuating and unsettled. By evening the city was in an uproar. A great mob of scholars and townsmen appeared in the streets cursing and damning the Presbyterians. The members of the Constitution Club had met at the King's Head Tavern to drink pros-

perity to the Royal Family, and had had a bonfire lighted
before the tavern. The mob surrounded the house and
bore away the burning wood. It next broke into the
Presbyterian Chapel, and tearing down the wainscot and
bearing out the benches and the pulpit, made a great
Jacobite bonfire at the head of High Street. The members of the Constitution Club took refuge in New College,
and, if we can believe the charge that was brought against
them, thence shot off several blunderbusses at a venture
among the people. The mob round the blazing pile
were heard to vow that the next night they would serve
the Quakers as they had served the Presbyterians. By
nine o'clock on the following evening—the evening of
May 29, a day for many a long year dear to Oxford—
the mob began to assemble again. This night it was the
Quakers whom they cursed and damned.

It was in vain that the great bell of Christ Church
rang out, as it had rung out for many a year before, and
would ring out for many a year to come, calling the
scholars within their colleges. What scholar was likely
on such a night as this to be asked troublesome questions by his Dean? They gutted the Quakers' Meeting-
house, as they had vowed, and then they gutted the Baptist
Chapel. They next broke into the dwelling house of a
widow—the daughter of an ancient Friend. A young

nobleman had been murdered, they said, and hidden somewhere thereabouts, and they were in search of his body. Finding neither young nobleman nor body, they broke all the windows and threw in some hundredweight of stones and dirt. Story was lodging with the widow's brother. The terrified Quakers crouched for safety under the staircase, and there the two men, with the frightened woman of the house and her little children, stayed while the rioters let fly their volley of stones. By two o'clock in the morning the riot was over, and some of the neighbours ventured to come in. From them Story learned 'the unreasonable reason,' as he calls it, of the mob's violence. Some of the Low Party, it was said, when dining at a tavern, 'had drunk healths and confusions,' and had talked of burning the late Queen's picture and Sacheverell's also. The Quakers at the last election had voted for the Low members, and in revenge the mob had wrecked their meeting-house and their homes. Story the next morning went to see the ruins. He stood on a slight rise in the ground, and seeing many scholars present, he said loud enough for them all to hear, 'Can these be the effects of religion and learning?' Several of them had shame enough left to hang their heads, but none answered.

The 1st of August of that year was appointed for a

thanksgiving day for His Majesty's happy accession. In these happier times for more than three long months of summer, nothing can happen at Oxford to trouble the calm repose of the Vice-Chancellor, the Proctors, and the Heads of Houses. But in the early part of last century the undergraduates, as I have shown, remained at Oxford in large numbers during the Long Vacation. Those in authority dreaded another riot; dreaded, no doubt, still more the angry displeasure of the Government. They accordingly published regulations for the observance of the day. The scholars were strictly forbidden to draw a mob together by giving drink. Neither were they to make bonfires in the street. Each College and Hall might at the public expense of the society make a bonfire. But the bonfires were to be lighted immediately after morning service at St. Mary's, at which time, it was said, the University bonfire was usually made before the church door. A bonfire lighted in the broad light of an August day would make but a sorry sight. It is not impossible that there was some touch of humour in the regulation. Though the Vice-Chancellor was accused of currying favour with the Government, yet the Heads of Houses, as a body, were not unwilling to cast ridicule on this Hanoverian thanksgiving. The day passed off quietly enough. Hearne says that ' the gene-

rality of people turned it into a day of mourning. The
bells only jambled, being pulled by a parcel of children
and silly people ; but there was not so much as one good
peal rung in Oxford.'

Meanwhile a regiment had been quartered in the
town, to overawe gownsmen and townsmen alike. It was
at this time, I imagine, that Dr. Trapp, the Fellow of
Wadham, wrote his famous epigram—

> Our royal master saw, with heedful eyes,
> The wants of his two Universities :
> Troops he to Oxford sent, as knowing why
> That learned body wanted loyalty :
> But books to Cambridge gave, as well discerning,
> That that right loyal body wanted learning.

Sir William Browne, when Johnson had repeated these
lines to him with an air of triumph, made, if we may
trust Mdme. Piozzi, the famous epigram in answer on the
spur of the moment—

> The King to Oxford sent his troop of horse
> For Tories own no argument but force ;
> With equal care to Cambridge books he sent,
> For Whigs allow no force but argument.

It was not, however, a troop of horse, but a regiment of
foot soldiers that on this occasion was quartered in
Oxford. The peace was not disturbed till October 30 in
the following year (1716). It was the Prince of Wales's

birthday, but, learned though the University was in dates generally, of that one date it was in profound ignorance. No less ignorant was the Mayor. Not a bell was rung in honour of the day. Major d'Offrainville, who was in command of the regiment, could not contain his indignation. He came into a coffee-house cursing and swearing, and said that not a bell had stirred that morning. A Bachelor of Arts of Brasenose College, who happened to be present, turned to his companion and innocently asked what day it was. 'It was the Prince's birthday,' the Major answered, 'and it was the disaffection of the governors, who were a pack of villains, which occasioned the bells not ringing.' 'Why,' asked the simple Bachelor, 'did not the Merton bells ring? No one could think that Merton, the stronghold of the Constitution Club, was disaffected.' 'No,' said the Major; 'that was a good, honest college.' He went on swearing, and said over and over again that he would send soldiers at night to break the windows of the colleges. This however the Major afterwards denied. He admitted that he had said that the colleges deserved to have their windows broken, but he had never said that he would send soldiers to break them. The same day he met one of the magistrates of the town, and told him that the townspeople deserved to have their windows broken also. At five o'clock in the afternoon, when it must have been growing dark,[1] the Major drew up his regiment all along High Street, from the Conduit that at that time stood before Carfax Church, to the East Gate by Magdalen College. The mob cried out 'Down with the Roundheads.' The Major, hearing the cry, turned his horse about, and seeing 'some one who had on the habit of a clergyman told him he was the rogue, and that if he could get at him he would break his head, or any disaffected person's head, as soon as he would a dog's, or words to that effect' (the Major's own evidence). The soldiers discharged their three rounds in honour of the day, the colours were lodged, and the regiment was dismissed. The officers, with some honest gentlemen of the Constitution Club, went to the Star Inn to finish up the day with a dinner. A bonfire had been made in front of the inn, by the Major's orders. After dinner, they all went out into the street, and round the fire drank healths to His Majesty, the Prince of Wales and the Royal Family, and to the pious memory of William III.

It must have been a strange sight in the Corn-market —North Street as it was then called—that November night. The blazing bonfire, with the soldiers standing round it glass in hand, drinking their loyal toasts ; in the background, a crowd of sullen townsmen and gownsmen,

[1] October 30, Old Style, is the same as November 11, New Style.

bent on mischief. No sooner had the officers gone back into their inn than a volley of stones shattered the windows. The soldiers who were in the crowd below, and had no doubt joined in the loyal and pious toasts, at once broke the windows of a Jacobite ironmonger on the other side of the street. The inn was a second time attacked by the mob, and the soldiers then began to break the windows of all the houses that were not illuminated. The Major went down into the street and ordered his men to drive away all the Jacobites. Mr. Wilson, a cutler, prayed that he might be allowed to stay, for he was an honest man, and had been so in the worst of times, whereupon the Major made him drink two or three glasses to His Majesty's health. He asked the cutler if there were many such men as he in the town. There were a few of them, he answered, and pointing towards a mercer, he said 'that is a man that suffered much in the bad times,' and then towards a barber's shop, 'that is another.' The Vice-Chancellor, attended by a man bearing a lanthorn and candle, came up to help to keep the peace. But the soldiers went up to the Vice-Chancellor and asked him if he carried any fire-arms, and continued whooping and hallooing, and one of them struck the lanthorn with a great stick, and beat out the candle.

The account that the soldiers gave differed not a little. A shot had been fired at them out of a window of St. John's College, and soon after, up came the Vice-Chancellor and several of the gownsmen. The soldiers asked why they fired at them thus ; whereupon one of them answered, 'we can fire for the king as well as you.' In another part of the town the mob seized one of the patrol, who thereupon fired his piece and shot the Mayor's mace-bearer through the hat. One man swore that he had heard the gentlemen of the Constitution Club hallooing out of the windows, and crying out, *A Marlborough, a Marlborough,* while those in the street cried out, *Ormond.*[1]

During the debate on the Mutiny Bill in the following spring, a peer complained of the conduct of the soldiery at Oxford during this riot. An address was moved to the Crown that all papers relating to that affair should be laid before the House. 'A great debate ensued.' The House voted by 65 to 33 that the Heads of the University and the Mayor were in fault, and that the conduct of the Major seemed well justified.

More than thirty years later, on the 23rd of February,

---

[1] The Duke of Ormond had been Chancellor of the University till his flight from the country the year before, on his impeachment for high treason.

1747-48, not two years after the battle of Culloden, there was another Jacobite riot in Oxford. It so happened that on the evening of that day one of the Canons of Windsor, the Rev. R. Blacow, was in Winter's Coffee House in Oxford. He was told that there were in the street at the door of the coffee-house some rioters shouting K—g J—s for ever, Pr— C—s for ever. It is amusing that the loyal Canon cannot bring himself to write such treasonable names in full. There had been that day an entertainment in Balliol College, a very hot-bed of Jacobites, to which had been invited among other out-college guests, Mr. Dawes, Mr. Whitmore, and Mr. Luxmoore. No doubt many a toast had been drunk to the king over the water. The guests, as soon as they left Balliol, had begun their treasonable cries. The Canon hurried into the street, and heard the rioters as they went down High Street not only bless King James and Prince Charles, but also d—n K—g G—e. He boldly laid hold of one of them, but his comrades desired him to let him go. Some of them even pulled off their clothes and struck the Canon. They then went down St. Mary Hall Lane, waving their caps and shouting the most treason-able expressions, where they met two soldiers. The gownsmen, being seven or eight in number, demanded the soldiers' swords, tore the coat of one of them and insisted on both crying King James for ever. The Canon tried to take refuge in Oriel College, for the rioters had now increased to forty in number. Some of them cried, D—n K—g G—e and all his assistants, and cursed the Canon in particular. Mr. Dawes laid hold of him, and then stripping to fight, cried out, 'I am a man who dare say, God bless K—g James[1] the Third, and I tell you my name is Dawes of St. Mary Hall. I am a man of an independent fortune, and therefore afraid of no man.' The Proctor came up at that moment and seized Mr. Dawes, who even when in the Proctor's hands shouted, 'G—d bless my dear K—g J—s.' Mr. Luxmoore made his escape, though the Proctor adjured him to stop by the solemn and peremptory command of *Siste per fidem.*[2]

The Canon called on the Vice-Chancellor and informed him of what he had seen. The Vice-Chancellor said that he was sorry for what had happened, but that nothing could prevent young fellows getting in liquor. He would severely punish them however. They should be delayed a year in taking their degree and they should

---

[1] The Canon in his narrative, sometimes by forgetfulness, gives the name in full.

[2] Note by Canon Blacow. Expulsion is due by statute for running off from the Proctor's *Siste per fidem.*

have an imposition of English to be translated into Latin. The Canon was not satisfied with this and required the Vice-Chancellor as a magistrate to receive his depositions. The Vice-Chancellor refused. 'In consequence of this,' says the Canon, ' the rioters were treated with general respect, and I was, as generally, hissed and insulted.'

Shortly after the riot the Assizes were held, and the Canon laid an account of what had happened before one of the judges. The judge said that he was to dine that afternoon with the Vice-Chancellor and he would talk the matter over with him. The same evening he told the Canon that he had desired the Vice-Chancellor to take the depositions and have the rioters brought before the Grand Jury at once. Nothing, however, was done. News of the riot had, however, reached the Court and messengers were sent down to arrest the three chief rioters. They were brought before the Court of King's Bench on May 6th for drinking the Pretender's health and other disorders, and were admitted to bail. They were tried in the following November. Luxmoore, after an eight-hours' trial, was acquitted. Whitmore and Dawes were found guilty and were sentenced 'To be fined five nobles [1] each ; to suffer two years' imprisonment in the

---

[1] A noble is equal to 6*s.* 8*d.*

King's Bench Prison, and to find securities for their good behaviour for seven years, themselves bound in £500 each, and their sureties in £250 each ; and to walk immediately round Westminster Hall with a libel affixed to their foreheads denoting their crime and sentence, and to ask pardon of the several courts.' The whole sentence was strictly carried out. Steps were taken to put the Vice-Chancellor himself on his trial for refusing to receive the depositions, but the matter was allowed to drop.

It was only a year before this that the University had presented a loyal address to the King on the suppression 'of the most wicked rebellion in favour of a popish pretender,' and had expressed a modest hope that 'the zealous loyalty of the clergy of the Church of England, whose education in part was our care, had its weight on this important occasion.'

The year after the riot Dr. King, the Principal of St. Mary Hall, 'the idol of the Jacobites,' delivered amidst the greatest applause a violent Jacobite speech at the opening of the Radcliffe Library. This speech made a great stir at the time, and even twenty years later John Wilkes, in a letter to the editor of the 'Political Register,' wrote, 'Methinks, Sir, I still hear the seditious shouts of applause given to the pestilent harangues of the late Dr.

King when he vilified our great deliverer, the Duke of Cumberland, and repeated with such energy the treasonable *redeat.*' With scarce an attempt at disguise he had, in a series of eloquent sentences, each of which began with *Redeat,* prayed for the return of the Pretender. The great Hero of Culloden, the Darling of the people, as he was styled, he had, indeed, treated with the greatest contempt.

'Learned men,' he said, 'we may acknowledge to be the pride of their age, the ornament of mankind, and the most illustrious heroes of the world ; and indeed, always to be preferred to those heroes, foreign ones I mean, for our own as is becoming I always except, who delight in the slaughter of mankind and the destruction of cities, and cruelly contrive the ruin of those they govern as well as of others . . . . Shall these pretend to be adored by the people? These expect us Oxonians to adore them, who are inveterate enemies to this celebrated University, whose glory they envy, and to letters themselves which they do not understand?' Dr. King was thinking, no doubt, of the king who cared nothing for 'Bainters and Boets.' 'He who was the first author of moulding an earthen vessel used for the vilest purposes, or of weaving a wicker basket, that man has deserved more from all nations than all the generals (except those who fought for their country like ours, whom on that account I distinguish)—I say than all the generals, emperors, nay conquerors, that now are or ever have been.'

He ends by praising 'our glorious Vice-Chancellor, whom they had accused' only last year at Westminster. A few years later Dr. King made another great speech at Oxford, at which Johnson in his Master's gown, that at his first coming was so new and handsome, clapped his hands till they were sore.

It was Dr. King who with his own hands delivered to Johnson his diploma of Master of Arts. Johnson, in his letter of thanks to the Vice-Chancellor, wrote : 'Ingratus (mihi videar) nisi comitatem qua vir eximius mihi vestri testimonium amoris in manus tradidit, agnoscam et laudem.' Dr. King has left it on record that Johnson was one of the three [1] men whom he had known in his long life, 'who spoke English with that elegance and propriety, that if all they said had been immediately committed to writing, any judge of the English language would have pronounced it an excellent and very beautiful style.'

[1] The other two were Atterbury, the exiled Bishop of Rochester, and Dr. Gower, Provost of Worcester College. Lord Chesterfield moreover says that 'Lord Bolingbroke's most familiar conversations, if taken down in writing, would bear the press without the least correction either as to method or style.'

Oxford for many a year stood as steadily by every-thing that was old as it had stood by the Jacobite's falling cause. The age, as Johnson said, was running mad after innovation. There was little fear lest Oxford should run. It had long ceased even to move. Yet it is strange that it was in Oxford of all places that the great Methodist movement began. Scarcely less strange is it that it was a student of Oxford, who by his 'Wealth of Nations' wrought a far greater change in the world's history than even Methodism with its host of preachers.

The University, as I have shown, did little as a body to encourage learning, still less to restrain idleness. The greater part of the Professors had for many years given up altogether even the pretence of teaching. They had nothing to gain by teaching, as Adam Smith pointed out, for they were secure in the enjoyment of a fixed stipend without the necessity of labour or the apprehension of control. There were, indeed, a few brilliant exceptions. Lowth by his lectures on the Poetry of the Hebrews, and Blackstone by his lectures on the English Constitution and Laws, did something to redeem the University from the reproach that had fallen on her. Lowth was proud of his University, and when Warburton reproached him with his education there, burst out into eloquent praise of his *Alma Mater.* 'I was educated in the University of Oxford. I enjoyed all the advantages, both public and private, which that famous seat of learning so largely affords. I spent many years in that illustrious society, in a well-regulated course of useful discipline and studies, and in the agreeable and improving commerce of gentlemen and of scholars; in a society where emulation without envy, ambition without jealousy, contention without animosity, incited industry and awakened genius; where a liberal pursuit of knowledge and a genuine freedom of thought was raised, encouraged, and pushed forward by example, by commendation, and by authority.'

Lowth was Professor of Poetry, and must have had not a little of the poet's fancy himself. At least we of the present age are bound to think so, who hold that it is a law of nature that where there are no examinations, much more where there are no competitive examinations, there learning cannot flourish. And yet Adam Smith must have studied hard in the seven years he spent at Balliol, for, to quote Dugald Stewart's words, 'How intimately he had once been conversant with the works of the Roman, Greek, French, and Italian poets appeared sufficiently from the hold which they kept of his memory, after all the different occupations and enquiries in which his maturer faculties had been employed.'

Blackstone, who was at Pembroke College only a few years after Johnson left, 'prosecuted his studies,' his biographer tells us, 'with unremitting ardour, and although the classics, and particularly the Greek and Roman poets, were his favourites, they did not entirely engross his attention. Logic, mathematics, and the other sciences were not neglected.' Wesley too studied hard ; and when he was Greek lecturer and moderator of the classes at Lincoln College, presided over six disputations in a week. 'However the students may have profited by them, they were of singular use to the moderator.'

Johnson, in one of his 'Idlers,' speaks of the 'one very powerful incentive to learning' to be found at either of the Universities—'the genius of the place. It is a sort of inspiring deity, which every youth of quick sensibility and ingenuous disposition creates to himself, by reflecting that he is placed under those venerable walls where a Hooker and a Hammond, a Bacon and a Newton, once pursued the same course of science, and from whence they soared to the most elevated heights of literary fame.' He extols, 'the conveniences and opportunities for study which still subsist in them, more than in any other place.' Yet his utterance is uncertain. When he writes that 'the number of learned persons in these celebrated seats is still considerable,' he shows that he looked back to a golden age of learning as well as of loyalty.

This number of the ' Idler' was written but five years after Gibbon had found the potations of the Fellows of his College so dull and deep and seductive, and his tutors and the Vice-Chancellor so forgetful of his religious training. Yet Johnson says, 'English Universities render their students virtuous, at least by excluding all opportunities of vice ; and by teaching them the principles of the Church of England, confirm them in those of true Christianity.'

A letter in the Bodleian Library, entitled 'Advice to a Young Student, by a Tutor,' shows that not all tutors were like the tutors of Magdalen. This letter was published in 1755, but it had been written thirty years earlier, shortly before Johnson entered. The scheme of studies it presents is not therefore merely the scheme of a young man with his Master's gown still fresh, whose requirements are as high as his acquirements are small. It is the scheme drawn up, indeed, by a tutor in his youth, but confirmed by the experience of many years. 'Studies,' he says, ' should be of three kinds. Philosophy, classical learning, and divinity. The mornings and evenings are to be set apart for philosophy ; the afternoons for classics ; while the Sundays and Church holidays are to be given to divinity.' He arranges a course of study for four years, and divides every year into periods of two months. He takes no notice of vacations, as if it were a matter of course that the student should remain at Oxford from the day he matriculates till the day he takes his degree. The whole scheme is so curious that I shall not hesitate to copy it, not giving, however, the list of the books on divinity. Johnson once distinguished between the learning of two different men. One had learning enough for a parson; the other had learning enough not to disgrace a bishop. If the young student read all the books on divinity that his tutor enjoined, he would, I should have thought, have had learning enough not to disgrace even an archbishop. The following is the scheme of his studies in philosophy and the classics.

BOOKS TO BE READ.

FIRST YEAR.

	Philosophical.	*Classical.*
Jan. and Feb.	Wingate's 'Arithmetic'.	Terence.
March and April	Euclid	'Xenophontis Cyri Institutio.'
May and June	Wallis's 'Logic' . .	Tully's 'Epistles.' Phædrus' 'Fables.'

	Philosophical.	*Classical.*
July and Aug.	Euclid	Lucian's 'Select Dialogues.' Theophrastus.
Sept. and Oct.	Salmon's 'Geography' .	Justin. Nepos.
Nov. and Dec.	Keil's 'Trigonometria' .	Dionysius' 'Geography.'

SECOND YEAR.

	Philosophical.	*Classical.*
Jan. and Feb.	Harris' 'Astronomical Dialogues' . . . Keil's 'Astronomy' .	Cambray 'On Eloquence.' Vossius' 'Rhetoric.'
March and April	Locke's 'Human Understanding' . . . Simpson's 'Conic Sections'. . . .	Tully's 'Orations.'
May and June	Milnes' 'Sectiones Conicæ'. . . .	Isocrates. Demosthenes.
July and Aug.	Keil's 'Introduction' .	Cæsar. Sallust.
Sept. and Oct.	Cheyne's 'Philosophical Principles'. . .	Hesiod. Theocritus.
Nov. and Dec.	Bartholin's 'Physics' . Rohaulti's „	Ovid's 'Fasti.' Virgil's 'Eclogues.'

THIRD YEAR.

	Philosophical.	*Classical.*
Jan. and Feb.	Burnet's 'Theory'.	Homeri 'Ilias.'
March and April	Whiston's 'Theory'	Virgil's 'Georgics.' „ 'Æneid.'
May and June	Wells' 'Chronology' Beveridge's „	Sophocles.
July and Aug.	'Ethices Compendium.' Puffendorf's 'Law of Nature'	Horace.
Sept. and Oct.	Puffendorf Grotius 'de Jure Belli'	Euripides.
Nov. and Dec.	Puffendorf Grotius	Juvenal. Persius.

FOURTH YEAR.

	Philosophical.	*Classical.*
Jan. and Feb.	Hutcheson's 'Metaphysics'	Thucydides.
March and April	Newton's 'Optics'.	„
May and June	„ „	Livy.
July and Aug.	Gregory's 'Astronomy'.	„

	Philosophical.	Classical.
Sept. and Oct.	Gregory's 'Astronomy'.	Diogenes Laertius.
Nov. and Dec.	„ „	· Cicero's 'Philosophical Works.'

The student is not to neglect English writers altogether. He is recommended ' to read the best authors, such as Temple, Collier, the "Spectator," and the other writings of Addison.'

It is strange that no book of Plato or Aristotle is to be found in this scheme. They are to be read in his fifth year, after he has taken his Bachelor's degree. Among the authors mentioned is Puffendorf. That he was at this time regularly read at Oxford is shown by a passage in one of Richard West's letters to the poet Gray. 'Adieu!' he says, 'I am going to my tutor's lectures on one Puffendorf, a very jurisprudent author as you shall read on a summer's day.'

West does not rate Oxford learning very highly. He had lately entered Christ Church. 'Consider me,' he writes, 'very seriously here in a strange country, inhabited by things that call themselves Doctors and Masters of Arts ; a country flowing with syllogisms and ale, where Horace and Virgil are equally unknown.' It was in the year 1735 that he thus wrote.

We may wonder if Mr. Bateman were still a tutor there, whom five years before Johnson on enquiry found to be the tutor of highest reputation in all the University. It was his lectures, if we can trust the story, that he used to get second-hand from his friend Taylor till the Christ Church men mocked at his worn-out shoes.

That young men, and young men of fashion, could respect learning even when they were not forced to pass examinations, is shown by an anecdote Horace Walpole told in his old age. He was at Cambridge with Gray from 1735 to 1738. He attended blind Professor Sanderson's mathematical lectures till the Professor honestly said to him, ' Young man, it would be cheating you to take your money; for you never can learn what I am trying to teach you.' ' I was exceedingly mortified,' said Walpole, 'and cried; for being a Prime Minister's son, I had firmly believed all the flattery with which I had been assured that my parts were capable of anything. I paid a private instructor for a year ; but at the year's end was forced to own Sanderson had been in the right.'

While many a student of these old days worked with far greater benefit to himself and with far better results than if he had been teased with a system of examinations, yet it cannot be doubted that the average of work done must have been far below the average of the present day.

The University, as I have shown, exercised no control over the college, and the degree was given as a matter of course when an undergraduate had resided his sixteen terms. Thirteen weeks residence in each year was all that was insisted on, and in the first and last of the four years even this short period might be cut down.

It is clear that at the time when the six Methodists were expelled the examination was a mere farce. Had there been any real examination to be undergone the danger to the Church would have been averted, for men so ignorant could never have taken their degree, and so could never have been ordained. Mr. Blatch, the gentleman of fortune, who had had no school learning, was allowed to stay on, because he had no intention of taking holy orders when he had finished his University course. That he would take his degree at the end of his four years there seemed to be no manner of doubt.

A curious book entitled 'The Ancient and Present State of the University of Oxford,' by Doctor John Ayliffe, Fellow of New College, published in the year 1723, shows what was required by the statutes for each degree. For the degree of Bachelor of Arts a student had first diligently to attend all public lectures. How he was to do this when the Professors had ceased to lecture, is nowhere stated. He had besides 'to do the other

statutable exercise, such as Generals, Juraments, Answer-
ing under Bachelor, &c.'

Generals are disputations on three logical questions,
from one o'clock in the afternoon till three. This exercise
could not be performed till the end of the third year of
residence. After the student had performed this exercise
he was created General or Senior Sophist. When a scholar
was created Senior Sophist, the Master of the Schools,
ascending the rostrum, made a short speech to him in
praise of Aristotle's Logic and exhorted him to the study
of good letters, and thereupon delivered Aristotle's Logic
into his hands.

In each of the remaining terms he was obliged to
dispute once at least. These disputations were called
Juraments, 'from the oath taken at the time of proceeding Bachelor that he had done all the statutable
exercise.'

Besides this he had 'to answer twice at Lent Determinations for an hour and a half under Bachelor . . . .
the respondent sitting opposite to the opponent under
the Bachelor's pew.' When he had fulfilled these requirements he could take his degree.

For the degree of Master of Arts he had ' to solemnly
determine in Lent, to answer at Quodlibet Disputations,
to dispute in Austins, speak two Declamations, and read

six solemn Lectures.' For the management of these Determinations and Disputations certain officers called Collectors were appointed, who were bound 'as soon as admitted to their office to go to their respective Halls and Colleges without any noise or disturbance ; and not to entertain any persons at all with compotations.'

The Collectors in disposing their classes with a view to the Disputations were bound 'to have special regard to persons of more eminent condition and quality, to place them so as they might have the opportunity of praying a Gracious Day.' On a Gracious Day the Disputations lasted only from nine till eleven, instead of from one till five.

'On Ash Wednesday, according to an ancient laudable custom, immediately after the Latin sermon preached to these Determiners there is a bell rings out.' The Deans of the Colleges with their Bachelors thereupon went to 'the Schools.' Three questions in Natural Philosophy were propounded for a discussion between the Dean of each College and each of his Bachelors. But the Bachelor apparently was allowed to answer by deputy, for when a Syllogism was propounded to him 'he thereupon prayed his Aristotle (for so is the senior responding bachelor called)' to answer for him. These Disputations lasted from one o'clock till five, 'when the first Determiner

in each School in the name of the rest surrounding, on
his bended knees ought to return thanks to the Dean and
the Aristotles under a certain form of words.'

These were followed by Disputations on logical questions, which the Bachelors were obliged to defend according to their great master Aristotle.   In Rhetoric, Politics,
and Moral Philosophy everyone was likewise bound to
defend Aristotle and the whole doctrine of the Peripatetics,
under pain that his answer shall not be taken *pro formâ*,
and that he shall be mulcted five shillings *toties quoties*.

All the Bachelors had to attend service at St. Mary's
on the vigil of Palm Sunday, when 'after the end of
prayers the junior Proctor makes a speech, rebuking all
errors committed in point of learning during the Lent,
as well as offences against good manners, especially
tumults, brawlings, and fightings if any shall have happened.'   They had next each to read six solemn lectures
in public without borrowing or transcribing from authors,
but purely of their own composition, and each of these
lectures was to last above half an hour.

They had moreover to go 'a circuiting.'   Mr. Erasmus
Philipps records in his diary : 'April 4.   Went a circuiting with Mr. Collins of our College.   This is an exercise
previous to a Master's Degree.'   A man was said to go a
circuiting when clothed in his proper habit and following

his Dean, bareheaded, with the bedels (or one of them at least) going before him he waited upon the Vice-Chancellor and the Proctors to supplicate their presence at a Congregation the next day that he might be presented for his degree. It was required that the Vice-Chancellor and Proctors should be waited upon on the same day and before the sun set.

They had lastly to dispute on three questions at the next Act or Commemoration as it is now called. Not every Commemoration was in those days a Public Commemoration.

'These academical jubilees,' writes Colley Cibber, 'have usually been looked upon as a kind of congratulatory compliment to the accession of every new Prince to the throne.' They had been more frequently held, however, after the Restoration, though, owing as he thinks to the dissensions of Whigs and Tories, they had again become uncommon.

A company of actors often went down to Oxford on such occasions, and Dryden wrote several of his prologues for the plays that were then performed. The comedians generally acted twice a day. Once quite early in the morning so that the play might be over before the hour of dinner, and once in the afternoon in time for the scholars to get back to their colleges before the great bell of Christ Church rang at nine o'clock for the gates to be shut. The actors found a more highly cultivated audience at Oxford than at London. 'A great deal of that false flashy wit and forced humour, which had been the delight of our Metropolitan multitude was only rated there at its bare intrinsic value.' Shakespeare and Jonson were now reverenced in Oxford as Aristotle once had been. · Addison alone among the play-writers of the day was allowed to have any merit. Thrice was 'Cato' acted during the Commemoration of 1712, and each time before a crowded house.

A great change has, indeed, come over Oxford. Plays are no longer acted during the great summer festival. But the undergraduate who once despised the false, flashy wit and forced humour of the hired actor, has now turned buffoon himself. The students who cannot for one short hour restrain their folly while strangers, men of worth and learning, are having honour done to them by the most venerable of Universities, would not have thronged to see 'Cato' acted, written though it was by one of the most illustrious of the sons of Oxford.

The Commemoration of old was not altogether free from scurrility. It suffered under but one buffoon, and that a licensed buffoon. 'An impudent fellow,' says

Ayliffe, ' of no reputation in himself, called a " Terræ-Filius," was allowed to sport and play with the reputation of others. This manner of sportive wit,' he adds, ' had its first original at the time of the Reformation, when the gross absurdities and superstitions of the Roman Church were to be exposed.' It was no small gain, however, that the Terræ-Filius, whose opponent was one of the pro-Proctors, had to carry on the disputation in Latin.

In the year 1733 a grand public Act was held.[1] Hearne commended the Vice-Chancellor ' for reviving our Acts ' and for excluding the players. But the old Jacobite was indignant that ' one Handel, a foreigner,' was allowed to come with ' his lousy crew—a great num-ber of foreign fiddlers.' Whether Hearne hated them as fiddlers or as Germans is not clear. Perhaps he hated them as both. More than one account is preserved of this Commemoration.

At the Act, whether it was public or was private, those who took the higher degrees, whether Masters or Doctors—inceptors as they were called—had, as I have said, to perform their final exercises. On the previous Saturday, ' in their Act habits, the bedels going before them, they went into all the schools, and by a bedel of each faculty gave an invitation in Latin to the several

[1] See page 42.

readers to be present at the performance of their exercise. They craved, moreover, a benediction of their professors, which they gave accordingly.' Perhaps the benedictions went some way to make up for the lectures which the professors had left off giving. The disputations were carried on in the schools and in the Sheldonian Theatre the following Monday. On that day the Vice-Chancellor, accompanied by the heads of houses, the doctors in their boots and robes, and the other members of the University properly habited, repaired to the theatre, where was a vast concourse of nobility and other persons of distinction of both sexes. There were eighty-four Masters of Arts created. There were besides nine Inceptors in Theology, six in Medicine, two in Law, and one in Philosophy. These had each to discuss three questions against an opponent. The opponents in divinity were mostly the heads of houses. In theology alone, therefore, on that Monday afternoon twenty-seven questions had to be discussed. It is not surprising that in this faculty the disputation lasted from one o'clock till between six and seven. In the other faculties it was finished by five. The following are examples of the questions :—

'An tota christiana fides contineatur in hac simplici propositione, Jesum esse Messiam?'

'An purgatio conveniat in secunda variolarum febre?'

'An ex præsumptionibus de crimine quis sit condem-
nandus?'

'An entium spiritualium proprietates concipiantur
analogice?'

The eighty-four inceptors in Arts had to dispute on
three philosophical questions ; but, happily for the
audience, one of these inceptors was appointed as
respondent for all. At this grand Commemoration of
1733 the Terræ-Filius, though he appeared in his
character, was not allowed to open his mouth. It were
greatly to be wished that the modern Terræ-Filius, with
his hundred mouths, could be silenced whenever it was
thought that buffoonery would be out of place.

It is worth noticing, as a proof of the favour shown
to rank, that of the thirty-five students who took part in
the ' Philological Exercises,' eleven were sons of men of
title. If those who had thus the honour of reciting in
public were fairly chosen, Savage must have been
singularly unjust when, about this time, he wrote his
celebrated line :

Some tenth transmitter of a foolish face.

A great crowd of country people had come to see this
unusual sight. On common occasions they were welcome

enough, but this year the crowd was so great that the gownsmen took it ill. 'They contrived,' said an eye-witness, 'so to place themselves, that as soon as the "Hem!" was given, the country people were set a-going in such a manner, that they trundled one another into the court whilst you could say "Bob Fergeson."' In what age, we may ask, did Jack Robinson begin to flourish? In the evening the Chevalier Handel, 'as some of the company had been but very scramblingly entertained at the disputations, tried how a little fiddling would sit upon them,' and gave a performance of his 'Esther.'

In each college a sumptuous and elegant supper—called the Act Supper—at the equal expense of all the inceptors, was given for the entertainment of the Doctors.

The next morning, all the inceptors being waited upon by the bedels, met at St. Mary's, and after the Litany was over, the bedels still waiting upon them, humbly and reverently presented their offerings at the altar.

There were then fresh disputations in the theatre. The first among the inceptor Masters had a book given him by the Senior Proctor—the Father of the Comitia, as he was styled; and was then by him created a Master

by a kiss and by putting on his cap. Next the Regius
Professor of Divinity addressed the inceptor Doctors.
'When he came to that part which related to their boots,
it was incumbent upon the Proctors to see that he
examined whether they had their boots on. By which is
intimated, some say, that they should be always ready for
the discharge of every part of their duty; others say that
the superior inceptors were allowed to wear upon this
festivity that which they are forbidden by statute to wear
generally, as too proud a fashion for the University.'
From Ayliffe we learn that in the congregation which
was held immediately after the Act, 'at the supplication
of the Doctors and Masters newly created, they are wont
to dispense with the wearing of boots and slop shoes, to
which the Doctors and Masters of the Act are obliged
during the Comitia.' When the Proctors were satisfied
that the Regius Professor of Divinity had properly examined whether the Doctors had their boots on, and
when the degrees had been all conferred, Handel gave a
performance of his new opera 'Athalia' before an
audience of 3,700 persons.

On the last day of the Commemoration, Father
Courayer, who had fled from France about seven years
before on account of a book he had written in defence of
the English ordination, returned thanks in his robes to

the University for the honour it had done him two years
before in presenting him with his degree.

Such was the Grand Public Act, or Commemoration,
of 1733. Johnson, no doubt, had witnessed one Act if
not more, and had seen the solemn procession of Heads
of Houses and Doctors, and had listened to the disputations
of the inceptors in each of the faculties. No Handel
had come in his time, however, nor had one come would
Johnson have cared to hear him. He knew no difference
between tweedle-dum and tweedle-dee.

There is one other scene at which it is likely that
Johnson was at times an attentive listener. The students
in those days were privileged to attend the assize courts,
and largely availed themselves of their privilege. Their
conduct there was anything but seemly.

In most country courts in those days there was, if we
may trust Lovell Edgeworth, not a little noise and confusion. At Oxford the din and interruption were beyond
anything he had ever witnessed. The young men were
not in the least solicitous to preserve decorum, and the
judges were unwilling to be severe upon the students.

Edgeworth says that he was present at a trial for
felony, when the foreman of the jury, who had not heard
the evidence or the summing up, asked him what verdict
he should give. The young student at once stood up to

inform the Judge. 'Sit down, sir,' said the Judge. Edgeworth begged to be heard. The Judge grew angry, and told him that his gown should not protect him. Edgeworth persisted, and the Judge ordered the sheriff to remove him. At last he made the Judge hear him, and 'at once received an apology and a few words of strong approbation.'

I have done my best to bring before my readers Oxford as it was when the rolls of Pembroke College first received the name of Samuel Johnson. I have, I hope, thrown some light also on the University as it was in later years, when the scholar who had been driven forth by poverty and neglect would now have been a welcome and an honoured guest in any of its colleges. It is but little that has been handed down to us of the incidents of his undergraduate days, and to that little I have not been able to add anything. All that was left to me to do was to give a picture of the general life of the students in his time. I have tried to show what were the habits, the feelings, and the tone of thought which, at an age when the character is most strongly affected for good or for evil, were brought to bear on this poor scholar, the story of whose life is, in the words of Lord Macaulay, 'likely to be read as long as the English exists either as a living or a dead language.'

CHAPTER II.

LORD MACAULAY ON JOHNSON.[1]

JOHNSON's character must have had a singular interest for Macaulay, as he has twice described it. The vigorous sketch that he dashed off in the days of his youth for the pages of the 'Edinburgh Review' is doubtless more widely known than the life that he wrote with such exquisite skill when he was now in the fulness of his powers. In the essay we seem to look upon the picture of a Tory painted by a Whig. In the life we have the portrait of one great man drawn by another great man. Even here there are great blemishes and great exaggerations. But, taken as a whole, it is an admirable piece of workmanship. In it Macaulay silently retracts not a few of the gross statements he had made in his earlier writing He no longer holds that 'as soon as Johnson took his

[1] In writing this chapter I have made use of articles contributed by me to the *Times*, September 19, 1874, and the *Pall Mall Gazette*, February 17, 1875.

pen in his hand to write for the public his style became systematically vicious.'　He no longer sneers at ' his constant practice of padding out a sentence with useless epithets till it became as stiff as the bust of an exquisite.' He can now see the beauty and the power of his writings. He thus describes his ' Life of Savage.'　' The little work, with all its faults, was a masterpiece.　No finer specimen of literary biography existed in any language living or dead ; and a discerning critic might have confidently predicted that the author was destined to be the founder of a new school of English eloquence.'

It is a pity that Macaulay had not the justice more openly to own his error.　His Essays are read in every quarter of the world.　They have been sold by thousands and tens of thousands, and wherever they are read there a grievous wrong is done to the memory of Johnson.　We remember how the old man, when he was ill, begged Miss Burney ' to stand by him and support him, and not hear him abused when he was no more and could not defend himself.'

Few people have memory enough, or judgment enough if they have the memory, to compare different accounts of the same man.　However inconsistent the accounts may be, they accept both as true, and remember in each that only which best fixes itself in the memory.

It may seem almost a hopeless matter to struggle against Macaulay's powerful mind and brilliant style. 'There is no appeal against character,' said Lord Chesterfield. Certainly there is very little hope of appeal against any character Macaulay has drawn. Yet the misstatements of which he is guilty are so gross that, if truth has the power that is commonly assigned to her, she ought to prevail.

It is doubly important now and then to examine with great minuteness some one or two of the almost countless likenesses that Macaulay has drawn. There is no man living who could follow him in all the width of his reading, and through all the stores of learning displayed by his powerful and ready memory. There are many men who can rival him, and even go beyond him, in the knowledge of some among the books and men and periods that he has described. Such men can test the accuracy of his workmanship on one point, and can thereby infer how far he is to be trusted in cases where they have not their own previous knowledge by which to judge, but only his statements on which to rely. I have in more than one case followed in his steps with no little labour and care. The result has been that, much as I wonder at his vast and varied gifts, I have, like many others, come to distrust the truthfulness of the characters he has so vigorously drawn. The first thing he aimed at was brilliancy, and to brilliancy he was not unwilling to make some sacrifice of truth. A hasty saying which was, perhaps, forgotten by the speaker almost as soon as uttered; a hasty action, which was quickly regretted and never repeated, are turned by him into the habits of a lifetime. Gibbon has justly censured the historian of the reign of the Emperor Justinian, by whom ' the partial injustice of a moment is dexterously applied as the general maxim of a reign of thirty-two years.' I shall have, in another chapter, to show in the case of Boswell how open Macaulay is to the same kind of censure. I shall now confine myself to his treatment of Johnson. I should weary my readers' attention if I were to point out all the errors into which he has fallen, and all the misstatements which he has made. I shall content myself with examining some—but only some —of those which are of the most importance. I shall try, moreover, to show one side of Johnson's character, which, neither in Macaulay nor in any other of his biographers, is seen with any fulness, and I shall end by attempting to prove that Johnson was a far happier man than is commonly supposed.

The character that Macaulay gives of Johnson might have been founded on a passage in one of Horace Walpole's letters, just as the character he gives of Boswell would seem to have been founded on a criticism by Gray.

Walpole writing[1] of 'Boswell's most absurd enormous book,'[2] which had just been published, says, 'The more one learns of Johnson, the more preposterous assemblage he appears of strong sense, of the lowest bigotry and prejudices, of pride, brutality, fretfulness, and vanity.' Macaulay says, 'the characteristic peculiarity of his intellect was the union of great powers with low prejudices.' In writing of that curious though quite intelligible mixture of credulity and incredulity which characterized Johnson, he says, 'Johnson was in the habit of sifting with extreme severity the evidence for all stories which were merely odd. But when they were not only odd but miraculous, his severity relaxed. He began to be credulous precisely at the point where the most credulous people begin to be sceptical. . . . He once said, half jestingly we suppose, that for six months he refused to credit the fact of the earthquake at Lisbon, and that he still believed the extent of the calamity to be greatly exaggerated. Yet he related with a grave face how old Mr. Cave of St. John's-gate saw a ghost, and how this ghost was something of a shadowy being. He

---

[1] *Letter to the Hon. H. S. Conway,* October 6, 1785. I am not sure if this letter had been published at the time when Macaulay wrote his review.

[2] *Journal of the Tour to the Highlands and Islands of Scotland.*

went himself on a ghost-hunt to Cock-lane, and was angry with John Wesley for not following up another scent of the same kind with proper spirit and perseverance.'

Now, before I consider the misrepresentations contained in the last two paragraphs, I will first examine into Johnson's general belief in apparitions. Boswell, in writing about the appearance of departed spirits, states that it is 'a doctrine which it is a mistake to suppose that Johnson himself ever positively held.' Johnson himself said, in speaking of apparitions, 'A total disbelief of them is adverse to the opinion of the existence of the soul between death and the last day ; the question simply is whether departed spirits ever have the power of making themselves perceptible to us. A man who thinks he has seen an apparition can only be convinced himself; his authority will not convince another, and his conviction, if rational, must be founded on being told something which cannot be known but by supernatural means.' In another passage he said, in considering whether there had ever been an instance of the spirit of any person appearing after death, 'All argument is against it, but all belief is for it.' In fact, his state of mind was not an unnatural one for a man who had a firm belief in another world. If we have any existence after death, it is surely only negative evidence which can disprove the existence of apparitions. If we still exist somewhere after death, there is no *à priori* impossibility of our existing on the earth. Johnson, indeed, was certainly likely to have admitted general evidence in proof of the appearance of a ghost which many men would have at once and rightly rejected. When, however, there was a possibility of testing any particular piece of evidence, he would have been the first to sift it with the utmost severity. This, indeed, he wanted John Wesley to do; and he was angry with him, not for not following up the scent with proper spirit and perseverance, as Macaulay says, but for believing in a ghost story without proper grounds. It is necessary to quote the whole passage from Boswell, so that my readers may see how strangely Macaulay has perverted it :—'Of John Wesley he said, "He can talk well on any subject." *Boswell* : " Pray, sir, what has he made of his story of a ghost?" *Johnson* : "Why, sir, he believes it, but not on sufficient authority. He did not take time enough to examine the girl. It was at Newcastle where the ghost was said to have appeared to a young woman several times, mentioning something about the right to an old house ; advising application to be made to an attorney, which was done ; and at the same time saying the attorney would do nothing, which proved to be the fact. 'This,' says John, 'is a proof that a ghost knows our thoughts.' Now (laughing) it is not necessary to know our thoughts to tell that an attorney will sometimes do nothing. Charles Wesley, who is a more stationary man, does not believe the story. I am sorry that John did not take more pains to enquire into the evidence for it." Miss Seward (with an incredulous smile) : "What, sir, about a ghost!" Johnson (with solemn vehemence) : "Yes, madam. This is a question which, after five thousand years, is yet undecided; a question, whether in theology or philosophy, one of the most important that can come before the human understanding."' We may, indeed, wonder that a man of Johnson's vigorous intellect should have refused to accept the general evidence against apparitions, which was strong enough even in his day. In the case of John Wesley's ghost, however, he was anything but credulous. In fact, as is shown by another passage, it was Boswell, and not Johnson, who wanted to follow up the scent. Boswell says, ' Mr. Wesley believed it, but Johnson did not give it credit. I was, however, desirous to examine the question closely.'

The account Macaulay gives of the ghost that Cave was said to have seen, though not so inaccurate, is still not fair. Boswell writes : 'Talking of ghosts, he said he knew one friend who was an honest man and a sensible man, who told him he had seen a ghost ; old Mr. Edward Cave, the printer at St. John's Gate. He said Mr. Cave did not like to talk of it, and seemed to be in great horror whenever it was mentioned. *Boswell* : " Pray Sir, what did he say was the appearance?" *Johnson* : " Why, Sir, something, of a shadowy being."' Macaulay says, ' he related with a grave face how old Mr. Cave saw a ghost.' Of the gravity of his face we are told nothing, but what he related was not what old Mr. Cave saw, but what old Mr. Cave said he saw. Well might Johnson say, ' Accustom your children constantly to a strict attention to truth, even in the most minute particulars ; if a thing happened at one window, and they, when relating it, say that it happened at another, do not let it pass, but instantly check them ; you do not know where deviation from truth will end.' As for the Cock-lane ghost, Johnson scarcely deserves more reproach than did Faraday when he took the trouble to expose the folly of table-turning. He thought, indeed, that it was possible for a ghost to appear in Cock-lane as anywhere else, while Faraday, from the beginning, saw through the modern absurdity. Johnson examined into the facts of the case and exposed the whole imposture in an account which he wrote for the *Gentleman's Magazine.* Later on, 'he expressed,' writes Boswell, 'great indignation at the imposture of the Cock-lane ghost, and related, with much satisfaction, how he had assisted in detecting the cheat, and had published an account of it in the newspapers.'

Scarcely less unfair is Macaulay when he says that Johnson 'declares himself willing to believe the stories of the second sight.' Johnson when he went to the Highlands, resolved to examine the question of the second sight. 'Of an opinion,' he writes, 'received for centuries by a whole nation, and supposed to be confirmed through its whole descent by a series of successive facts, it is desirable that the truth should be established or the fallacy detected.' He found that 'the islanders of all degrees, whether of rank or understanding, universally admitted it, except the ministers.' He enquired into the question as far as he was able, but ends by saying, 'I never could advance my curiosity to conviction; but came away at last only willing to believe.' Is this the habit of mind of a man who 'begins to be credulous precisely at the point where the most credulous people begin to be sceptical?' A superstitious man always believes what he is willing to believe, and advances his curiosity to conviction just as fast as his wishes lead him. His judgment says to his inclination, 'I believe. Help thou my unbelief,' and his inclination at once renders the required aid. Johnson no doubt longed to find, as one who knew him said, 'some positive proof of communication with another world.' With all his faith in the immortality of the soul, there can be little doubt that he would have eagerly welcomed any further proof. Had his faith, indeed, been as free from all doubts as that of many men, it is not likely that he would have so fiercely resented any attempt, however slight, to question the evidences of Christianity. 'Every man,' he once said, 'who attacks my belief diminishes in some degree my confidence in it, and therefore makes me uneasy ; and I am angry with him who makes me uneasy.' It was this strong desire to add one more prop to his belief that made him willing to believe in the appearance of spirits and second sight. But as I have said, whenever he came in each case to look into the evidence, his reason was too powerful to suffer any indulgence to be shown to his desires.

To pass to another of his 'low prejudices.' 'It is remarkable,' Macaulay writes, 'that to the last Johnson entertained a fixed contempt for all those modes of life and those studies which tend to emancipate the mind from the prejudices of a particular age or a particular nation. Of foreign travel and of history he spoke with the fierce and boisterous contempt of ignorance. "What does a man learn by travelling? Is Beauclerk the better for travelling? What did Lord Charlemont learn in his travels, except that there was a snake in one of the pyramids of Egypt?"' Any one reading this passage and seeing the inverted commas would at once believe that he was reading Johnson's own words. He is really reading but an abridgment of them, and an abridgment in which the sense has been greatly altered. I must again give his words as reported by Boswell :—

' "Time may be employed to more advantage from nineteen to twenty-four almost in any way than travelling. When you set travelling against mere negation, against doing nothing, it is better to be sure ; but how much more would a young man improve were he to study during those years ! Indeed, if a young man is wild, and must run after bad company, it is better this should be done abroad, as. on his return, he can break off such connections, and begin at home a new man, with a character to form and acquaintance to make. How little does travelling supply to the conversation of any man who has travelled ! how little to Beauclerk !" *Boswell* : "What say you to Lord —— (Charlemont) ?" *Johnson* : "I never but once heard him talk of what he had seen, and that was of a ·large serpent in one of the pyramids of Egypt." *Boswell* : " Well, I happened to hear him tell the same thing, which made me mention him." ' Croker adds in a note, ' His lordship was, to the last, in the habit of telling this story rather too often.'

Johnson, in this passage, does not condemn travelling in general. He says, and most men would agree with him, that the years between nineteen and twenty-four should not be spent, as was in his time so commonly the case, in mere travelling. He goes on to say that good talkers who have travelled talk little the better because they have travelled. But it is not needful to enlarge on the way in which his meaning has been wrested. It is open to every one to see. So far from having a fierce and boisterous contempt of travel, Johnson had very early shown a great eagerness for it and this eagerness lasted till old age. When he was an undergraduate at Pembroke he was, as my readers will remember, overheard saying to himself, ' Well, I have a mind to see what is done in other places of learning. I'll go and visit the universities abroad. I'll go to France and Italy. I'll go to Padua. And I'll mind my business. For an Athenian blockhead is the worst of all blockheads.' It was not till he was an old man that he could afford to gratify this eagerness.

The tour to the Hebrides was a greater undertaking than a tour to Iceland in the present day, and he was sixty-four when he set out on it. 'On our return to Edinburgh,' says Boswell, 'everybody accosted us with some studied compliment,' while Robertson advanced to Dr. Johnson repeating a line of Virgil. 'I am really ashamed,' said Johnson, 'of the congratulations which we receive. We are addressed as if we had made a voyage to Nova Zembla and suffered five persecutions in Japan.' In his sixty-eighth year he was eager for a trip to the Baltic. He writes: 'Boswell shrinks from the Baltic expedition, which, I think, is the best scheme in our power. What we shall substitute, I know not. He wants to see Wales; but, except the woods of Bachycraigh, what is there in Wales that can fill the hunger of ignorance or quench the thirst of curiosity?' He had been the year before full of eagerness for a tour to Italy with the Thrales. He said, 'Mr. Thrale is to go by my advice to Mr. Jackson (the all-knowing), and get from him a plan for seeing the most that can be seen in the time that we have to travel. We must, to be sure, see Rome, Naples, Florence, and Venice, and as much more as we can. (Speaking with a tone of animation.)' The tour was put off. Boswell goes on to say: 'He said, "I am disappointed, to be sure; but it is not a great disappointment." I wondered to see him bear with a philosophical calmness what would have made most people peevish and fretful. I perceived that he had so warmly cherished the hope of enjoying classical scenes that he could not easily part with the scheme; for he said, "I shall probably contrive to get to Italy some other way."' Later on, in a letter to Mrs. Thrale, he says, 'I hope you have no design of stealing away to Italy before the election; nor of leaving me behind you; though I am not only seventy, but seventy-one.'

On another occasion Boswell says: 'He talked with an uncommon animation of travelling into distant countries; that the mind was enlarged by it, and that an acquisition of dignity of character was derived from it. He expressed a particular enthusiasm with respect to visiting the wall of China. I catched it for the moment, and said I really believed I should go and see the wall of China had I not children, of whom it was my duty to take care. "Sir," said he, "by doing so, you would do what would be of importance in raising your children to eminence. There would be a lustre reflected upon them from your spirit and curiosity. They would be at all times regarded as the children of a man who had gone to view the wall of China. I am serious, Sir."'

Johnson's manners, if we are to trust Macaulay, were almost savage. 'His active benevolence,' he says, 'contrasted with the constant rudeness and the occasional ferocity of his manners in society. . . . For the suffering which a harsh word inflicts upon a delicate mind he had no pity ; for it was a kind of suffering which he could scarcely conceive.' Mr. Carlyle, in a few pages, has most nobly and beautifully vindicated Johnson's claim to ' a merciful, tenderly affectionate nature.' It is rather, however, with the greater matters that he has dealt. I shall attempt to show that in smaller matters also Macaulay has not done Johnson justice.

There is no doubt that though his tenderness of heart was always great, yet his manners in the last twenty years of his life were not a little softened. He never complained of the world, yet for many a year he must have felt that his labour was shamefully underpaid. A sense of injustice—the sight, ever before the eyes, of the unworthy idler getting filled with good things while the worthy labourer is sent empty away—does not sweeten the temper or soften the manners. Even at this time of his life, however, he was far from deserving the harsh judgment that Macaulay has passed on him. But when his modest pension had put an end to that struggle with poverty which, without a moment's breathing space, he had carried on for more than thirty years ; still more, when the Thrales had made their house his home, a change came over him. As he himself said,

'In my younger days, it is true, I was much inclined to treat mankind with asperity and contempt, but I found it answered no good end. I thought it wiser and better to take the world as it goes. Besides, as I have advanced in life, I have had more reason to be satisfied with it. Mankind have treated me with more kindness, and of course I have more kindness for them.'

Madame Piozzi herself, on whom Macaulay has largely drawn, says, 'I saw Mr. Johnson in none but a tranquil, uniform state, passing the evening of his life among friends who loved, honoured, and admired him.' Her words must not be pressed too closely, for beyond a doubt she was more than once a witness of violent outbursts of temper. Nevertheless, her testimony is clear. She made Johnson's acquaintance when he was fifty-five years old. 'It should seem,' writes Macaulay, 'that a full half of Johnson's life, during about sixteen years, was passed under the roof of the Thrales.' The tranquil, uniform state in which he lived for so many years contrasts curiously with the manners that were 'almost savage' and the constant rudeness which are laid to his charge. When he was rude, even when he was violent, there was so much 'method in his madness,' such wit, such humour, that these outbursts of passion were never forgotten. Other men are violent and silly; he was violent, and kept his wits more than ever about him. The wit of his rudeness passed from mouth to mouth, while the gentleness of his every-day life afforded no matter for talk, and so was scarcely known beyond his friends.

How tranquil he commonly was, at all events in his later years, there is other evidence besides that of Madame Piozzi to show. Boswell says, 'that by much the greatest part of his time he was civil, obliging, nay, polite in the true sense of the word ; so much so that many gentlemen who were long acquainted with him never received or even heard a strong expression from him.'

This is confirmed by the statement of Mr. Barclay (Mr. Thrale's successor in the brewery), who had seen not a little of Johnson, and who said that he 'had never observed any rudeness or violence on his part.' 'Few men,' said Miss Reynolds, who had known Johnson in the days of his greatest poverty, 'in his ordinary disposition or common frame of mind could be more inoffensive than Dr. Johnson. . . . Peace and goodwill towards man were the natural emanations of his heart.'

Miss Burney was present at one of the outbursts of temper. 'He had,' she said, 'been long provoked, and justly enough.' Yet 'he did, to own the truth, appear unreasonably furious and grossly severe.' She adds, ' I never saw him so before, and I heartily hope I never shall again.' But by this time she had known him at least five years, and she had known him most intimately for no less than three years. She had spent a great deal of time with him at Streatham. Yet this was the first violent outburst that she has recorded. Towards her he was all gentleness and tenderness. She came to him, indeed, ready to love him from the affection her father bore him. He has recorded 'the politeness and urbanity' that Johnson showed him when he was young and un-known—'politeness and urbanity,' he says, 'which may be opposed to some of the stories which have been lately circulated of his natural rudeness and ferocity.' When Dr. Burney's daughters first met Johnson, and were amazed at his figure and his habits, they asked their father why he had not prepared them 'for such uncouth, untoward strangeness, he laughed heartily, and said he had entirely forgotten that the same impression had been at first made upon himself, but had been lost even on the second interview.'

Miss Burney is never tired of recording his kindness to her. He once met her at dinner, when he was suffer-ing greatly. He was little apt to complain, but he said more than once, 'Ah! you little know how ill I, am.' 'Yet he was,' she says, 'excessively kind to me in spite of all his pain.' In her diary are to be found such records as the following : 'The dear Dr. Johnson was more pleased, more kind, and more delightful than ever.' 'He was charming both in spirits and in humour. I really think he grows gayer and gayer daily, and more ductile and pleasant.' 'He was, if possible, more instructive, entertaining, good-humoured, and exquisitely fertile than ever.' Those who can be charged with either constant rudeness or anything like savageness of manners are rude and savage above all to the weak. But Miss Burney says, 'He was always indulgent to the young, he never attacked the unassuming, nor meant to terrify the diffident.' He himself said that he looked upon himself as 'a very polite man;' and, indeed, to anyone who would look below the surface he had 'the noble universal politeness of a man that knows the dignity of men and feels his own.'[1] But his politeness was seen also by those who in such matters did not look deep.

Boswell, in recording Johnson's first introduction to Mrs. Boswell, writes, 'as no man could be more polite when he chose to be so, his address to her was most courteous and engaging.' 'When Dr. Johnson,' says Madame Piozzi, 'had a mind to compliment any one, he did it with more dignity to himself and better effect upon

[1] Mr. Carlyle. Boswell's *Life of Johnson.*

the company than any man.' So far from being indifferent to politeness, he had a great regard for it. 'He did not much like any of the contrivances by which ease has been lately introduced into society instead of ceremony.' When he entered a room and 'everybody rose to do him honour, he returned the attention with the most formal courtesy.' When any lady visited him he would, even in his old age, whatever was the state of the weather, attend her down a very long entry to her coach. The character Macaulay gives of him is after all only an expansion and an exaggeration of a comical speech by some Irish gentleman whom Miss Burney met. 'Dr. Johnson is not much of a fine gentleman, indeed ; but a clever fellow—a deal of knowledge—got a deuced good understanding.'

Nothing was farther from the truth than Macaulay's statement that 'for the suffering which a harsh word inflicts upon a delicate mind he had no pity ; for it was a kind of suffering which he could scarcely conceive.' He himself said in Miss Burney's presence that he was always sorry when he made bitter speeches, and never did it but when he was insufferably vexed. Mr. Murphy bears witness to the truthfulness of this statement. 'When the fray was over he generally softened into repentance, and by conciliating measures took care that no animosity should be left rankling in the breast of his antagonist.' Of this defect he seems to have been conscious.   In a letter to Mrs. Thrale he says, 'Poor Baretti ! do not quarrel with him ; to neglect him a little will be sufficient.   He means only to be frank and manly and independent, and perhaps, as you say, a little wise.   Forgive him, dearest lady, the rather, because of his misbehaviour I am afraid he learned part from me. I hope to set him hereafter a better example.'

Miss Burney records how on one occasion, ' when he was pursuing an antagonist with unabating vigour and dexterity, recollecting himself, and thinking, as he owned afterwards, that the dispute grew too serious, with a skill all his own, he suddenly and unexpectedly turned it to burlesque.'

One evening when he had treated Goldsmith with rudeness he noticed that he was sitting silently, brooding over his reprimand.   ' He said aside to some of us—" I'll make Goldsmith forgive me," and then called to him in a loud voice, "Dr. Goldsmith, something passed to-day where you and I dined : I ask your pardon." Goldsmith answered placidly, "It must be much from you, Sir, that I take ill."'

Even more strongly did he show his sorrow for his rude treatment of Dean Bernard.   He had told him at a dinner-table that in his character there was great room for improvement. He soon followed the ladies into the drawing room, leaving the dean still at table. 'Sitting down by the lady of the house, he said, " I am very sorry for having spoken so rudely to the dean .... and I am the more hurt on reflecting with what mild dignity he received it." When the dean came up into the drawing room, Dr. Johnson immediately rose from his seat, and made him sit on the sofa by him, and with such a beseeching look for pardon and with such fond gestures .—literally smoothing down his arms and knees—tokens of penitence which were so graciously received by the dean as to make Dr. Johnson very happy.'

'One evening in the drawing room at Streatham, a young gentleman,' says Madame Piozzi, called to him suddenly, and I suppose he thought disrespectfully, in these words : 'Mr. Johnson, would you advise me to marry?' 'I would advise no man to marry, sir, (returns for answer in a very angry tone Dr. Johnson), who is not likely to propagate understanding,' and so left the room. Our companion looked confounded, and, I believe, had scarce recovered the consciousness of his own existence, when Johnson came back, and drawing his chair among us, with altered looks and a softened voice, joined in the general chat, insensibly led the conversation to the subject of marriage, where he laid himself out in a dissertation so useful, so elegant, so founded on the true knowledge of human life . . . . that no one ever recollected the offence, except to rejoice in its consequences.'

It would be easy to bring forward other instances to prove that Johnson could both conceive the suffering which he had inflicted by a harsh word, and had not only pity for it, but was ready to do all he could to make amends. Macaulay in one passage shows how little he understood the real tenderness of Johnson's nature. He is talking of the school he had started in Staffordshire. 'His appearance,' he writes, 'was so strange, and his temper so violent, that his school-room must have resembled an ogre's den.' Johnson would, no doubt, have often been irritable, but that he could have ever been violent to the boys in his charge, I greatly doubt. He had suffered himself under a master who was what he called 'wrong-headedly severe,' and though his discipline would have been strict, yet he would never have been cruel or unjust.

His love of little children was, as Boswell says, great. He used to show it 'upon all occasions, calling them "pretty dears," and giving them sweetmeats.' Madame Piozzi says that 'he was exceedingly disposed to the general indulgence of children, and was even scrupulously and ceremoniously attentive not to offend them : he had strongly persuaded himself of the difficulty people always find to erase early impressions, either of kindness or resentment, and said, 'he should never have so loved his mother when a man, had she not given him coffee she could ill afford, to gratify his appetite when a boy.' 'If you had had children, sir,' said I, 'would you have taught them anything?' 'I hope,' replied he, 'that I should have willingly lived on bread and water to obtain instruction for them; but I would not have set their future friendship to hazard for the sake of thrusting into their heads knowledge of things for which they might not perhaps have either taste or necessity. You teach your daughters the diameters of the planets, and wonder when you have done that they do not delight in your company.' Madame Piozzi further says that ' the re-membrance of what had passed in his own childhood made Mr. Johnson very solicitous to preserve the felicity of children ; and when he had persuaded Dr. Sumner to remit the tasks usually given to fill up boys' time during the holidays, he rejoiced exceedingly, and told me that he had never ceased representing to all the eminent school-masters in England the absurd tryanny of poisoning the hour of permitted pleasure by keeping future misery before the children's eyes.'

On one occasion hearing that Dr. Burney, with whom he was at that time by no means intimate, was going to Winchester to place his youngest son in the college, he at once 'offered to accompany the father to Winchester that he might himself present the son to the head master.' The offer was gratefully accepted. His tenderness to poor children was very touchingly shown. 'As he returned to his lodging, at one or two o'clock in the morning, he often saw poor children asleep on thresholds and stalls, and he used to put pennies into their hands to buy them a breakfast.' This he did, as Mr. Croker has pointed out, 'at a time when he himself was living on pennies.' Certainly he would have made one of the strangest ogres that children have ever seen.

'Want of tenderness Johnson always alleged was want of parts, and was no less a proof of stupidity than depravity.' Benevolence, any amount of benevolence, Macaulay would have allowed him, but very little tenderness. And yet it would be easy to multiply the instances I have already adduced, that beneath the rough outside there was a heart almost tremulous with sensibility. Of his friend Dr. Bathurst 'he hardly ever spoke without tears in his life.' Speaking of Dr. Hodges, who, 'during the whole time of the plague continued in London, administering medical assistance, he used to relate with tears in his eyes how he was suffered to die for debt in a gaol.' One day a lady who was travelling in a post-chaise with him, and was relating to him some story of sadness, 'heard him heave heavy sighs and sobs, and turning round she saw his dear face bathed in tears.' Once with pretended sharpness he reproved Hannah More for reading 'Les Pensées de Pascal.' 'I was beginning to stand upon my defence, when he took me with both hands, and with a tear running down his cheeks, "Child," said he, with the most affecting earnestness, "I am heartily glad that you read pious books by whomsoever they may be written."' How strikingly was his consideration for the feelings of others shown when he always went himself to buy food for his sick cat, and would not send his man-servant, the negro Frank, that the man's 'delicacy might not be hurt at seeing himself employed for the convenience of a quadruped.'

Besides this tenderness there was a liveliness, a comicality, we might even say a joviality in Johnson's character which is not at all shown in the pages of Macaulay, and but little even in those of Boswell. It was at Streatham that this side of his character was most shown, and of the life at Streatham Boswell knew very little. He did his best to get an account of it, but he failed. He went down to Windsor and asked Miss Burney for her help.

' My help?' said Miss Burney.

' Yes, Madam; you must give me some of your choice little notes of the Doctor's; we have seen him long enough upon stilts; I want to show him in a new light. Grave Sam, and great Sam, and solemn Sam, and learned Sam—all these he has appeared over and over. Now I want to entwine a wreath of the Graces across his brow; I want to show him as gay Sam, agreeable Sam, pleasant Sam; so you must help me with some of his beautiful billets to yourself.'

It was a pity that Miss Burney would not yield, for the notes she could have given Boswell would, when worked into ' The Life,' have thrown a great light on Johnson's character. The scenes that she describes at Streatham show Johnson in his happiest mood. The days, indeed, did come when she had ' long and melancholy discourses with him about our dear deceased master whom, indeed, he regrets incessantly;' but while Thrale still lived—Thrale whose face for fifteen years had never been turned upon him but with respect or benignity— she had had little but lively scenes and lively talk to record. Her letters and her diary bear her out to the full when she writes that ' Dr. Johnson has more fun and comical humour and love of nonsense about him that almost anybody I ever saw.' The humour of ' Evelina ' had tickled him greatly, and he played upon the characters in a most amusing manner. 'He got those incomparable Branghtons quite by heart, and recited scene after scene of their squabbles and selfishness and forwardness, till he quite shook his sides with laughter. He got into such high spirits that he set about personating Mr. Smith himself. We all thought we must have died no other death than that of suffocation, in seeing Dr. Johnson handing about anything he could catch or snatch at, and making smirking bows, saying he was all for the ladies—everything that was agreeable to the ladies, &c., "except," says he, "going to church with them; and as to that, though marriage, to be sure, is all in all to the ladies, marriage to a man—is the devil."' The reader who does not know him in this happy state must first read 'Evelina,' and next the first two volumes of Madame d'Arblay's 'Diary.' In reading these books he will certainly maintain that Johnson was in one instance wrong when he asserted that 'the progress which the understanding makes through a book has more pain than pleasure in it.'

In the society of women of quick understandings and pleasant manners he was seen in his liveliest moods; and of their society he never tired. He once went to a party at Miss Monckton's house, about the time when Mrs. Siddons was becoming famous. 'How

these people talk of Mrs. Siddons !' said the Doctor.
'I came hither in full expectation of hearing no name
but the name I love and pant to hear,—when from one
corner to another they are talking of that jade Mrs. Siddons; till at last wearied out I went yonder into a corner
and repeated to myself Burney ! Burney ! Burney !
Burney !' 'Ay Sir,' said Mr. Metcalfe, 'You should have
carved it upon the trees.'   'Sir, had there been any trees,
so I should, but, being none, I was content to carve it
upon my heart.'

Hannah More's 'Memoirs' tell of the same liveliness.
One evening she and Johnson had 'a violent quarrel till
at length laughter ran so high on all sides that argument
was confounded in noise ; the gallant youth at one o'clock
in the morning set us down at our lodgings.'   Another
time she writes, 'I have got the headache to-day, by
raking out so late with that gay libertine Johnson.'
According to Madame Piozzi, Mr. Murphy, who was no
bad judge, 'always said Johnson was incomparable at
buffoonery ; and I verily think if he had had good eyes,
and a form less inflexible, he would have made an
admirable mimic.'

Even in his earlier days when life went very hard with
him, there was the same liveliness in him, though it was
not so often called forth.   In the winter of 1749 he formed

a club that met in Ivy Lane every Tuesday evening. 'Thither he constantly resorted, and,' says the surly 'unclubable' Hawkins, who was one of the members, 'he had a disposition to please and be pleased.' 'In the talent of humour,' Hawkins adds, 'there hardly ever was his equal, except perhaps among the old comedians, such as Tarleton, and a few others mentioned by Cibber. By means of this he was enabled to give to any relation that required it the graces and aids of expression, and to discriminate with the nicest exactness the characters of those whom it concerned.' He drank nothing but lemonade, but 'in a short time after assembling he was transformed into a new creature.'

One morning at Streatham everyone had been urging Miss Burney to write a comedy. 'While Mrs. Thrale was in the midst of her flattering persuasions the Doctor, see-sawing in his chair, began laughing to himself so heartily as to almost shake his seat as well as his sides. We stopped our confabulation, in which he had ceased to join, hoping he would reveal the subject of his mirth ; but he enjoyed it inwardly without heeding our curiosity —till at last he said he had been struck with a notion that Miss Burney would begin her dramatic career by writing a piece called "Streatham." He paused and laughed yet more cordially, and then suddenly commanded a

pomposity to his countenance and his voice, and added
—"Yes ! Streatham, a Farce."' It is pleasant to think
that had the farce been written, the old man now in his
seventieth year, whose life, to use his own words, had
been 'radically wretched,' would nevertheless have most
naturally found in it his place by his mirthfulness.

To Johnson's powers of conversation Macaulay does
full justice. He quotes the observation of Mr. Burke that
Johnson appears far greater in Boswell's books than in his
own.   Great though he there appears, we must remember
that that talk of his which has been handed down to us
is the merest fragment of the great utterances of his long
life. Of the seventy-five years that Johnson lived, he and
Boswell spent not above two years and a quarter in the
same neighbourhood.   If we exclude the time they were
together in the tour to the Hebrides, which does not, of
course, fall within the 'Life,' during scarcely two years in
all were they within reach of each other.   In these two
years there were very many days, even some weeks, in
which they did not meet, and often when they did meet,
Boswell did not make the effort to record what was said.
Then, too, Johnson was in his fifty-fourth year when
Boswell first met him.   He was already, at that time, the
most powerful talker, if not that the world has ever known
—at least that the world is ever likely to know of.   It

would be absurd, of course, to compare Johnson's genius
with Shakespeare's, and yet he talks as well as some of
the best of Shakespeare's characters. ' He wrote, indeed,
well ; though not so well as the men of his own age
thought. Yet it would be difficult to find a better
written biography than the 'Life of Savage.' His
letters, too, are written with simplicity and admirable
force.

It is not in his writings, however, but in his talk, that
Johnson lives. It is his lost talk that we regret more
than a decade of Livy, or a library of Cyclic poets. It is
sad to think that a man who talked so much, so wisely,
and so well, should have been ever reproaching himself
with his indolence and his waste of time. Like Socrates,
he taught by talking ; and so long as he talked, neither in
his own mind, nor in his listeners, was there any indolence. Doubtless he was not aware of all the influence
he had on the men of his own time by his conversation ;
far less, of course, could he have looked forward to the
influence he should have on men as yet unborn. He
knew that Boswell kept notes of what he said, and meant
to write his life ; but he did not know how fully those
notes would prove to have been kept, and how admirably
the Life was to be written. He showed on one occasion how many more he thought he should reach by his

writings than by his talk, when he likened himself to a physician, who, after he had practised long in a great city, retires to a small town, and takes less practice. 'Now, Sir, the good I can do by my conversation bears the same proportion to the good I can do by my writings that the practice of a physician, retired to a town, does to his practice in a great city.' Had he known how vast an audience his strong, wholesome conversation was to reach, he would have seen that if, according to the monkish saying, toiling is praying, so in some cases talking is toiling.

The more familiar we are with Boswell, the more are we convinced that Johnson was a far happier man, at all events, in his latter days, than is commonly thought. Mr. Forster has shown in his 'Life of Goldsmith' how strong a cast is given by Boswell to one side of Johnson's character. The melancholy that undoubtedly existed in his hero's temperament is also, we have little doubt, brought too much into the foreground by his biographer. Boswell himself, at times, revelled in me-lancholy, and was as proud of it as Dogberry was of his losses. Johnson wrote to him that he hoped he had got rid of all this hypocrisy of misery. But it was not so willingly dropped. Doubtless, Boswell often had his real moments of misery. A man who shortens his life by drinking, as Boswell did, has at times something worse than the hypocrisy of misery. Then, too, we form our notions of Johnson's unhappiness from the sad entries which are to be found in his diaries. He hated solitude; and it was, we should remember, in the hours of solitude that these entries were made. Many a man, who enjoys a fair share of happiness, would often say with Johnson, 'When I survey my past life, I discover nothing but a barren waste of time, with some disorders of body and disturbances of the mind very near to madness.' Happily, most men keep such thoughts to themselves. This diary was never intended to be read by others;[1] and, perhaps, we should form a juster estimate of his character had the whole of it, and not merely a part, perished in the flames to which in his last illness he committed so many of his papers. 'Whenever,' he says, 'any fit of anxiety or gloominess, or perversion of mind, lays hold upon you, make it a rule not to publish it by complaints, but exert your whole care to hide it; by endeavouring to hide it, you will drive it away.' It is a pity that his own fits of gloominess were not more successfully hidden.

[1] Johnson recommended me to keep a journal of my life, full and unreserved. . . . He counselled me to keep it private, and said I might surely have a friend who would burn it in case of my death.—Boswell's *Life of Johnson* (July 14, 1763).

The unhappiness of his home life is commonly exaggerated.[1]   Mrs. Williams, his blind companion, though petulant, yet, as Boswell tells us, 'had valuable qualities, and her departure left a blank in his house.'   Levett was no less missed,—that 'faithful adherent for thirty years;' that 'old friend who lived with me in the house, and was useful and companionable.'   When they were both gone, Johnson, now near the close of his life, wrote:—'I have now no middle state between clamour and silence, between general conversation and self-tormenting solitude.'   Mrs. Desmoulins, her daughter, and Miss Carmichael, who certainly, if they lessened the silence, did not increase the harmony or the happiness of the household, were its inmates only some five years or so.   A long time enough, no doubt; but happily during their residence Johnson mixed very much in general society.

It was not the fear of death alone that made Johnson cling so fast to life.   He loved life scarcely less strongly than he dreaded death.   He had in his early life and in his later manhood struggles enough to undergo and miseries enough to encounter.   By the death of his wife he had felt how, to quote his own words, 'the continuity of being is lacerated, the settled course of sentiment and

[1] See page 168.

action is stopped, and life stands suspended and motion-less, till it is driven by external causes into a new channel.' But then, as Boswell says, 'it pleased God to grant him almost thirty years of life after this time; and once, when he was in a placid frame of mind, he was obliged to own to me that he had enjoyed happier days, and had had many more friends since that gloomy hour than before.' 'Grief has its time,' he once said.

The evening when Boswell found him in Mr. Hector's house, some twenty years after his wife's death, 'sitting placidly at tea with his first love, Mrs. Careless,' he said, 'If I had married her, it might have been as happy for me.' He would still maintain that a man never is happy in the moment that is present—'never'—and this excep-tion he made when hard pressed on the subject—'but when he is drunk.' Even in a rapidly driven post-chaise, than which life, as he said, has not many better things, a man, he maintained, is not happy, for 'you are driving rapidly from something or to something.'

Doubtless he was suffering greatly at the time when Mr. Thrale found him giving way to such an uncontrolled burst of despair regarding the world to come that he tried to stop his mouth by placing one hand before it, and be-fore leaving him desired Mrs. Thrale to prevail on him to quit 'his close habitation in the court,' and come with them

to Streatham. And yet it was somewhere about this time that we have the pleasant scene in Neville's Court, Trinity College, described in the 'New Monthly Magazine.' I hope that we may rely on the truthfulness of the narrative, for the sake of the following pleasant anecdote :—
' In the height of our convivial hilarity, our great man exclaimed, "Come, now, I'll give you a test ; now I'll try who is the true antiquary among you. Has any one of this company ever met with the 'History of Glorianus and Gloriana?'" Farmer, drawing the pipe out of his mouth, followed by a cloud of smoke, instantly said, "I've got the book." "Gi' me your hand, gi' me your hand," said Johnson. "You are the man after my own heart." And the shaking of two such hands, with two such happy faces attached to them, could hardly, I believe, be matched in the whole annals of literature.'

Johnson knew as well as any one the means by which to keep this melancholy at a distance. He did not make of it the mystery that Boswell did. 'He recommended,' though he did not always practise, 'constant occupation of mind, a great deal of exercise, and moderation in eating and drinking. He observed that labouring men, who work hard and live sparingly, are seldom or never troubled with low spirits.' Just before he was found in that melancholy state by Thrale he had not stirred out of his room, as Mrs. Thrale writes, 'for many weeks together, I think months.'

Leigh Hunt, in his autobiography, tells us that he himself had suffered much in the same way, and had been cured by regular and steady walking. Johnson lived nearly twenty years after the day when he first met Thrale, and during these twenty years he had no violent attack of hypochondria. Boswell when he first went to Streatham and found that, 'though quite at home, he was yet looked up to with an awe tempered by affection, and seemed to be equally the care of his host and hostess, rejoiced at seeing him so happy.'

The mere exercise of the remarkable powers of mind that he possessed must have been to him a source of great happiness. He had the pleasure of doing a thing well, and the scarcely smaller pleasure of reflecting that he had done a thing well. Thirty years after he had brought out his 'Dictionary' he could say, 'Yes, sir, I knew very well what I was undertaking, and very well how to do it; and I have done it very well.' It could not have been rarely, too, that on the morrow of some great talk, Boswell found him highly satisfied with his colloquial powers the evening before. 'Well, we had good talk,' must have been often what he thought, if not often what he said.

It may have been true with him, as he said, that 'the whole of life is but keeping away the thought of death;' and yet, while it was Burke and Goldsmith and Garrick and Reynolds who helped him to keep the thought away, life may have been pleasant enough. What a happy picture does Boswell paint of the dinner at his lodgings in Old Bond Street, when 'Garrick played round Johnson with a fond vivacity, taking hold of the breasts of his coat, and, looking up in his face with a lively archness, complimented him on the good health which he seemed to enjoy, while the sage, shaking his head, beheld him with a gentle complacency.'

If, as he maintained, 'a tavern chair is the throne of human felicity,' it was a throne on which he was ever sitting. 'I can scarcely recollect,' says the Rev. Dr. Maxwell, the assistant preacher at the Temple, 'that he ever refused going with me to a tavern, and he often went to Ranelagh, which he deemed a place of innocent recreation. He declaimed all the morning, then went to dinner at a tavern, where he commonly stayed late, and then drank his tea at some friend's house, over which he loitered a great while.' 'He often used to quote, with great pathos,' Dr. Maxwell goes on to say, 'those fine lines of Virgil:—

Optima quæque dies miseris mortalibus ævi
Prima fugit,' &c.

Happily there was for Johnson, as we have shown, more of sentiment than of reality in the lines. His best days were to come last. What a pleasant picture we have of him, too, as he drove along in the post-chaise to Twickenham, when 'he was in such good spirits that everything seemed to please him, and, as Boswell writes, shaking his head and stretching himself at his ease in the coach, and, smiling with much complacency, he turned to me and said, "I look upon myself as a good-humoured fellow." When he was merry I never knew a man,' says Boswell, ' laugh more heartily.' Who does not remember Johnson 'shaking his sides and laughing' when Goldsmith was talking of the skill of the writer of fables, who had made the little fishes talk like little fishes? 'Johnson,' said Garrick, 'gives you a forcible hug, and shakes laughter out of you whether you will or not.'

What a scene rises up before us when Boswell tells us how, on coming from Scotland and driving to Thrale's house in the Borough, he found Johnson and Mrs. Thrale at breakfast. 'In a moment he was in a full glow of conversation, and I felt myself elevated as if brought into another state of being. Mrs. Thrale and I looked at each other while he talked, and our looks expressed our congenial admiration and affection for him. I shall ever recollect this scene with great pleasure.' But there is an almost endless number of similar pleasant scenes which rise up in the memory.

Johnson, moreover, if often dissatisfied with himself, was never dissatisfied with the world or the age in which his life was cast. 'Sir, I have never complained of the world, nor do I think that I have reason to complain. It is rather to be wondered at that I have so much.' 'He was never querulous, never prone to inveigh against the present times, as is so common when superficial minds are on the fret. On the contrary, he was willing to speak favourably of his own age, and, indeed, maintained its superiority in every respect, except in its reverence for government.'

If he was not always happy, he, nevertheless, steadily aimed at happiness. 'Life admits not of delays,' he writes to Boswell; 'when pleasure can be had, it is fit to catch it. If you and I live to be much older, we shall take great delight in talking over the Hebridean journey.' In recording, too, their visit to the silk mill at Derby, Boswell writes, 'I had learnt from Dr. Johnson during this interview not to think with a dejected indifference of the works of art and the pleasures of life, because life is uncertain and short ; but to consider such indifference as a failure of reason, a morbidness of mind ; for happiness should be cultivated as much as we can.'

His own theoretical or hypothetical mode of cultivating it, he once set forth as follows :—'If I had no duties, and no reference to futurity, I would spend my life in driving briskly in a post-chaise with a pretty woman, but she should be one that could understand me and would add something to the conversation.' In his eager search after all kinds of knowledge much happiness must have lain. 'There is the same difference,' he would say, 'between the learned and the unlearned as between the living and the dead.'

His thirst for knowledge was not quenched by old age. Not six months before his death he asked Dr. Burney to teach him the scales of music. When close upon three-score and ten, having picked up in the drawing-room of Mr. Dilly's house in the Poultry the account of the late Revolution in Sweden, he, not only disregarding the company, 'seemed to read it ravenously as if he devoured it,' but in the dining-room 'he kept it wrapt up in the table-cloth in his lap during the time of dinner, from an avidity to have one entertainment in readiness when he should have finished another.'

A short time before his death, when most men

would have been looking forward to the end as an escape from bodily suffering, he writes to Boswell :—'I hope still to see you in happier times to talk over what we have often talked, and perhaps to find new topics of merriment or new incitements to curiosity.' 'Such,' we read, 'was his intellectual ardour even at this time that he said to one friend, "Sir, I look upon every day to be lost in which I do not make a new acquaintance."' In June, less than five months before his death, he was dining at General Paoli's, where he was eating so heartily that, Boswell says, 'I was afraid he might be hurt by it ; and I whispered to the General my fear, and begged he might not press him. "Alas !" said the General, " see how very ill he looks ; he can live but a very short time. Would you refuse any slight gratification to a man under sentence of death ? There is a humane custom in Italy by which persons in that melancholy situation are indulged with having whatever they like best to eat and drink, even with expensive delicacies."' Yet only a few days later, receiving from Lord Eliot a copy of a rare book which he happened never to have seen, 'he told Sir Joshua Reynolds that he was going to bed when it came, but was so much pleased with it that he sat up till he read it through, adding, with a smile (in allusion to Lord Eliot's having recently been raised to the peerage),

" I did not think a young lord could have mentioned to me a book in the English history that was not known to me." '

A little earlier than this he had recorded, 'I read a book in the " Æneid" every night ; so it was done in twelve nights, and I had great delight in it.' Harassed though his body was by asthma and dropsy, yet such was its natural vigour that less than a month before his death we find him writing, 'I came in the common vehicle easily to London from Oxford.'

Even when his body was at its worst, his mind, at all events, never knew the approach of age. Mr. Burke applied to him the words of Cicero : 'Intentum enim animum tanquam arcum habebat, nec languescens succumbebat senectuti.' He was attacked one night with paralysis, and for a while lost the power of speech. In describing afterwards how the paralytic stroke fell upon him, he says, 'I was alarmed, and prayed God that, however he might afflict my body, he would spare my understanding. This prayer, that I might try the integrity of my faculties, I made in Latin verse. The lines were not very good, but I knew them not to be very good. I made them easily.' That very evening before he had retired he felt himself, he writes, 'light and easy, and began to plan schemes of life.'

Just one year before his death he was establishing a new Club in Essex Street, Strand. He writes to ask Sir Joshua to join, and says 'the company is numerous, and, as you will see by the list, miscellaneous. The terms are lax and the expenses light. We meet thrice a week, and he who misses forfeits two-pence.' If his house in Bolt Court was lonely, why he would seek for company abroad. He would never allow that he was old. ' I value myself upon this—that there is nothing of the old man in my conversation.' 'Don't let us discourage one another,' was his reply to his college friend Edwards, when on meeting Johnson Edwards said, 'Ah, Sir, we are old men now.'

Later on, when his infirmities forced him to acknowledge that old age had come upon his body, he said, 'He that lives must grow old, and he that would rather grow old than die has God to thank for the infirmities of age.' Six months before his death, as we can learn from Boswell, he had dined out at least six times in nine days, besides spending one evening at the Essex Street Club. 'Of these days and others,' writes Boswell, 'on which I saw him, I have no memorials, except the general recollection of his being able and animated in conversation, and appearing to relish society as much as the youngest man.'

It was this perfect preservation of the powers of his mind that rendered death so terrible to him to the last. 'I struggle hard for life,' he writes, 'I try to hold up my head as high as I can;' and again, 'I will be conquered; I will not capitulate.' Some one told him of a wonderful learned pig, and when 'a person who was present proceeded to remark that great torture must have been employed ere the indocility of the animal could have been subdued, "Certainly" (said the Doctor), "but" (turning to me), "how old is your pig?" . I told him three years old. "Then," said he, "the pig has no cause to complain ; he would have been killed the first year if he had not been educated, and protracted existence is a good recompense for very considerable degrees of torture."' Who can forget the stern strength of mind the old man showed in the last day of his life when, thinking that the surgeons, out of fear of giving him pain, would not cut deep enough, he called for a case of lancets and operated upon himself ? Nay even, 'soon after he got at a pair of scissors that lay in a drawer by him, and plunged them deep into the calf of each leg.'

The longer he lived the more attractive did the world seem to him. He had kept his friendship in constant repair, to quote his own expressive words. The retired and uncourtly scholar whose shoes had been laughed at by the Christ Church men, who had come to London poor and unknown, whose surly virtue had often wanted a friend ; who 'in the gloom of solitude,' had thirty years before brought out his great work, now found himself courted by the great, whose rank, if only joined with decency of life, he had always so deeply respected. The friends of his daily life were some of the greatest men that England could then boast of; who, great though they were, looked upon him not as their equal but as their chief. What more splendid homage was ever paid to any man than to him, to whom when Burke and Reynolds and Gibbon and Sheridan wished to present a petition, they only ventured to send it in the form of a Round Robin? He relished fame, and he was famous.

'He called to us,' as Boswell writes in describing a Club meeting a short while before his death,—'he called to us with a sudden air of exultation as the thought started into his mind, "Oh! gentlemen, I must tell you a very great thing. The Empress of Russia has ordered the 'Rambler' to be translated into the Russian language ; so I shall be read on the banks of the Wolga. Horace boasts that his fame would extend as far as the banks of the Rhone ; now the Wolga is farther from me than the Rhone was from Horace." *Boswell*: " You must certainly be pleased with this, Sir." *Johnson*: "I am pleased, Sir, to be sure. A man is pleased to find he has succeeded in that which he has endeavoured to do."' London life had lost to him none of its charms. 'When a man is tired of London, he is tired of life ; for there is in London all that life can afford.' And when in the last autumn that he was ever to see, he had gone into the country in the hope that change of air and scene might do something for him, worn with suffering it is not to the rest of the grave or to some better world that he looks forward. 'The town,' he writes, 'is my element ; there are my friends, there are my books, to which I have not yet bidden farewell ; and there are my amusements.' He had, too often in his long life, with good reason to own himself 'a man of sorrows and acquainted with grief.' Yet we please ourselves with the strong belief that he who had so large a share of some of the noblest qualities with which man is endowed, had also no small share of that happiness which here on earth can fall to the lot of man.

CHAPTER III.

MR. CARLYLE ON BOSWELL.[1]

IN the whole of literature there is scarcely a stronger contrast to be found than that which exists between the two celebrated reviews of Boswell's 'Life of Johnson.' Lord Macaulay was, I think, carried by his love of paradox and his hatred of Tories as far wrong in one direction, as Mr. Carlyle by his love of hero-worship and his utter indifference both to Whigs and Tories was carried in another direction. There are those who imagine that between two opposite characters that are given of the same man a kind of balance can be struck, which shall not be far removed from the truth. Character, however, admits of such infinite variety that it may well happen that the truth lies not between any two opposing views, but in some altogether different direction. Though the study of both Boswell and Johnson as drawn by

[1] Reprinted (with alterations) from the *Saturaay Review*, November 28, 1874.

these two great writers is very interesting, yet I doubt whether in their pages there is to be found, even by a man who is well skilled in weighing arguments and balancing opposing statements, an accurate estimate of the two men.

Macaulay had represented Boswell as everything that was contemptible and mean. It was no hard matter to upset this outrageous view; and Mr. Carlyle has done it most thoroughly. Even he, in some points, has not done full justice to Boswell's character. In one respect, however, he has exaggerated his merits. 'Loyalty, discipleship,' he writes, 'all that was ever meant by *Hero-worship*, lives perennially in the human bosom, and waits, even in these dead days, only for occasions to unfold it, and inspire all men with it, and again make the world alive! James Boswell we can regard as a practical witness, or real *martyr*, to this high, everlasting truth.' Now the more hidden the hero is, the less recognised by the world, the greater is the merit of the disciple who discovers him and establishes his worship. Mr. Carlyle, I hold, exalts Boswell's merits by lowering the position which Johnson held at the time when the two first became acquainted. 'At the date,' he writes, 'when Johnson was a poor, rusty-coated " scholar," dwelling in Temple Lane, and indeed throughout their whole intercourse afterwards, were there not chancellors and prime ministers enough ; graceful gentlemen, the glass of fashion ; honour-giving noblemen ; dinner-giving rich men ; renowned fire-eaters, swordsmen, gownsmen ; Quacks and Realities of all hues—any one of whom bulked much larger in the world's eye than Johnson ever did ?'

In another passage he says : ' His mighty "constellation," or sun, round whom he, as satellite, observantly gyrated, was, for the mass of men, but a huge, ill-snuffed tallow-light.'   Again he writes : ' Nay, it does not appear that vulgar vanity could ever have been much flattered by Boswell's relation to Johnson. Mr. Croker says Johnson was, to the last, little regarded by the great world.'   Anyone who should read the review without knowing the Life would certainly infer that Boswell was the first to discover to the world a great man hidden away in obscurity and poverty. Now by the year 1763, when the disciple first met his master, Johnson was at the head of the literary world. He had published ' Irene,' ' London,' the ' Life of Savage,' the Dictionary, the ' Vanity of Human Wishes,' the ' Rambler,' the ' Idler,' and ' Rasselas.' His edition of Shakespeare he had been engaged on for some years, and he completed it two years later, before Boswell's return from the Continent. He was no longer the poor, rusty-coated scholar, for the year before he had had granted to him his pension of £300 a year.[1] It was granted, it will be remembered, in the most honourable way possible, 'solely as the reward of his literary merit, without any stipulation whatever, or even tacit understanding that he should write for the Administration.' Boswell's own allowance from his father was but £240 a year; so that of the two men, Johnson, in the early part of their acquaintance at all events, had the larger income. We have not very full information as to the society in which Johnson mixed, and the regard in which he was held before the time when Boswell made his acquaintance. But I have gathered together a few facts, which I will briefly lay before my readers.

When Boswell was only a boy of twelve years old, a gentleman of a higher lineage and an older family than he could boast of had come up to London to worship at

---

[1] How large a sum this pension must have been in his eyes we can judge from a passage in his *Life of Savage*. He describes how Lord Tyrconnel received the poet into his family, and engaged to allow him a pension of £200 a year. He goes on to tell how Savage became at once all the rage. ' His presence was sufficient to make any place of public entertainment popular, and his approbation and example constituted the fashion. So powerful is genius when it is invested with the glitter of affluence.'

the feet of the author of the 'Rambler.' Bennet Langton, the son of the Lincolnshire squire whose 'ancestor signed Magna Charta first, as Primate of all England,' had, I should imagine, to use Mr. Carlyle's words, 'been nurtured in an atmosphere of heraldry' scarcely less than Boswell. He could show a pedigree, engrossed on a piece of parchment about ten inches broad and from twelve to fifteen feet long. He not only visited Johnson in London, but quite early in their acquaintance invited him down to his father's Hall in Lincolnshire. Through him, too, Johnson became acquainted with Topham Beauclerk, the grandson of the Duke of St. Albans. With these two young Oxonians Johnson was living on terms of the greatest intimacy many years before he knew Boswell.

Writing of the year 1752, Boswell says, 'The circle of his friends at this time was extensive and various, far beyond what had been generally imagined ;' while Hawkins, speaking of about the same time, says, 'His acquaintance was sought by persons of the first eminence in literature.' Men of rank were reckoned among his friends, as the Earl of Cork and Orrery and Lord Southwell. Bubb Doddington, afterward Lord Melcombe, wrote to him to say that 'if Mr. Johnson was inclined to enlarge the circle of his acquaintance, he should be glad to be admitted into the number of his friends.' So early as the year 1748, in the print that is still preserved of the company which that summer visited Tunbridge Wells, we find Johnson and his wife represented, in company with Speaker Onslow, Mr. Pitt (Lord Chatham), and Mr., afterwards Lord, Lyttelton. As Mr. Croker remarks, 'in that assemblage neither Johnson nor his wife exhibit an appearance of inferiority to the rest of the company.' The reference to the figures, by the way, in the facsimile of the print is said to be in Richardson's own writing. How comes it then that we find Dr., and not Mr., Johnson? Johnson received his degree from Dublin in 1765, and Richardson died in 1761.

It was in the year 1755 that Lord Chesterfield by his attempts to flatter him provoked the celebrated letter. When he was accused of having treated Johnson with rudeness by keeping him waiting in his ante-chamber, he said he 'would have turned off the best servant he ever had, if he had known that he denied him to a man who would have been always more than welcome.' In the same year Johnson received from Oxford the honorary degree of Master of Arts, while the Academy at Florence presented him with a copy of their 'Vocabulario' in return for a copy of his Dictionary presented to it by 'his friend the Earl of Cork and Orrery,' at the same

time that the French Academy sent him their 'Diction-
naire.' A year or two later Smollett, writing on his
behalf to Wilkes, describes him as that great Cham of
literature. When his pension was granted Lord Bute
behaved in the handsomest manner. In the same year
that he received his pension, Boswell says that in a trip
which he took with Reynolds to Devonshire 'he was entertained at the seats of several noblemen and gentlemen in
the West of England.' At Plymouth 'the Commissioner
of the Dockyard paid him the compliment of ordering the
yacht to convey him and his friend to Eddystone.' At
Exeter, 'that very eminent divine, the Rev. Zachariah
Mudge, Prebendary of Exeter, preached a sermon pur-
posely that Johnson might hear him.' Boswell, when he
comes to the time of his own introduction to his hero, says
that 'Sir David Dalrymple, now one of the Judges of Scotland, by the title of Lord Hailes, had contributed much to
increase my high opinion of Johnson, on account of his
writings, long before I attained to a personal acquaintance
with him.' Sir David writes to congratulate Boswell on
making Johnson's acquaintance, and says, ' I envy you the
free and undisguised converse with such a man.' He goes
on to say, ' May I beg you to present my best respects to
him, and to assure him of the veneration which I entertain for the author of the "Rambler" and of "Rasselas"?'

On one of the early days of their acquaintance, Boswell 'found tall Sir Thomas Robinson (the elder brother of the first Lord Rokeby) sitting with Johnson.' Boswell another day told Johnson how 'Sir James Macdonald, who united the highest reputation at Eton and Oxford with the patriarchal spirit of a great Highland chieftain, had said that he had never seen Johnson, but he had a great respect for him, though at the same time it was mixed with some degree of terror.' Mr. Dempster, long M.P. for Fife, 'was so much struck,' Boswell says, writing of the same period, 'even with the imperfect account I gave him of Dr. Johnson's conversation, that to his honour be it recorded, when I complained that drinking port and sitting up late with him affected my nerves for some time after, he said, " One had better be palsied at eighteen than not keep company with such a man." '

It was in the same year that the Countess de Boufflers, one of the leaders of French society, who was now on a round of visits in England, breakfasting with Walpole, dining with the Duke of Grafton, supping with Beauclerk, paid her visit to Johnson in Inner Temple Lane. All readers of Boswell will remember how Johnson, a moment or two after the lady had left his rooms, eager to show himself a man of gallantry, hurried down the staircase in violent agitation, and in the strangest of costumes, seized her hand and conducted her to her coach. Some years before this Dr. Maxwell, the assistant preacher at the Temple, had described the levee of morning visitors that he held. 'He seemed to me,' he wrote, 'to be considered as a kind of public oracle, whom everybody thought they had a right to visit and consult. Though the most accessible and communicative man alive,' he goes on to add, 'yet when he suspected he was invited to be exhibited, he constantly spurned the invitation.'

In 1764, the year after Boswell first met Johnson, the Club was founded. 'When the society was not more than fifteen years old,' I quote from Mr. Forster's 'Life of Goldsmith,' 'the Bishop of St. Asaph wrote to Mr. William Jones, "I believe Mr. Fox will allow me to say that the honour of being elected into the Turk's Head Club is not inferior to that of being the representative of Westminster or Surrey. The electors are certainly more disinterested ; and I should say they were much better judges of merit, if they had not rejected Lord Camden and chosen me."' The Bishop of Chester was blackballed on the same night as the ex-Lord Chancellor.

In 1765, Johnson paid a visit to Cambridge. Mr. Turner, who twenty years later published an account of this visit, says : ' I admire his prudence and good sense in not appearing that day (Sunday) at St. Mary's, to be the general gaze during the whole service. Such an appearance at such a time and place might have turned, as it were, a Christian church into an idol temple.' The writer, after saying that Johnson 'seemed studious to preserve a strict incognito,' goes on to add : ' Had he visited Cambridge at the Commencement, or on some public occasion, he would doubtless have met with the honours due to the bright luminary of a sister University; and yet even these honours, however genuine and desirable, the modesty of conscious excellence seems rather to have prompted him to avoid.' In the same year ' Trinity College, Dublin, surprised Johnson with a spontaneous compliment of the highest academical honours by creating him Doctor of Law.'

In 1767, by which year Boswell had still seen very little of Johnson, occurred the interview with the King in the library at the Queen's house. ' His Majesty having been informed of his occasional visits, was pleased to signify a desire that he should be told when Dr. Johnson came next to the library. Accordingly, the next time that Johnson did come, as soon as he was fairly engaged with a book, on which, while he sat by the fire, he seemed quite intent, Mr. Barnard stole round to the apartment where the King was, and, in obedience to his Majesty's commands, mentioned that Dr. Johnson was then in the library. His Majesty said he was at leisure, and would go to him.' In the course of the conversation that followed, the King, it will be remembered, asked him if he was then writing anything. 'Johnson said he thought he had already done his part as a writer. "I should have thought so, too (said the King), if you had not written so well." Johnson observed to me upon this (writes Boswell) that "No man could have paid a handsomer compliment, and it was fit for a king to pay. It was decisive."'

At one period of his life, and probably not much later than the time when Boswell made his acquaintance, 'Johnson was a good deal with the Earl of Shelburne.' Boswell himself does not seem to know when it was that the intimacy had existed. We may infer, therefore, that it was at least somewhat early in the friendship of Johnson and his biographer, if not, indeed, before the friendship began.

I have shown, I think, that at the time when Boswell became intimate with Johnson the position his hero held in the world was very far from being inconsiderable. It would not be difficult to go on and upset Mr. Croker's statement, which Mr. Carlyle seems to adopt, that Johnson was to the last little regarded by the great world.

In his tour to the Hebrides he was welcomed by the great people wherever there were great people to welcome him. Setting aside the Scotch judges, many of whom were men of good family and received him hospitably, and the Scottish lairds, whom Mr. Carlyle describes as the hungriest and vainest of all bipeds yet known, but who were as warm in their welcome as the judges, he was hospitably received by the Earl of Errol, the Duke of Argyle, the Earl of Loudoun, and the Countess of Eglintoun. 'The Earl of Errol put Dr. Johnson in mind of their having dined together in London.' At Inverary 'the Duke placed Dr. Johnson next to him at dinner. The Duchess was very attentive to him. He talked a great deal, and was so entertaining that Lady Betty Hamilton, after dinner, went and placed her chair close to his, leaned upon the back of it, and listened eagerly. He did not know all the while how much he was honoured.' When the Earl of Loudoun heard that Johnson would dine with him, Boswell's servant reported that 'he jumped for joy.' 'We were received with a most pleasing courtesy by his Lordship, and by the Countess his mother, who in her ninety-fifth year had all her faculties quite unimpaired.' At the Countess of Eglintoun's 'in the course of our conversation it came out that she was married the year before Dr. Johnson was born, upon which she graciously said to him that she might have been his mother, and that she now adopted him; and when we were going away she embraced him, saying, "My dear son, farewell." ' In London ' he associated,' as Boswell tells us, ' with persons the most widely different in manners, abilities, rank, and accomplishments. He was at once the companion of the brilliant Colonel Forrester of the Guards, who wrote "The Polite Philosopher," and of the awkward and uncouth Robert Levett; of Lord Thurlow and Mr. Sastres, the Italian master; and has dined one day with the beautiful, gay, and fascinating Lady Craven, and the next with good Mrs. Gardiner, the tallow-chandler on Snow Hill.' Mr. Fitzgerald, in his edition of Boswell, quoting from Rogers's ' Table Talk,' says : ' Mr. Rogers was told by Lady Lucan that her mother, Lady Spencer, used to say, "Now, child, we have nothing to do to-night; let us bring home Dr. Johnson to dinner." ' Boswell says that ' at the house of Lord and Lady Lucan he often enjoyed all that an elegant house and the best company can contribute to form happiness.' But Bennet Langton's account of the party at Mrs. Vesey's, where the company, in which there were two duchesses, half a dozen or so of lords and ladies, whom he names, and ' others of note both for their station and understanding, began to collect round Johnson till they became not less than four, if not five, deep,' is in itself proof enough that Johnson was regarded by the great.

I cannot admit, then, the claim made for Boswell that he, and he alone, last century was a real martyr to the high, everlasting truth that hero-worship lives perennially in the human bosom. If the age in which he lived was ' a decrepit, death-sick era, when Cant had first decisively opened her poison-breathing lips to proclaim that God-worship and Mammon-worship were one and the same, that Life was a Lie,' &c., it was at all events the age of Goldsmith, Burke, Reynolds, and the gentle Bennet Langton, each of whom rivalled Boswell in the high esteem and the deep affection which they felt for Samuel Johnson.

CHAPTER IV.

LORD MACAULAY ON BOSWELL.[1]

IT is strange how a man of Macaulay's common sense, wide reading, and knowledge of the world could have fallen into such a rhetorical passion with Boswell. It would be almost as reasonable if a writer were to set about to belabour the memory of Sir Toby Belch as a man who had lost all self-respect.

Boswell, I should have thought, had sufficiently guarded himself against such an attack by the story he applies to himself in his dedication of the 'Life' to Sir Joshua Reynolds. He complains that he had been misunderstood when, in his 'Tour to the Hebrides,' in his eagerness to display the fertility and readiness of Johnson's wit, he freely showed to the world its dexterity, even when he himself was the object of it.

[1] In writing this chapter I have made some use of articles published in the *Saturday Review*, June 20, 1874, and the *Pall Mall Gazette*, October 13, 1875.

He goes on to say, 'It is related of the great Dr. Clarke that, when in one of his leisure hours, he was unbending himself with a few friends in the most playful and frolicksome manner, he observed Beau Nash approaching; upon which he suddenly stopped. "My boys," said he, "let us be grave; here comes a fool."' It is well for the world that Boswell had none of that second sight in which he was very willing to believe, or he might have spoiled his book by often stopping suddenly in his narrative with the exclamation, 'Let me be grave! I see coming from afar an Edinburgh Reviewer.'

His faults—and they were certainly very great—were not such as to raise either anger or contempt. A correspondent of Malone's described him well when he said 'he was an amiable, warm-hearted fellow, and there was a simplicity in him very engaging.' Hume, who was no bad judge of a man, wrote of him as 'a young gentleman very good humoured, very agreeable, and very mad.' Adam Smith, if we may trust Boswell, had told him when he was quite a young man that he was 'happily possessed of a facility of manners.' Rousseau recommended him to Pascal Paoli, and Paoli, after he had had him as his guest, in writing to him told him he should be desirous to keep up a correspondence with him. Hannah More speaks of him as 'a very agreeable, good-natured man.' Cumber-

land calls him 'the pleasant tourist to Corsica. . . . I
loved the man,' he writes; 'he had great convivial
powers, and an inexhaustible fund of good humour in
society.' Miss Burney, angry though she was with him
for revealing to the world 'every weakness and infirmity of
the first and greatest good man of these times,' and resolved
though she was to show him 'a forbidding reserve and
silence,' yet found her resolution overcome. 'He is so
open and forgiving for all that is said in return, that he
soon forced me to consider him in a less serious light, . . .
and before we parted we became good friends. There is
no resisting great good humour, be what will in the opposite scale.' Beauclerk, the courtly Topham Beauclerk,
who, according to Macaulay,[1] used Boswell's name as a
proverbial expression for a bore, was nevertheless very
zealous for his election into the Club. It was at his house
that Boswell's friends dined on the day of the election,
and went off in a body to vote for him, leaving him 'in a
state of anxiety which even the charming conversation of
Lady Di Beauclerk could not entirely dissipate.'

Sir Joshua Reynolds was the last man to have been a
friend to the vile sycophant whom Macaulay describes.
Boswell, in dedicating his great work to Reynolds, boasts

---

[1] Macaulay, no doubt, was thinking of the passage in a letter
from Beauclerk to the Earl of Charlemont, that I quote on page 311.

'with honest pride' that between the two there had been a long and uninterrupted friendship. And he was justified in making this boast, for Reynolds had been no less eager than Johnson for his election into the Club. It was to him, no doubt, that many years later was due his appointment as Secretary for Foreign Correspondence to the Royal Academy. He gave him during his lifetime one of the portraits that he had painted of Johnson, and in his will he left him £200, 'to be expended, if he thought proper, in the purchase of a picture at the sale of his paintings, and to be kept for his sake.' Dr. Barnard, Bishop of Killaloe, when he was appointed chaplain to the Royal Academy, writing to Reynolds, said, 'Tell my brother Boswell that I expect his congratulations.'

Dr. Barnard was a wit who could hold his place even when in company with Johnson and Burke. He would never have asked for the congratulations of 'a man of the meanest and feeblest intellect.' Was Johnson likely to have endured a man of the meanest and feeblest intellect for twenty minutes? But his friendship with Boswell lasted more than twenty years. 'He described him,' writes Macaulay, 'as a fellow who had missed his only chance of immortality by not having been alive when the "Dunciad" was written.'[1] But are all Johnson's hasty

[1] 'Johnson repeated to us in his forcible, melodious manner, the

utterances to be taken as so many deliberate judgments? Did he really look upon Fielding as a blockhead, a barren rascal; or upon Reynolds as a man too far gone in wine; or upon Dean Percy as a man who had done with civility; or upon Beauclerk as a man who was very uncivil; or upon Garrick as a fellow who exhibited himself for a shilling—a Punch who had no feelings? Did he really think that Dean Barnard deserved to be openly told that in him there was great room for improvement; or that Goldsmith deserved to be no less openly told that he was impertinent?

In his 'Life of Savage' he has himself shown how unreasonable it is to give too much weight to such utterances as these. 'A little knowledge of the world, he writes, 'is sufficient to discover that such weakness is very common, and that there are few who do not sometimes, in the wantonness of thoughtful mirth, or the heat of transient resentment, speak of their friends and benefactors with levity and contempt.'

If, to use Boswell's own expression, he at times gored

concluding lines of the *Dunciad*. While he was talking loudly in praise of those lines, one of the company ventured to say, "Too fine for such a poem: a poem on what?" *Johnson* (with a disdainful air) : "Why, on *dunces*. It was worth while being a dunce then. Ah, Sir, hadst *thou* lived in those days!"'—Boswell's *Johnson*, October 16, 1769.

him and tossed him, he often spoke of him in a very different way. In his 'Journey to the Western Islands' he writes: 'I was induced to undertake the journey by finding in Mr. Boswell a companion whose acuteness would help my inquiry, and whose gaiety of conversation and civility of manners are sufficient to counteract the inconveniencies of travel in countries less hospitable than we have passed.' In his letters to Mrs. Thrale, who, as he must have known, did not like Boswell, he speaks of 'his good humour and perpetual cheerfulness.' 'It is very convenient to travel with him, for there is no house where he is not received with kindness and respect.' Mrs. Boswell 'had the mien and manners of a gentlewoman.' Yet 'she is in a proper degree inferior to her husband; she cannot rival him, nor can he ever be ashamed of her.' In letters written in later years he tells how Boswell 'is with us in good humour, and plays his part with his usual vivacity.' 'He has been gay and good humoured in his usual way.'

Johnson, no doubt, was, as Madame D'Arblay says, 'really touched by Boswell's attachment. It was indeed surprising, and even touching,' she goes on to say, 'to remark the pleasure with which this great man accepted personal kindness even from the simplest of mankind, and the grave formality with which he acknowledged it even to the meanest. Possibly it was what he most prized because what he could least command, for personal partiality hangs upon lighter and slighter qualities than those which earn solid approbation.' But no amount of personal attachment from such a man as Macaulay describes could have won Johnson's friendship. 'On men and manners,' as he justly says, 'Johnson had certainly looked with a most observant and discriminating eye. . . . It is clear, from the remains of his conversation, that he had more of that homely wisdom which nothing but experience and observation can give than any writer since the time of Swift.'

It was certainly with an observant and a discriminating but not with a scornful eye that Johnson had looked on men and manners, and it was because he had so looked that he could see Boswell's merits and enjoy Boswell's society. He could find good in everything. His mind was large enough to be tolerant of that which was immeasurably beneath him. He was like some lofty and wide-spreading tree, beneath whose branches the grass can grow which the thick shrub would choke. The range of his knowledge was wide, and he was always eager to make it still wider.

No less wide was the range of his friendships, and scarcely less eager was his desire to extend it. 'Let us keep our friendships in repair,' he wrote in his old age. He despised no one who knew anything that he himself did not know, or who had any share of common sense, or ordinary intelligence. Swift one day overheard a gentleman regretting that he should have chanced to come to the house where among the guests was so great a scholar and a wit. 'A plain country squire,' the gentleman said, 'will have but a bad time of it in his company, and I don't like to be laughed at.' Swift stepped up to him and said, 'Pray, Sir, do you know how to say *yes* or *no* properly?' 'Yes, I think I have understanding enough for that.' 'Then give me your hand—depend upon it you and I will agree very well.'

Johnson and the plain country squire would have agreed still better. 'It was never,' as Madame Piozzi says, 'against people of coarse life that his contempt was expressed; while poverty of sentiment in men who considered themselves to be company for *the parlour*, as he called it, was what he would not bear.' It might have been said of him what he said of Burke: 'Take up whatever topic you please, he is ready to meet you.' One evening when he had been with Burke and had had by far the largest share in the talk, Burke in his modesty owned that it was enough for him to have rung the bell to him. When a clergyman complained of the want of society in the country where he lived and said 'They talk of runts[1];' a lady, who was by and who knew Johnson well, said, 'Sir, Mr. Johnson would learn to talk of runts.'

With all his prejudices he was, so far as men are concerned, one of the most unprejudiced of men. He had in a high degree the power of finding out in each man his better part. He was on a level with Burke and Gibbon, Reynolds and Garrick, but blind Miss Williams and old Mr. Levett were not beneath him.

Macaulay sneers at the inmates of his house—'this strange menagerie,' as he calls them—'Miss Williams whose chief recommendations were her blindness and her poverty,' 'the old quack doctor named Levett,' and the others who 'continued to torment him and to live upon him.' But in both of them he found in no small degree that eagerness after knowledge which he himself had in so large a degree. 'My house has lost,' he wrote when Levett died, 'a man who took interest in everything, and therefore ready at conversation.' When death the following year swept off Miss Williams, he wrote, 'had she had good humour and prompt elocution, her universal curiosity and comprehensive knowledge would have made her the delight of all

---

[1] 'Runt, in the Teutonick dialects, signifies a bull or a cow, and is used in contempt by us for small cattle.'—Johnson's *Dictionary*.

that knew her.' Hannah More writing of Miss Williams whom she had met for the first time, said : ' She is engaging in her manners ; her conversation lively and entertaining.'

He felt their loss deeply. 'The amusements and consolations of languor and depression,' he wrote to Mrs. Thrale, 'are conferred by familiar and domestick companions which can be visited or called at will, and can occasionally be quitted or dismissed. . . . Such society I had with Levett and Williams; such I had where—I am never likely to have it more.' The last passage is very striking. He is thinking of the home at Streatham that was now broken up, and he puts it and his ' strange menagerie' on a level.

Macaulay was not able to understand the pleasure that Johnson found in such companions as these. Still less was he able to understand the pleasure that he found in Boswell. But Macaulay was a man of 'imperfect sympathies.' He was not a humourist himself and he was quite free from those harmless follies which are so commonly joined with humour. He never, we may be sure, enjoyed a quiet laugh at himself. He never smiled at his own inconsistencies. Had he known Goldsmith, he would have scorned him almost as much as he scorned Boswell. He could never have burst into tears, as Burke did, when he heard of Goldsmith's death, nor laid aside his pen for the day, as Reynolds laid aside his brush. He could never have liked 'an inspired idiot.'

In some lines that I have somewhere read the beauty of a woman is described as so great that

> The beggars drew into shadow as she passed
> And covered up their sores with deeper sense of ill.[1]

The clearness of Macaulay's mind was so great, so wide were the partitions that divided his wit from madness, that a man whose folly and whose genius were hopelessly tangled together might well in like manner have covered himself up, if he had known how, from the gaze of that keen but unsympathetic eye. To like a man, Macaulay had first to respect him. Could he have wandered like Don Quixote through the world, he would rather have been accompanied by a consistent Whig, who said nothing because he had nothing to say, than by Sancho Panza with all his humour and his folly. He could never laugh at a man and laugh with him at the same time. So little, indeed, was he formed for understanding a man of Boswell's character, that when we examine the gross caricature that he would pass off as his portrait, we have, indeed, a feeling of pity—but the pity is for Macaulay not for Boswell.

---

[1] I quote from recollection, and likely enough my quotation is imperfect.

'Servile and impertinent, shallow and pedantic, a bigot and a sot, bloated with family pride, and eternally blustering about the dignity of a born gentleman, yet stooping to be a talebearer, an eavesdropper, a common butt in the taverns of London ; so curious to know everybody who was talked about, that Tory and High Churchman as he was, he manœuvred, we have been told, for an introduction to Tom Paine ; so vain of the most childish distinctions that, when he had been to court, he drove to the office where his book was printing without changing his clothes, and summoned all the printer's devils to admire his new ruffles and sword ; such was this man ; and such he was content and proud to be.'

'I would your grace would take me with you !' we may exclaim as Falstaff did when he heard himself described by Prince Hal, 'Whom means your grace?' And with some change in the words, we may go on to say, 'No, my good Lord, banish Whig, banish Tory, banish Edinburgh Reviewer, but for Jemmy Boswell banish not him thy reader's company, banish not him thy reader's friendship ; banish Jemmy and banish all the world.' For with all his failings and with all his faults, despise him as much as we please, yet we cannot help liking the man and almost looking upon him as a friend. He is delightful because he is Boswell, and to abuse him for being

Boswell is to abuse him for being delightful. He was more than half aware of his own weaknesses and absurdities, and a fool who knows his own folly is no longer a fool. In his preface to his book on Corsica he writes, 'For my part I should be proud to be known as an authour; and I have an ardent ambition for literary fame; for of all possessions I should imagine literary fame to be the most valuable. A man who has been able to furnish a book which has been approved by the world has established himself as a respectable character in distant society, without any danger of having that character lessened by the observation of his weaknesses. To preserve an uniform dignity among those who see us every day is hardly possible; and to aim at it must put us under the fetters of a perpetual restraint. The authour of an approved book may allow his natural disposition an easy play, and yet indulge the pride of superiour genius, when he considers that by those who know him only as an authour he never ceases to be respected. Such an authour when in his hours of gloom and discontent may have the consolation to think that his writings are at that very time · giving pleasure to numbers, and such an authour may cherish the hope of being remembered after death, which has been a great object to the noblest minds in all ages.'

Boswell, unfortunately for his reputation, had by no

means the art of preserving even in his writings 'an uniform dignity.' This Goldsmith had, though perhaps among those who saw him every day he, more even than Boswell, exposed his weaknesses. As Sir Joshua said of him, 'admirers in a room whom his entrance had struck with awe, might be seen riding out upon his back.'

Boswell was always giving the world something to laugh at, but it was a good-natured laugh that he raised. When he was barely one and twenty he and his friend Erskine published a series of letters that had passed between them. He was in such a hurry for fame that he could not wait till he had written a book, but when we read the letters we are only amused. He no more excites our anger than did Goldsmith when he showed himself off in his bloom-coloured coat. He is in these Letters, as Hume says, very good humoured, very agreeable and very mad.

Erskine laughs at him ; he ridicules the solemnity of his small nose, his dark face which beamed a black ray upon him, the rotundity of his Bath great-coat, his person little and squat, the pomatum which gives his hair a gloss, the grandeur of his pinchbeck buckles. He had taken him, he says, sometimes for the witches' cauldron in Macbeth ; sometimes for an enormous ink-bottle ; sometimes for a funeral procession ; now and then for a chimney sweeper, and not unfrequently for a black-pudding. He knows, he tells him, his aversion at being thought a genius or a wit. He is aware he hates flattery, and yet, in spite of his teeth, he will tell him that he is the best poet and the most humorous letter-writer he knows. He ridicules his wish to become a soldier, and reminds him that 'we find in all history, ancient and modern, lawyers are very apt to run away.'

A man cannot, indeed, boast much of his dignity who publishes such jests on himself. But he shows at all events his good humour. He is wise enough to stand a laugh against himself. He had had the impudence to publish an Ode to Tragedy written by a gentleman of Scotland and dedicated to James Boswell, Esq. Erskine's curiosity is aroused, and he eagerly writes for information. 'I must now ask like the "Spectator," is this Ode-writing gentleman of Scotland fat or lean, tall or short, does he use spectacles? What is the length of his walking-stick?'

Boswell with some humour replies: 'The author of the Ode to Tragedy is a most excellent man: he is of an ancient family in the west of Scotland, upon which he values himself not a little. At his nativity there appeared omens of his future greatness. His parts are bright, and his education has been good. He has travelled in post-chaises miles without number.

He is fond of seeing much of the world. He eats of every good dish, especially apple-pie. He drinks old hock. He has a very fine temper. He is somewhat of an humourist and a little tinctured with pride. He has a good manly countenance, and he owns himself to be amorous. He has infinite vivacity, yet is observed at times to have a melancholy cast. He is rather fat than lean, rather short than tall, rather young than old. His shoes are neatly made, and he never wears spectacles. The length of his walking-stick is not as yet ascertained ; but we hope soon to favour the republic of letters with a solution of this difficulty, as several able mathematicians are employed in its investigation, and for that purpose have posted themselves at different given points in the Canongate, so that when the gentleman saunters down to the Abbey of Holyrood House in order to think on ancient days, on King James the Fifth, and on Queen Mary, they may compute its altitude above the street according to the rules of geometry.'

In the account he gives of his Tour to Corsica, there is the same display of vanity as harmless as it is amusing. To his great satisfaction it was generally believed that he was on a public mission. 'The more I disclaimed any such thing, the more they persevered in affirming it ; and I was considered as a very close young man.   I therefore just allowed them to make a minister of me, till time should undeceive them. . . . The *Ambasciadore Inglese*—the English ambassadour—as the good peasants and soldiers used to call me, became a great favourite among them.   I got a Corsican dress made, in which I walked about with an air of true satisfaction. . . . They were quite free and easy with me.   Numbers of them used to come and see me of a morning, and just go in and out as they pleased.   I did everything in my power to make them fond of the British, and bid them hope for an alliance with us.   They asked me a thousand questions about my country, all of which I chearfully answered as well as I could.'

In another passage he says, 'At Bastelica, where there is a stately spirited race of people, I had a large company to attend me in the convent.   I liked to see their natural frankness and ease ; for why should men be afraid of their own species?   They just came in making an easy bow, placed themselves round the room where I was sitting, rested themselves on their muskets, and immediately entered into conversation with me.'   We are pleasantly reminded by his condescension how a few years later on he said, 'For my part I like very well to hear honest Goldsmith talk away carelessly.'

Paoli treated him with great ceremony, and whenever

he chose to make a little tour he was attended by a party of guards. 'One day,' he writes, 'when I rode out I was mounted on Paoli's own horse, with rich furniture of crimson velvet, with broad gold lace, and had·my guards marching along with me. I allowed myself to indulge a momentary pride in this parade, as I was curious to experience what could really be the pleasure of state and distinction with which mankind are so strangely intoxicated.' I wonder, by the way, if Boswell ever read the Book of Esther without being filled with envy of Mordecai. How he would have delighted to be led along the street in royal apparel, with the Prime Minister or the Lord Chancellor walking by his side and proclaiming before him, 'Thus shall it be done to the man whom the King delighteth to honour.' When first he was to appear before Paoli, 'I could not help being,' he says, 'under considerable anxiety. My ideas of him had been greatly heightened by the conversations I had held with all sorts of people in the island, they having represented him to me as something above humanity.' But a few pages later on he writes: 'My time passed here in the most agreeable manner. I enjoyed a sort of luxury of noble sentiments. Paoli became more affable with me. I made myself known to him.'

Wonderfully amusing is the account he gave of himself, when he had thus made himself known. ' This kind of conversation led me to tell him how much I had suffered from anxious speculations. With a mind naturally inclined to melancholy, and a keen desire of inquiry, I had intensely (Oh, Bozzy ! Bozzy ! you bounced there, and you know you did) applied myself to metaphysical researches, and reasoned beyond my depth on such subjects as it is not given to man to know. I told him I had rendered my mind a camera obscura—that in the very heat of youth I felt the *non est tanti*, the *omnia vanitas* of one who has exhausted all the sweets of his being, and is weary with dull repetition. I told him that I had almost become for ever incapable of taking a part in active life.'

One good, at all events, resulted from this visit, for he says : ' From having known intimately so exalted a character my sentiments of human nature were raised ; while, by a sort of contagion, I felt an honest ardour to distinguish myself and be useful, as far as my situation and abilities would allow ; and I was, for the rest of my life, set free from a slavish timidity in the presence of great men—for where shall I find a man greater than Paoli ? ' It was, no doubt, this happy freedom from slavish timidity which a year or two later gave him courage to write to the great Chatham, and ask, ' Could your lordship find time to honour me now and then with a letter ?'

As he had delighted in the experience of the pleasure of state and distinction, so another day he made trial of Arcadian simplicity. On almost every day of his life but this he was, as every one knows, only too fond of good eating and the bottle. But on this day, in describing a trip he was taking, he says, 'When we grew hungry we threw stones among the thick branches of the chestnut trees which overshadowed us, and in that manner we brought down a shower of chestnuts with which we filled our pockets, and went on eating them with great relish ; and when this made us thirsty we lay down by the side of the first brook, put our mouths to the stream, and drank sufficiently. It was just being for a while one of the *prisca gens mortalium*, the primitive race of men, who ran about in the woods eating acorns and drinking water.'

Macaulay says that Boswell ' has reported innumerable observations made by himself in the course of conversation. Of those observations we do not remember one which is above the intellectual capacity of a boy of fifteen.' Had he read 'The Tour to Corsica' he must have allowed that in the following conversation Boswell showed a good deal of wit.

'While I stopped to refresh my mules at a little village, the inhabitants came crowding about me as an ambassador going to their general. When they were informed of my country, a strong black fellow among them said: " English ! They are barbarians ; they don't believe in the great God." I told him, " Excuse me, Sir. We do believe in God, and in Jesus Christ too." "And in the Pope?" "No." "And why?" This was a puzzling question in these circumstances ; for there was a great audience to the controversy. I thought I would try a method of my own, and very gravely replied, " Because we are too far off." A very new argument against the universal infallibility of the Pope. It took, however ; for my opponent mused awhile, and then said, " Too far off ? Why, Sicily is as far off as England. Yet in Sicily they believe in the Pope." " Oh !" said I, " we are ten times farther off than Sicily." " Aha !" said he ; and seemed quite satisfied.'

All this vanity that Boswell thus early showed would in a Malvolio, or a Mr. Collins such as Miss Austen drew, be intolerable ; but vanity when it is joined with good nature, a lively temperament, and an active mind, often amuses, and even pleases rather than offends.

But he had no liveliness of temperament, no activity of mind, if we may trust Macaulay. ' He was, if we are to give any credit to his own account or to the united testimony of all who knew him, a man of the meanest and feeblest intellect.' Yet this 'Tour to Corsica' was not the act of an intellect that was either mean or feeble. He was, he says, the first Briton[1] who had had the curiosity to visit Corsica, and a trip to Corsica in those days was as great a feat as a trip to Mount Ararat in these days. 'Your countrymen,' said Paoli, 'will be curious to see you. A man come from Corsica will be like a man come from the Antipodes.' The Mediterranean still swarmed with Turkish corsairs, and Corsica itself swarmed with brigands. 'Come home,' wrote Johnson to him, 'and expect such welcome as is due to him whom a wise and noble curiosity has led where perhaps no native of this country ever was before.' The enthusiasm that led him there was, perhaps, wild ; but enthusiasm is not the failing of the meanest intellects. Scarcely less noble was the enthusiasm which led him, a young

---

[1] He was not, indeed, quite the first Briton to go to Corsica. Curiously enough, he found in a town occupied by the French, an Englishwoman of Penrith in Cumberland. When the Highlanders marched through that country in the year 1745, she had married a soldier of the French picquets in the very midst of all the confusion and danger, and when she could hardly understand one word he said. What a strange story might have been written of that woman's adventures, if Boswell had had the powers of De Foe, and had taken the trouble to learn all the circumstances of her life.

man of two and twenty, fond, only too fond, of pleasures, and freshly arrived in London, to sit up four nights in one week recording in his journal all that he could remember of what Johnson had said to him in the day.

But he had more than enthusiasm ; he had sound literary judgment. When he came to write his book on Corsica he showed that he knew very well the right way to set about the work he had taken in hand. He says, 'From my first setting out on this tour I wrote down every night what I had observed during the day, throwing together a great deal, that I might afterwards make a selection at leisure.' His method might be studied with great advantage by most of the authors of voyages and travels. He not only makes it quite clear what it is that he has seen himself and what it is that he knows only on the authority of others ; but more than this, he keeps each narrative quite apart from the other. He first of all gives a history of Corsica and then the journal of his tour.

The criticism which Johnson passed on the different parts of the book is thoroughly sound. 'Your history,' he writes, 'is like other histories ; but your journal is in a very high degree curious and delightful. There is between the history and the journal that difference which there will always be found between notions borrowed from without and notions generated within. Your history was copied from books ; your journal rose out of your own experience and observation. You express images which operated strongly upon yourself, and you have impressed them with great force upon your readers. I know not whether I could name any narrative by which curiosity is better excited or better gratified.'

But what is Johnson's judgment worth in the case of books ?—for according to Macaulay 'the judgments which he passed on books are in our time generally treated with indiscriminate contempt.'

The judgment that Macaulay passed on the ' Life of Johnson,' is sure to be treated with contempt by anyone who gives himself the trouble to think how rare and how great are the powers that a man must have who is to write a book that will live for all time.

A sentence in one of Gray's Letters, which contains one of the earliest criticisms that we have on Boswell, has in brief all that Macaulay has said at length. In writing to Horace Walpole of the ' Tour to Corsica,' which had just come out, Gray says, ' Mr. Boswell's book I was going to recommend to you when I received your letter ; it has pleased and moved me strangely—all (I mean) that relates to Paoli. He is a man born two thousand years after his time ! The pamphlet proves what I have always maintained, that any fool may write a most valuable book by chance, if he will only tell us what he heard and saw with veracity. Of Mr. Boswell's truth I have not the least suspicion, because I am sure he could invent nothing of this kind.'

Gray, like Macaulay, does not remember that the merit of a book quite as much depends on what is left out as on what is put in. A veracious fool, like anyone else, knows and sees a great deal. It demands sound taste and literary skill to seize and retain only what is interesting, and to put on one side even interesting matter, if it would interfere with the general plan of the work. Gray himself showed how well he understood this when he struck out from his Elegy almost the most beautiful stanza[1] of all, merely because he thought it caused too long a break. He did not, indeed, live to see the 'Life of Johnson' published. If he had, he would, I fear, have failed to discover that Boswell's judgment on this point was not much inferior to his own. And yet, perhaps, he would have found scarcely a passage that he would willingly have struck out, and

---

[1] There scatter'd oft, the earliest of the year,
   By hands unseen are show'rs of violets found ;
The redbreast loves to build and warble there,
   And little footsteps lightly print the ground.

scarcely a passage that does not bear on the hero of the story.

But in the varied society he kept Boswell must have heard many a good thing which could easily enough have been worked into his book, though it would not properly have belonged to it. In the conception he formed of the task that lay before him, and in the self-restraint with which he acted up to the rule he had laid down, he showed remarkable literary taste and literary power. And yet how strangely this is lost sight of, is shown not only by Macaulay's criticism, but also by the way in which his criticism is taken as just and sound by men of real ability.

Some few years ago Mr. George Henry Lewes wrote a preface to a kind of abridgment of Boswell. He admires the Life so much that he says, ' it is for me a sort of test-book ; according to a man's judgment of it I am apt to form my judgment of him. . . . It is a work which has delighted generations, and will continue to delight posterity. . . . Yet even the staunchest admirers of Boswell's Life must admit that it is three times as long as need be.' He had himself entertained the notion of ' re-writing Boswell,' intending ' to preserve all that constitutes the essential merits of his work, and merely to adapt it to the more exigent tastes of our day.'

Happily for Mr. Lewes's reputation, 'scientific pursuits absorbed,' he writes, 'all my energy, and left me neither time nor strength to turn to literature.' We shall next have some artist proposing to repaint Hogarth, preserving of course all that constitutes the essential merits of his pictures ; or adapting Gil Blas to the more exigent tastes of the day. When the celebrated Round Robin was laid before Dr. Johnson, in which he was asked by his friends to write Goldsmith's epitaph in English and not in Latin, we are told that 'upon seeing Dr. Warton's name to the suggestion, he observed to Sir Joshua, "I wonder that Joe Warton, a scholar by profession, should be such a fool." He said too, "I should have thought Mund Burke would have had more sense." ' Lord Macaulay and Mr. Lewes are both scholars by profession; yet they both raise our wonder.

The question, after all, lies in a nut-shell. Is this wonderful biography due, and due alone, as Macaulay says, to the fact that Boswell had not only a quick observation and a retentive memory, but was also a dunce, a parasite, and a coxcomb? Is it, as Mr. Lewes says, 'nothing more than the thin soup of Boswellian narrative and comment in which the solid meat of Johnson was dished up?' Might not Boswell, with good reason, have made the same proud boast as Johnson

made when speaking of the greatest of all his works:
'Yes, Sir, I knew very well what I was undertaking,
and very well how to do it, and have done it very well'?

I have spoken of Boswell's admirable literary taste.
But he shows also at times a dramatic power of which
even Goldsmith need not have been ashamed. How
few scenes there are in any play which, even when acted
before us on the stage by the best actors, seem half so
life-like as the dinner at Messieurs Dilly's in the Poultry,
where Wilkes and Johnson met. Does anyone suppose
that the wonderful merits of that scene are due merely to
Boswell's skill in reporting conversations? Could Goldsmith himself, if he had lived to be present at that first
of all dinners, have told the story better, even with the
help of Boswell's notes? How happy is Boswell when
he writes : ' I was persuaded that if I had come upon
him with a direct proposal, " Sir, will you dine in company with Jack Wilkes?" he would have flown into a
passion, and would probably have answered, " Dine with
Jack Wilkes, Sir ! I'd as soon dine with Jack Ketch !"'
How humourous is the touch when he describes his
exultation at having at last got the great man off :
' When I had him fairly seated in a hackney-coach with
me, I exulted as much as a fortune-hunter who has got
an heiress into a post-chaise with him to set out for

Gretna Green.'   Does he not show almost such an insight into the comic side of human nature as we find in Addison, when he describes the way in which Wilkes by means of politeness and of roast-veal overcomes the great man's surly virtue?   The dexterity that Boswell displayed in thus bringing these two men together surely shows a great readiness of wit.   As Burke pleasantly said, ' there was nothing equal to it in the whole history of the *corps diplomatique.'*

It is less to be wondered at that Boswell could give a dramatic turn to such a scene as this, as he had himself great powers as an actor.   Hannah More was once made 'umpire in a trial of skill between Garrick and Boswell, who could most nearly imitate Johnson's manner. She gave it for Boswell in familiar conversation, and for Garrick in reciting poetry.'   The man who could even in one point beat Garrick in his own art surely had powers which Macaulay should not have failed to discover and acknowledge.

Miss Burney also tells us that his imitations of Johnson, though comic to excess, yet did not turn Johnson into ridicule by caricature.   To imitate a man of strongly marked character, and yet not to caricature him, requires not only keenness of observation but also a certain delicacy of mind.

That love, I might almost say that passion, for accuracy, that distinguished Boswell in so high a degree does not belong to a mind that is either mean or feeble. Mean minds are indifferent to truth, and feeble minds can see no importance in a date. He had been urged by his friends to make here and there in his book on Corsica, 'a change in Paoli's remarkable sayings.' He had steadily refused, for ' I know,' he writes, ' with how much pleasure we read what is perfectly authentic.'

He had set up Johnson as his idol. The Life that he was on the point of bringing out he everywhere spoke of as the *magnum opus*. But he had not the weakness of most worshippers, who think to make their idol greater by carefully hiding its faults. Hannah More begged him ' to mitigate some of Johnson's asperities. He said roughly he would not cut off his claws, nor make a tiger a cat to please anybody.' Eager though he was for fame, yet he would not bring out his book till he had made it as perfect as he could. Hawkins, Murphy, and Madame Piozzi had all brought out their books, but Boswell was not to be hurried. Johnson had been dead nearly seven years before the Life appeared. Whoever has read the book as a student reads it, knows that he had a right to boast that he had spared no pains to ascertain with a scrupulous authenticity, even the most minute of the innumerable detached particulars of which it consists. Genius has been defined, if I remember rightly, as an infinite capacity for taking trouble in small matters. If this is genius, Boswell certainly had his share of it.

In the record that Boswell gives of Johnson's conversation, Macaulay allows him no other merit but that of a retentive memory. But more than once in reading the Life, the question has forced itself upon me, How much of Johnson's reported conversation is his own and how much Boswell's? Whenever Boswell pretends to give Johnson's exact words, does he, even though he omits a great deal, show in what he gives the literal accuracy of a shorthand reporter? Or, on the other hand, while the thoughts are altogether Johnson's, is some part of the language in which they are expressed Boswell's? An answer to this may to some extent be found in a passage of the Life which, so far as I know, has escaped the notice of the commentators. Of the year 1780, Boswell writes :—

' Being disappointed in my hopes of meeting Johnson, so that I could hear none of his admirable sayings, I shall compensate for this want by inserting a collection of them, for which I am indebted to my worthy friend Mr. Langton. Very few articles of this collection were committed to writing by himself, he not having that habit. I however found, in conversation with him, that a good store of Johnsoniana was treasured in his mind. The authenticity of every article is unquestionable. For the expressions, I, who wrote them down in his presence, am partly answerable.'

It is quite clear from this that Boswell had, to use his own word, 'Johnsonised' the stories with which Mr. Langton supplied him. His friend gave him the substance of what Johnson had said, and Boswell then gave it a Johnsonian turn. So Johnson himself in his early life had given an oratorical turn to the notes of the Parliamentary debates that had been taken down for him by Guthrie. Johnson no doubt, even at his first start, made a far greater change than ever Boswell did, for he could have supplied, and in fact generally did supply, the greatest speakers, not only with words, but also with facts and arguments.

Now Boswell, with all his great merits, was utterly incapable of imitating Johnson in the substance of what he said. Of that neither he was capable, nor was Garrick, nor Goldsmith, nor Reynolds, nor Burke. As Gerard Hamilton said on Johnson's death, 'He has made a chasm, which not only nothing can fill up, but which nothing has a tendency to fill up. Johnson is dead. Let us go to the next best.   There is nobody ; no man can be said to put you in mind of Johnson.'   But yet, just as Garrick, with his little body, could in a most ludicrous way take off Johnson's huge frame, so Boswell had, I have little doubt, a considerable power of taking off his style. He did not, I believe, trust solely to his memory, tenacious though it was, when he was reproducing Johnson's conversation.   If his memory did not preserve the exact words, he would draw on his imagination for them.

A considerable light was thrown on this question by the publication of some 'loose quarto sheets in Boswell's writings inscribed on each page Boswelliana.'   In these sheets are found twenty-five anecdotes about Johnson, at least twenty-one of which are given also in the Life. Fifteen or sixteen of these twenty-one must have been recorded in the first ten weeks of the acquaintance of the two men.   During this time Boswell kept his journal with the greatest diligence.   It was then that he sat up, working at it four nights in one week.

I cannot pretend to offer any thoroughly satisfactory explanation of the fact that Boswell kept double records —if, indeed, he did keep double records—of the same

<hr>

¹ *Boswelliana. The Commonplace Book of James Boswell.* Edited by the Rev. Charles Rogers, LL.D.   London : Printed for the Grampian Club.   1874.

story. It may have been the case that when he first met Johnson, while he was bent on recording his conversations, he was intending at the same time to form a general collection of good sayings, and that thus he entered certain stories in both collections. It may also be the case—and this I think much more likely—that the loose sheets on which ' Boswelliana' are recorded were, in certain cases, the only notes, or at all events the first notes, he had taken of Johnson's sayings. Be the explanation what it may, the curious fact remains, that though the stories in both collections are in substance the same, yet most of them differ more or less verbally. If I am justified in assuming that the stories given in this collection that are common to both books were recorded in the ' Boswelliana' at the time they were heard, then we have a clear proof that Boswell, to a certain extent, changed the sayings of Johnson which he had collected.

It may be objected that this is at variance with the high character for accuracy which he claims for himself, and which is so generally and so justly allowed him. And there would be certainly some force, though not much, in the objection. His reports of Johnson's talk must of necessity have often been very imperfect. Complete accuracy was therefore impossible. He aimed at giving them what I have called a Johnsonian turn, knowing that he would thereby give a truer picture of Johnson. Whether what was said told for his hero or against his hero, mattered nothing to him. He left for the most part the facts as he found them, and made only changes in words. And yet one or two of the changes are greater than we should have expected, assuming, that is to say, as I am now assuming, that in 'Boswelliana' we have in each case the original record.

Perhaps the most striking instance is to be found in the two following stories from 'Boswelliana.' 'Mr. Sheridan, though a man of knowledge and parts, was a little fancifull (*sic*) in his projects for establishing oratory and altering the mode of British education. Mr. Samuel Johnson said, "Sherry, cannot abide me, for I allways (*sic*) ask him, Pray, Sir, what do you propose to do?" (From Mr. Johnson.)'

The second anecdote is as follows : 'Boswell was talking to Mr. Samuel Johnson of Mr. Sheridan's enthusiasm for the advancement of eloquence. "Sir," said Mr. Johnson, "it won't do. He cannot carry through his scheme. He is like a man attempting to stride the English Channel. Sir, the cause bears no proportion to the effect. It is setting up a candle at Whitechapel to give light at Westminster." '

Now there is good internal evidence that these two

anecdotes, as well as all the earlier ones, were recorded at the time they were heard. For in every one of them Boswell calls his friend Mr. Samuel Johnson, and not Dr. Johnson or Johnson. Boswell was abroad from August 1763 to February 1766. In his absence Johnson was complimented by the University of Dublin with the degree of Doctor of Laws, and Boswell, in the Life, writes : ' I returned to London in February, and found Dr. Johnson in a good house in Johnson's Court.' In none of the later anecdotes of ' Boswelliana ' do we find ' Mr. Samuel Johnson.' In the Life, however, these two stories about Mr. Sheridan are not only run into one, but they are also not a little altered. Boswell writes : ' He now added, " Sheridan cannot bear me. I bring his declamation to a point. I ask him a plain question, What do you mean to teach ? Besides, Sir, what in-fluence can Mr. Sheridan have upon the language of this great country by his narrow exertions ? Sir, it is burning a farthing candle at Dover to show light at Calais." '

While the first of the stories seems to me to have been not a little improved, the latter has suffered to a far greater extent. Whitechapel and Westminster not only contrast far better than Dover and Calais, but they are sufficiently near to keep the absurdity from being too gross.

In the ' Boswelliana ' we have the following anecdote :

'Boswell asked Mr. Samuel Johnson what was best to teach a gentleman's children first. "Why, Sir," said he, " there is no matter what you teach them first. It matters no more than which leg you put first into your bretches (*sic*). Sir, you may stand disputing which you shall put in first, but in the meantime your legs are bare. No matter which you put in first, so that you put 'em both in, and then you have your bretches on. Sir, while you think which of two things to teach a child first, another boy in the common course has learnt both." (I was present.)'

This is thus given in the Life in a much more pithy form : ' We talked of the education of children; and I asked him what he thought was best to teach them first. *Johnson* : " Sir, it is no matter what you teach them first, any more than what leg you shall put into your breeches first. Sir, you may stand disputing which is best to put in first, but in the meantime your breech is bare. Sir, while you are considering which of two things you should teach your child first, another boy has learnt them both."'

If in ' Boswelliana ' we have a report in the rough of what Johnson on this occasion said, Boswell may surely claim some small degree of merit for the more pointed way in which it is given in the Life.

In reporting one of the numerous attacks which Johnson made on Ossian, Boswell in the Life considerably weakens its force. He says that ' Dr. Blair asked Dr. Johnson whether he thought any man of a modern age could have written such poems? Johnson replied, " Yes, Sir, many men, many women, and many children."' In the 'Boswelliana' the story is thus told : ' Doctor Blair asked him if he thought any man could describe these barbarous manners so well if he had not lived at the time and seen them. " Any man, Sir," replied Mr. Johnson, " any man, woman, or child might have done it."'

At the same time that he has weakened what Johnson said by changing 'any' into 'many,' he has made it in another way a greater exaggeration ; for Johnson had not said (if we are to trust to the authority of ' Boswelliana ') that any child could have written the poems, but that any child could have described the barbarous manners.

Here is another story which is certainly more pointed as given in the Life than as it thus stands in ' Boswelliana ' : ' Boswell told Mr. Samuel Johnson that a gentleman of their acquaintance maintained in public company that he could see no distinction between virtue and vice. "Sir," said Mr. Johnson, " does he intend that we should believe that he is lying, or that he is in earnest? If we think him a liar, that is not honouring him very much. But if we think him in earnest, when he leaves our houses let us count our spoons."'

How much better is this told in the Life: 'Why, Sir, if the fellow does not think as he speaks, he is lying; and I see not what honour he can propose to himself from having the character of a liar. But if he does really think that there is no distinction between virtue and vice, why, Sir, when he leaves our houses let us count our spoons.'

Anyone who cares to study Boswell critically would find in a comparison of the other anecdotes not a little to interest him. But I will not run the risk of wearying my readers by quoting any more. I have, I hope, sufficiently shown that there are strong grounds for thinking that Boswell's merits, as a mere reporter of Johnson's talk, are not quite what they were thought to be.

As a writer, I have claimed for him, against the authority of one of the greatest writers of our age, a high place indeed. Macaulay, indeed, allows that 'his writings are likely to be read as long as the English exists, either as a living or as a dead language.' But while he grants him immortality, he refuses him greatness. Nay, even he belabours him with somewhat the same kind of fury as certain savage nations belabour their gods, who are at the same time the object of their adoration. Johnson, he will allow, was both a great and a good man, but Boswell, who has made known to us and to all time both the greatness and the goodness of Johnson, was himself most mean and vile. And yet we might almost fancy the two friends as they wandered through the Elysian Fields, and were pleased with the report each new comer brought of the fame 'The Life of Samuel Johnson' has here on earth, saying with a slight change in the words of the poet :—

> And it seems as I retrace the story line by line,
> That but half of it is his, and one half of it is mine.

I am fully aware of Boswell's failings and weaknesses as a man ; but grievous though they were, they do not make me for a moment forget the great debt under which we all lie to the author of the immortal Life. It is not likely that I should forget. He has carried me through many an hour of sickness and depression, and in the days of my health and strength has supplied me with an occupation in which I have found an interest that never fails.

CHAPTER V.

THE MELANCHOLY OF JOHNSON AND COWPER.[1]

IN Cowper's Letters we find a criticism on Johnson's diary which, though of no great interest in itself, is curious enough when we consider the man by whom it was written. He had not seen the whole of the diary, but merely some extracts from it in one of the newspapers. He says : 'It is certain that the publisher of it is neither much a friend to the cause of religion nor to the author's memory ; for by the specimen of it that has reached us, it seems to contain only such stuff as has a direct tendency to expose both to ridicule. His prayers for the dead, and his minute account of the rigour with which he observed church fasts, whether he drank tea or coffee, whether with sugar or without, and whether one or two dishes of either, are the most important items to be found in this childish register of the great Johnson, supreme dictator in the

---

[1] Reprinted (with alterations) from the *Pall Mall Gazette*, September 4, 1875.

chair of literature and almost a driveller in his closet—a melancholy witness to testify how much of the wisdom of this world may consist with almost infantine ignorance of the affairs of a better.' He goes on to refer to the diary of the Quaker of Huntingdon, over which Johnson himself, as was afterwards known from Boswell, had laughed so heartily; and he says that 'it contained much more valuable matter than the poor Doctor's journal seems to do.' To another correspondent he writes : 'Poor man! one would think, that to pray for his dead wife, and to pinch himself with church fasts, had been almost the whole of his religion. I am sorry that he, who was so manly an advocate for the cause of virtue in all other places, was so childishly employed, and so supersti- tiously too, in his closet.'

It is clear, I may notice in passing, that the extracts that Cowper had seen were not a fair sample of the whole diary. They had been selected, no doubt, to cast ridicule on Johnson's character, and the selection was only too easy. It is not with this point, however, that I intend to deal. As I was reading these letters—the letters of the best of English letter writers, if we may accept Southey's estimate—I could not but be affected with the melancholy state to which superstition had helped to reduce so fine a mind. In many points I was ever finding myself reminded of Johnson and of the gloom which so often hung round him, when, to my amazement, I found the one sufferer thus sitting in judgment on the other. Utterly unconscious that passages in his own letters would affect his readers in much the same way as Johnson's diary had affected him, Cowper is as full of pity for this supreme dictator in the chair of literature as we are for the poet. An extreme High Churchman, indeed, may see nothing pitiable in Johnson's records, any more than an extreme Low Churchman may in Cowper's. To a man of common sense there is but little to choose between them.

Compared with Johnson's entries about his tea and coffee, with sugar or without, the following extract from one of Cowper's letters does not strike me as showing a spark more of real sense : 'At present I am tolerably free from it (a nervous fever)—a blessing for which I believe myself partly indebted to the use of James's powder in small quantities, and partly to a small quantity of laudanum taken every night, but chiefly to a manifestation of God's presence vouchsafed to me a few days since.' In an earlier letter, in describing how Mrs. Unwin had narrowly escaped being burned to death when saying her prayers, he writes : 'It is not possible, perhaps, that so tragical a death should overtake a person actually engaged in prayer.' In another letter he tells a cock-and-bull story of an apparition that Johnson would have sifted with his usual severity, even though he saw no impossibility in a ghost story being true. How melancholy, too, is the frame of mind which could lead one so gentle thus to write such a verse as the following for the use of children :—

> Thanks for Thy word, and for Thy day ;
> And grant us, we implore,
> Never to waste, in sinful play,
> The holy Sabbaths more.

We may well compare with this Johnson's outburst against a friend who lamented the enormous wickedness of the times, because some birdcatchers were busy on Streatham Common one fine Sunday morning.[1] Between the superstition of the two men there was not, indeed, much to choose. Of the two, however, I should prefer Johnson's, for on the whole it sat on him more easily. He

---

[1] Mdme. Piozzi says : 'He ridiculed a friend who, looking out on Streatham Common from our windows one day, lamented the enormous wickedness of the times, because some birdcatchers were busy there one fine Sunday morning. "While half the Christian world is permitted," said he, "to dance and sing, and celebrate Sunday as a day of festivity, how comes your puritanical spirit so offended with frivolous and empty deviations from exactness ? Whoever loads life with unnecessary scruples, Sir," continued he, "provokes the attention of others on his conduct, and incurs the censure of singularity without reaping the reward of superior virtue." '

could find plausible excuses for shaking off at times some of the burdens he had bound on his own shoulders.   He once dined twice abroad in Passion week, as Boswell tells us, and thus ingeniously defended himself : ‘Why, Sir, a bishop’s calling company together in this week is, to use the vulgar phrase, not *the thing.*   But you must consider, laxity is a bad thing; but preciseness is also a bad thing; and your general character may be more hurt by preciseness than by dining with a bishop in Passion week. There might be a handle for reflection. It might be said, “He refuses to dine with a bishop in Passion week, but was three Sundays absent from Church.”’

It is an interesting question how far the gloom, both of Johnson and of Cowper, was due to religious belief, and how far religious belief was due to gloom.   If the dread of a future state had not constantly hung over each man, would he still have lived so much in a state of morbid melancholy?   This is a question rather for the physician to decide than for a layman.   I believe that under the most hopeful and encouraging of all creeds both men would at times have been distressed with melancholy, though at the same time I feel sure that their melancholy was greatly increased by the gloomy views they held.   It is plain that in Cowper’s case his friend Mr. Newton did him, and through him the world, as grievous a wrong as a thoroughly sincere and conscientious man of considerable ability often has a chance of doing. It is true that, before he knew Mr. Newton, Cowper had tried to make away with himself, but after that sad time he had regained his tranquillity and cheerfulness of mind. It was owing to the teaching and mismanagement of his pastor that this most loving and gentle of men lived year after year in the full belief that God had utterly rejected him, and that, as he was passing away from the world, he exclaimed, 'I feel unutterable despair.'

Johnson, indeed, at one time was in a scarcely less miserable state. In the early days of his acquaintance with the Thrales, 'he lamented to us,' as Madame Piozzi tells us, 'the horrible condition of his mind, which he said was nearly distracted; and though he charged us to make him odd, solemn promises of secrecy on so strange a subject, yet when we waited on him one morning, and heard him in the most pathetic terms beg the prayers of Dr. Delap, who had left him as we came in, I felt excessively affected with grief, and well remember my husband involuntarily lifted up one hand to shut his mouth, from provocation at hearing a man so wildly proclaim what he could at last persuade no one to believe; and what, if true, would have been so very unfit to reveal.' Some years later he said to Boswell, with some truth, 'I inherited a vile melancholy from my father, which has made me mad all my life, at least not sober.'

His dread of a future state, great though it was, nevertheless was far more tempered by reason than Cowper's. A few months before his death, in a gloomy conversation in which he joined after supper in Pembroke College, in answer to Boswell's question, 'May not a man attain to such a degree of hope as not to be uneasy from the fear of death?' he replied, 'A man may have such a degree of hope as to keep him quiet. You see I am not quiet, from the vehemence with which I talk; but I do not despair.' Cowper's misery led him to write: 'I feel— I will not tell you what—and yet I must—a wish that I had never been, a wonder that I am, and an ardent but hopeless desire not to be.' Into such a wish as this Johnson could never have entered. Much as he dreaded the next world, he dreaded annihilation still more. 'Mere existence,' he said on one occasion—and he expressed, we have no doubt, his settled belief—'is so much better than nothing, that one would rather exist even in pain than not exist.' He went on to say, in answer to an objection that was raised, 'The lady confounds annihilation, which is nothing, with the apprehension of it, which is dreadful. It is in the apprehension of it that the horror of annihilation consists.'

Both men were quite well aware that their melancholy could be to no small extent overcome by exercise, occupation, and attention to diet. Johnson, in writing to Boswell, says, 'I believe it is best to throw life into a method, that every hour may bring its employment, and every employment have its hour. . . . I have not practised all this prudence myself, but I have suffered much from want of it.' In his diary he records, 'by abstinence from wine and suppers I obtained great and sudden relief, and had freedom of mind restored to me.' Cowper often connects his mental feelings with the state of his digestion ; and it is worth while noting that Swift, whose case in many points resembles theirs, fills his letters with the doings of his stomach, and the meat and drink that give it the least trouble. While Swift's motto was *Vive la bagatelle*, and while in literary trifling, in gardening, and in riding he sought to break what Johnson calls 'the gloomy calm of idle vacancy,' and while Cowper had a greater variety of occupation both for in-doors and out-of-doors, Johnson had little but company on which to fall back. He did, indeed, now and then trim and water a vine that grew up his house in Bolt Court; and he delighted in chemical experiments till Mr. Thrale put an end to them, at Streatham at least, 'being persuaded that Johnson's short sight would have occasioned his destruction in a moment, by bringing him close to a fierce and violent flame.' He regretted that he had not learned to play at cards, and he once made the attempt to learn knotting. 'Next to mere idleness,' he said, 'I think knotting is to be reckoned in the scale of insignificance; though I once attempted to learn knotting; Dempster's sister endeavoured to teach me it, but I made no progress.' It is strange that he never took to smoking. 'I cannot account,' he said, in speaking of it, 'why a thing which requires so little exertion, and yet preserves the mind from total vacuity, should have gone out. Every man has something by which he calms himself; beating with his feet or so.'

There was the following difference between the two men. 'A vacant hour,' wrote Cowper, 'is my abhorrence.' Accordingly he took care that there should be no vacant hours. Every moment of his time was filled up, and to his correspondents he often complains that he can scarcely find leisure in which to write to them. Johnson, who suffered at times scarcely less than Cowper in his vacant hours, had not, nevertheless, resolution enough to overcome his natural indolence. 'He always felt,' he said, 'an inclination to do nothing.' Cowper, though he greatly stood in need of money to supply his very modest wants, yet needed not the inducement of money to set him writing.

In fact almost all his original poetry, in ignorance of its value, he made a present of to his publisher. He was paid, no doubt, for his translation of Homer; but he began it without hope of reward, and he would have finished it, though it took him many years, even had he not earned a penny by it. He had strength of mind to use the best cure he could find for his melancholy, and verse-making for a long time was the best. Johnson, on the contrary, maintained that no one but a fool would write unless he were paid for it. 'It has been said that there is pleasure in writing, particularly in writing verses. I allow you may have pleasure from writing after it is over, if you have written well; but you don't go willingly to it again. I know, when I have been writing verses, I have run my finger down the margin to see how many I had made, and how few I had to make.' Even of reading he said: 'The progress which the understanding makes through a book has more pain than pleasure in it.' Yet he was one of the most rapid of readers as he was one of the most rapid of writers.

Both men at one time undertook literary work for which they were very ill fitted, and which, in consequence, weighed very heavily on them. There is no doubt that Cowper's last attack of insanity was greatly brought on by the engagement into which he had entered to edit

Milton; while Shakespeare for many a year weighed most heavily on Johnson. A man of his strict honesty must have suffered greatly from the thought that he had been paid for work which it seemed he would never finish, long before Churchill taunted him in the lines—

> He for subscribers baits his hook,
> And takes your cash; but where's the book?

There is one point of resemblance between Cowper and Johnson which, likely enough, took its rise from the same cause. Boswell, in his 'Tour to the Hebrides,' says : 'Having taken the liberty, this evening, to remark to Dr. Johnson that he very often sat quite silent for a long time, even when in company with only a single friend, which I myself had sometimes sadly experienced, he smiled, and said, " It is true, Sir. Tom Tyers described me the best. He once said to me, 'Sir, you are like a ghost; you never speak till you are spoken to.'"' This habit of his was often remarked on. He very rarely, in fact, was the first to begin a conversation, nor, when he began to speak, was it on a subject of his own choosing. This habit of talk was shown, indeed, the first evening he spent at Oxford, when he was only a lad of nineteen. 'He sat silent till, upon something which occurred in the course of conversation, he suddenly struck in and quoted Macrobius.'

Cowper, in writing of himself, says : 'The effect of such continual listening to the language of a heart hopeless and deserted is, that I can never give much more than half my attention to what is started by others, and very rarely start anything myself. My silence, however, and my absence of mind make me sometimes as entertaining as if I had wit.'

Johnson, indeed, could give all his attention to what was started by others if it once roused his interest, but he, no doubt, too often, like Cowper, was listening to the language of a heart, if not hopeless and deserted, yet in a very despondent state. His absence of mind, too, was entertaining, and his habit of talking to himself occasioned some merriment. 'I was certain,' writes Boswell, 'that he was frequently uttering pious ejaculations, for fragments of the Lord's Prayer have been distinctly overheard. His friend, Mr. Thomas Davies, of whom Churchill says, "That Davies hath a very pretty wife," when Johnson muttered "Lead us not into temptation," used with waggish and gallant humour to whisper Mrs. Davies, "You, my dear, are the cause of this."'

The society of lively women told equally well on each. What Mrs. Thrale did for Johnson, the same, though in a far less degree, for they were far less with him, did Lady Austen and Lady Hesketh do for Cowper.

Without in the least forgetting all he owed to Mrs. Unwin, we may with some confidence say that, had he never known Mr. Newton, and had Lady Hesketh always lived with him, he might, as his death drew near, have owned with Johnson that he had enjoyed far more real happiness in his latter than in his earlier years.

For many years these two men lived very near to each other without ever meeting. Two of the unhappiest men in London—for so at about one and the same time they were—were indeed very close neighbours. Johnson was living in Inner Temple Lane when Dr. Adams, the tutor of his old college, visited him and found him 'in a deplorable state, sighing, groaning, talking to himself, and restlessly walking from room to room. He then used this emphatical expression of the misery which he felt: "I would consent to have a limb amputated to recover my spirits." It was in his chambers in the Inner Temple that only a few months earlier Cowper, first with laudanum and then with his garter, had tried to end his life, which had become too miserable for him any longer to bear. It was, moreover, at the same period of life that they were first attacked with melancholy. Cowper was but twenty when he was, as he says, 'struck with such a dejection of spirits as none but those who have felt the same can have the least conception of. Day and night I was upon the rack, lying down in horror and rising up in despair.' At the very same age Johnson 'felt himself overwhelmed with a horrible hypochondria, with perpetual irritation, fretfulness, and impatience, and with a dejection, gloom, and despair which made existence misery.'

It is strange that of these two melancholy men the one should have written one of the most diverting of histories, the 'History of John Gilpin,' and that the other should have lived to be the material out of which has been formed one of the liveliest of books, Boswell's 'Life of Samuel Johnson.' But humour and melancholy commonly go hand-in-hand, and men who have done most to lighten the sadness of others, too often themselves have passed through life 'as 'twere with a defeated joy.'

CHAPTER VI.

LORD CHESTERFIELD AND JOHNSON.

THERE is a well-known passage in one of 'Lord Chester-field's Letters to his Son,' which is commonly supposed to have been aimed at Johnson. Boswell says 'the character of a respectable Hottentot in "Lord Chesterfield's Letters" has been generally understood to be meant for Johnson, and I have no doubt that it was.' Murphy does not even raise a doubt on the question, neither does Hawkins. But Johnson himself said that the character was not meant for him, but for George Lord Lyttelton; and Lord Hailes, according to Boswell, 'maintained with some warmth that it was not intended as a portrait of Johnson, but of a late noble lord distinguished for abstruse science (probably, says Mr. Croker, the second Earl of Macclesfield).' I shall be able, I believe, to prove almost beyond a doubt that Boswell, Murphy, and Hawkins were wrong. Whoever it was that Lord Chester-field meant, it certainly was not Johnson. To establish my position I must quote the passage at length.

'There is a man whose moral character, deep learning, and superior parts I acknowledge, admire, and respect; but whom it is so impossible for me to love, that I am almost in a fever whenever I am in his company. His figure (without being deformed) seems made to disgrace or ridicule the common structure of the human body. His legs and arms are never in the position, which, according to the situation of his body, they ought to be in; but constantly employed in committing acts of hostility upon the Graces. He throws anywhere but down his throat whatever he means to drink; and only mangles what he means to carve. Inattentive to all the regards of social life, he mistimes or misplaces everything. He disputes with heat and indiscriminately, mindless of the rank, character, and situation of those with whom he disputes; absolutely ignorant of the several gradations of familiarity or respect, he is exactly the same to his superiors, his equals, and his inferiors, and therefore by a necessary consequence absurd to two of the three. Is it possible to love such a man? No. The utmost I can do for him is to consider him as a respectable Hottentot.'

Now in this passage itself there is good evidence to be found that Chesterfield was thinking of anyone rather than Johnson. As Boswell himself said to Johnson, 'there was one trait which unquestionably did not belong to him—"he throws his meat anywhere but down his throat."' He certainly was not the man to scatter his food. 'When at table he was totally absorbed in the business of the moment; his looks seemed riveted to his plate.' No man, moreover, was less open than Johnson to the charge of being 'absolutely ignorant of the several gradations of familiarity or respect.' He had, as every reader of Boswell knows, a high respect for rank. 'I have great merit,' he said, 'in being zealous for subordination and the honours of birth; for I can hardly tell who was my grandfather.' His respect for the dignitaries of the Church is well known, and his bow to an archbishop was described 'as such a studied elaboration of homage, such an extension of limb, such a flexion of body as have seldom or ever been equalled.' In his interview with the king he exactly acted up to one of Lord Chesterfield's directions to his son. 'Were you,' he writes to the young man, 'to converse with a king you ought to be as easy and unembarrassed as with your own *valet de chambre*; but yet every look, word, and action should imply the utmost respect.' What 'a nice and dignified sense of true politeness' did Johnson show, as Boswell has pointed out, when on some one asking him whether he had made any reply to a high compliment the king had paid him, he answered: 'No, Sir.

When the king had said it, it was to be so. It was not for me to bandy civilities with my sovereign.' Nothing, moreover, is farther from the truth than that he was 'inattentive to all the regards of social life.' Even Madame Piozzi, who was, to a great extent, an unfriendly witness, says that 'no one was so attentive not to offend in all such sort of things as Dr. Johnson; nor so careful to maintain the ceremonies of life.'

Nevertheless Chesterfield's portrait, though a gross caricature, might have been meant for Johnson. To prove that it was not, I will first consider the circumstances under which it was drawn. The letter in which it is given opens with the epigram in Martial—

> Non amo te, Sabidi, nec possum dicere quare,
> Hoc tantum possum dicere, non amo te.

Chesterfield goes on to show 'how it is possible not to love anybody and yet not to know the reason why . . . . 'How often,' he says, 'have I, in the course of my life, found myself in this situation with regard to many of my acquaintance whom I have honoured and respected, without being able to love.' He then goes on to instance the case of the man whom he ends by describing as a respectable Hottentot. It is clear that he is writing of a man whom he knows well and who has some claim upon his affections. Twice he says that it is

impossible to love him, and he clearly implies thereby
that this man was in some respect or other on such a
footing with him as to render it likely that he would have
loved him.

This letter was written in February 1751. On what
footing did Johnson stand with Chesterfield at that time?
Four years earlier Johnson, at the suggestion of Dodsley
the bookseller, had dedicated to his lordship the plan of
his great Dictionary. Chesterfield at this time was the
head of the world of fashion, and was moreover one of
the two Secretaries of State. Johnson had for years felt,
and was for years to feel, ' what ills the scholar's life assail.'
Only three years before this dedication he had dined behind the screen at Cave's house, when he was too shabbily
dressed to be seen, and had heard his ' Life of Savage '
praised by Mr. Harte, who, two years afterwards, was appointed tutor to Lord Chesterfield's son. Nine years after
the dedication he was under arrest for five pounds eighteen
shillings and was only freed by a loan from Richardson.
The two men—the great nobleman and the poor author—
were in the year 1747 wide as the poles asunder. Johnson
was laying the foundation of his fame, but he was not yet
famous. He had written the ' Parliamentary Debates,' but
they were not known to be his. His poem of ' London '
and his ' Life of Savage ' were as yet the books on which

his fame mainly rested. The work that he was now taking in hand was, to quote his own words, generally considered as a task that might 'be successfully performed without any higher qualities than that of bearing burthens with dull patience, and beating the track of the alphabet with sluggish resolution.' It was from one of his poor lodgings 'in the courts and alleys in and about the Strand and Fleet Street' that Johnson went to pay his respects to his noble patron the great Minister of State. He saw but little of him, and certainly never enjoyed his hospitality, for Johnson himself has stated that Chesterfield never saw him eat in his life. He received from him in return for his dedication a present of ten pounds. He soon grew weary of the neglect with which he was constantly received, and certainly never visited him after the beginning of the year 1748. 'Seven years, my lord,' he wrote on February 7, 1755, 'have now past since I waited in your outward rooms, or was repulsed from your door.' He had done all that he could. The honour that he had paid to Chesterfield was, indeed, a great one, when he addressed to him that fine piece of writing, in which he sets forth the plan on which was slowly to be built up one of the noblest monuments in our language. He had done all that he could; 'and no man is well pleased to have his all neglected, be it ever so little.'

It is clear then that Chesterfield had at no time seen much of Johnson, and that in the year 1751, when he wrote the letter to his son, he had not seen him for three years. Croker, in a note on Johnson's statement that Chesterfield never saw him eat, says : 'Nor did we—and yet we know that Chesterfield's picture, if meant for Johnson, was not overcharged.' We know of Johnson's mode of eating, but how should Chesterfield have known? how, above all, should he have known so early as the year 1751?

Here is the very key to the error into which Boswell and Hawkins have fallen. Had Chesterfield's letter been published when it was written, no one in all likelihood would have so much as dreamt that Johnson was aimed at. But it did not come before the world till twenty-three years later, when Johnson's quarrel with Chesterfield was known to everyone, when Johnson himself was at the very head of the literary world, and when his peculiarities had become a matter of general interest. His famous letter to Chesterfield had been seen as yet by very few, but that he had written a letter of great power and great severity was well known. Lord Hardwicke in his eagerness to read it had used, and used in vain, the intervention of the Bishop of Salisbury. Johnson had refused the Bishop's request, saying with a smile : 'No, Sir, I have hurt the dog too much already.'

From the beginning of 1748 to the end of 1754 Chesterfield had no dealings of any kind with Johnson. He later on attempted to excuse his neglect 'by saying that he had heard he had changed his lodgings, and did not know where he lived.' Johnson certainly changed his lodgings very often. In the first eleven years of his residence in London he had at least eleven different lodgings. But Chesterfield could, of course, at any time have learnt from Dodsley where he was to be found. By the end of 1754 the Dictionary was almost ready for publication, and Chesterfield no doubt had heard how admirably Johnson had performed his task. There was not a man in the kingdom, he must have felt, but would have had high honour done to him by having his name for ever associated with such a work. He had, no doubt, forgotten all about Johnson in the seven long years, during which he had been tugging at the oar. But a great man's smile goes a long way ; his good word goes still farther. 'He attempted therefore, in a courtly manner to soothe and insinuate himself with the sage . . . . and further attempted to conciliate him by writing two papers in "The World" in recommendation of the work.'

Boswell thinks that some of the 'studied compliments' in these papers are 'so finely turned that if there had been no previous offence, it is probable that Johnson would have been highly delighted.' We very much doubt, however, whether Johnson, pleased though he might have been with a passage here and there, would not have been offended, and most justly and highly offended, with the papers as a whole. He would have felt under small obligations when the anonymous writer hopes his readers will not suspect him 'of being a hired and interested puff of this work ; I most solemnly protest,' his lordship goes on to say, 'that neither Mr. Johnson, nor any bookseller or booksellers concerned in the success of it, have ever offered me the usual compliment of a pair of gloves or a bottle of wine.' It is, no doubt, a pretty piece of irony for a wealthy nobleman solemnly to protest that he has not been bribed by a poor author. But we cannot but think of Johnson's stubborn honesty, we cannot but call to mind how years later on, in far happier days, he burst into a passion of tears when he read his own noble poem in which he so touchingly described the poor scholar's hard life. We do not forget that this poem was written in 1749, the year after he had for the last time waited in Lord Chesterfield's outward rooms, or been repulsed from his door. The pert, flippant tone in which the second of the two papers is written would have pleased him, if possible, still less.

A man who has laboured hard till the eleventh hour, and has borne the heat and burthen of the day, is not likely to be over-pleased when a fine fellow in a laced coat strolls in with a genteel air, and begins to praise his work, and in gloved hands to pat him on the back.

But Chesterfield did worse than this. He displeased Johnson in a point where he always made his displeasure be most heavily felt. In the last year of his life, at a time of great weakness and depression, the old man boasted that obscenity had always been repressed in his company. Who can picture then the indignation that he must have felt at the support that Chesterfield brought to his book? This great patron of literature, by way of recommending a work of so much learning and so much labour, tells a foolish story of an assignation that had failed 'between a fine gentleman and a fine lady.' The letter that had passed between them had been badly spelt and they had gone to different houses. 'Such examples,' writes his lordship, 'really make one tremble; and will, I am convinced, determine my fair fellow-subjects and their adherents to adopt and scrupulously conform to Mr. Johnson's rules of true orthography.' 'What!' we can imagine Johnson exclaiming, 'shall the fellow turn me into a guide to the brothels?'

In one of his Letters Chesterfield has happily described his own conduct, and has fully justified Johnson's indignation. 'The insolent civility,' he says, 'of a proud man is, if possible, more shocking than his rudeness could be ; because he shows you by his manner that he thinks it mere condescension in him ; and that his goodness alone bestows upon you what you have no pretence to claim.' With good reason did Johnson exclaim when he read Chesterfield's papers in 'The World,' 'I have sailed a long and painful voyage round the world of the English language, and does he now send out two cock-boats to tow me into harbour ?'

Mr. Croker is almost lost in astonishment at 'the magnanimity of good taste and conscious rectitude' which Lord Chesterfield displayed, when he let Johnson's letter lie open on his table for anyone to read. But his motives are clear enough to anyone but Mr. Croker. He was only acting up to the advice which he had himself given his son, as his guide in a like case. 'When things of this kind happen to be said of you,' he wrote, 'the most prudent way is to seem not to suppose that they are meant at you, but to dissemble and conceal whatever degree of anger you may feel inwardly ; and should they be so plain that you cannot be supposed ignorant of their meaning, to join in the laugh of the company against yourself; acknowledge the hit to be a fair one, and the jest a good one, and play off the whole thing in seeming good humour ; but by no means reply in the same way ; which only shows that you are hurt, and publishes the victory which you might have concealed.'

He exactly acted up to this when he read Johnson's letter to Dodsley and 'said, "This man has great powers," pointed out the severest passages, and observed how well they were expressed.' He must have felt that he was overmatched, and that the wiser course for him was to show no resentment.

If we may trust Hawkins, he even made further efforts to conciliate Johnson. He sent to him Sir Thomas Robinson 'to apologize for his lordship's treatment of him, and to make him tenders of his future friendship and patronage.' Robinson declared that were his own circumstances other than they were, he would himself settle five hundred pounds a year on him. 'And who are you,' asked Johnson, 'that talk thus liberally?' 'I am,' said he, 'Sir Thomas Robinson, a Yorkshire baronet.' 'Sir,' replied Johnson, 'if the first peer of the realm were to make me such an offer, I would show him the way down stairs.'

It is not unlikely that Chesterfield really made this attempt. He knew what is commonly called the world well, and he had made man, as he often boasted, his chief study. He had told his son that 'people in high life are hardened to the wants and distresses of mankind as surgeons are to their bodily pains.' He had assured him, that if he wanted to succeed with them, he must apply to 'other sentiments than those of mere justice and humanity. . . . Their love of ease must be disturbed by unwearied importunity, or their fears wrought upon by a decent intimation of implacable, cool resentment.' Johnson, he might have said to himself, had waited upon him and had gained nothing. He had now tried what the other course would effect. Implacable and cool though his resentment threatened to be, he had as yet given but a decent intimation of it. He had not published his letter to the world.

But Johnson was not to be won over. He had taken Chesterfield's measure, and he ever afterwards spoke of him in terms of the greatest contempt. 'This man,' said he, 'I thought had been a lord among wits ; but I find he is only a wit among lords.' He even changed, as Boswell tells us, a word in one of the couplets of the Vanity of Human Wishes. It had run :—

> Yet think what ills the scholar's life assail,
> Toil, envy, want, the *garret*, and the jail.

Henceforth, in remembrance of what he had endured from Lord Chesterfield, the line ran :—

> Toil, envy, want, the *Patron*, and the jail.

The proofs that I have already brought forward that Chesterfield was not thinking of Johnson when he drew the character of a respectable Hottentot, seem to me conclusive. But further evidence is to be found in the letters themselves. I have no doubt that once again he described the same person, and I have as little doubt, that he had twice described him before. We must remember that these Letters were not written for publication, and were not published till after the writer's death. There is in them therefore not a little repetition, as might be expected, seeing that they spread over a space of thirty years. The first of these passages is in a letter dated September 22nd O. S. 1749 :—

‘You have often seen, and I have as often made you observe, L.'s distinguished inattention and awkwardness. Wrapped up, like a Laputan, in intense thought, and possibly sometimes in no thought at all (which, I believe, is very often the case of absent people,) he does not know his most intimate acquaintance by sight, or answers them as if he were at cross-purposes. He leaves his hat in one room, his sword in another, and would leave his shoes in a third, if his buckles, though awry, did not save them ; his legs and arms, by his awkward management of them, seem to have undergone the *question extraordinaire* ; and his head always hanging upon one or other of his shoulders, seem to have received the first stroke upon a block. I sincerely value and esteem him for his parts, learning, and virtue; but for the soul of me I cannot love him in company.'

The second passage is in a letter written sometime in November of the same year :—

'Should you be awkward, inattentive and *distrait*, and happen to meet Mr. L. at my table, the consequences of that meeting must be fatal; you would run your heads against each other, cut each other's fingers instead of your meat, or die by the precipitate infusion of scalding soup.'

The last passage is in a letter dated May 27, O. S. 1753 :—

'I have this day been tired, jaded, nay tormented, by the company of a most worthy, sensible, and learned man, a near relation of mine, who dined and passed the evening with me. This seems a paradox, but is a plain truth; he has no knowledge of the world, no manners, no address. . . . It would be endless to correct his mistakes, nor would he take it kindly; for he has considered everything deliberately, and is very sure that he is in the right. Impropriety is a characteristic, and a never failing one, of these people. Regardless, because igno- rant, of custom and manners, they violate them every moment. They often shock, though they never mean to offend ; never attending either to the general character, or the particular distinguishing circumstances of the people to whom, or before whom they talk ; whereas the knowledge of the world teaches one that the very same things which are exceedingly right and proper in one company, time, and place, are exceedingly absurd in others.'

We have in all these passages the same character throughout. There are the same parts, the same learning, the same virtue, the same awkwardness, the same absence of mind, the same indifference to the rank, character, and situation of those with whom he disputes. There is also the same claim upon Lord Chesterfield's affection, and the same impossibility of bestowing it. It is clear, I hold, that the respectable Hottentot was not Samuel Johnson, but Mr. L., Lord Chesterfield's relation.

CHAPTER VII.

LORD CHESTERFIELD'S LETTERS.

THOUGH Johnson had spoken with the utmost scorn of 'Lord Chesterfield's Letters to his Son,' yet he once admitted that 'they might be made a very pretty book. Take out the immorality and it should be put into the hands of every young gentleman.'

However much the book would be improved as a piece of morality, its chief interest as a work of art and as a study of manners would be gone. In it, as it at present stands, we have set forth at great length and with great minuteness the whole art of living as practised and taught by a man who at one time held a great place in England. Horace Walpole, who is no mean authority on such a point, says that 'the work is a most proper book of laws for the generation in which it is published, and has reduced the folly and worthlessness of the age to a regular system.' He sums it up as 'the whole duty of man adapted to the meanest capacities.' But the more faithful a picture the book gives of the times in which it was written, the more it would suffer if any parts of it were cut out. There is no doubt that it contains a great many shrewd remarks, a great deal of lively writing, and not a few wise sayings. But the real interest of the book is lost if it is not taken as a whole. Chesterfield held that 'the trade of a courtier is as much a trade as that of a shoemaker.' He is never weary of repeating this truth in one form or other. His son is his apprentice. He, himself is a master who knows the whole craft. He has for years made man and the world his study. His day, indeed, is passing by. He has played his part, and on the whole has played it very well. But he has retired in time, *uti conviva satur.* It should never be said of him—

Superfluous lags the veteran on the stage.

But he can make a still better player of his son. He himself is an old traveller, well acquainted with all the by-ways as well as with the great roads. He cannot misguide from ignorance. His only remaining ambition is to be the minister of his son's rising ambition. There is only one thing in the world so far as he knows that is not to be acquired by application and care, and that is poetry. But everything else he can have if he will. Every one must do something that deserves to be written, or write something that deserves to be read. 'Can there,' he asks of his son when he is a schoolboy of fourteen, 'Can there be a greater pleasure than to be universally allowed to excel those of one's own age and manner of life?' Earlier still does he try to teach him the lesson of ambition. Where would he, a boy of nine, run to hide himself if Master Onslow, a youth of the same age, should deservedly obtain a place in school above him? Master Onslow apparently did get above him, for the father later on writes that he knows very well his son will not be easy till he has got above Master Onslow. He must do everything well, however trifling it may be. If he plays at pitch and cricket, let him play better than any boy in Westminster. When Chesterfield is appointed Secretary of State, he writes to tell the lad that, if he will work, he may very possibly be his successor, though not his immediate successor. But everything must be 'steadily directed to this end. He, as his father, had done and was doing his best.' He had not spoilt his son by over-fondness or over-severity. Nineteen fathers in twenty, and every mother who had loved him as well as he did, would have ruined him. But no weaknesses of his own had warped his education, no parsimony had starved it, no rigour had deformed it. Sound and extensive learning was the foundation that he had meant to lay, and he had laid it. He had given him the best masters. He had put him at Westminster School, and before the boy had seen his fifteenth birthday he had sent him abroad under the care of a sound scholar to study in Lausanne, Leipzig, Berlin, Turin, Rome, and Paris.

He used from the very first to write to the lad as if he were almost a man. He was right, he said, in seeing the curiosities in the several places he visited. But he was to remember that seeing is the least material object of travelling ; hearing and knowing are the essential points. Not once in the course of his letters is there any mention of the beauties of nature. He might form a taste if he pleased for painting, sculpture, and architecture, for these were liberal arts, and a real taste and knowledge of them became a man of fashion very well. But the steeples, the market places, and the signs he must leave to the laborious researches of Dutch and German travellers.

George Fox himself could scarcely have spoken with greater contempt of the steeple-house than did Chesterfield of the steeple. His son's destination, he was to remember, was the great and busy world; his immediate object was the affairs, the interests, the history, the constitutions, the customs and the manners of the several parts of Europe. In whatever country he might be, he was to learn all he could about its strength, its revenue, and its commerce ; and this part of political knowledge could not be learnt from books, but could only be had by inquiry and conversation. He was never to waste a single moment. He was not, indeed, to pass all the day in studying, but he was to be always doing something. He was never to sit idle and yawning. Rather let him read a jest-book than do that. He might have his share in pleasures. He might go to public spectacles, assemblies, cheerful suppers, and even balls ; but even these require attention, or the time is lost. He must be curious, attentive, inquisitive as to everything.

There was hardly any place or any company where knowledge might not be gained. Almost everybody knows some one thing, and is glad to talk upon that one thing. Seek and you will find, in this world as well as in the next.

His chief study was to be the world ; that country which nobody ever knew by description, which is utterly unknown to the scholar, though he talks and writes of it as he sits in the dust of his closet. 'You must look into people,' he writes to this lad of fourteen, 'as well as at them. Almost all people are born with all the passions to a certain degree ; but almost every man has a pre-vailing one to which the others are subordinate. Search every one for that ruling passion; pry into the recesses of his heart, and observe the different workings of the same passion in different people. And, when you have found out the prevailing passion of any man, remember never to trust him where that passion is concerned. Work upon him by it if you please, but be upon your guard yourself against it, whatever professions he may make.'

He returns to this again and again. A year later he bids him observe the little habits, the likings, the antipathies, and the tastes of those whom he would gain. Let them, if they sup with him, find their favourite dish, and let them be informed that it has been provided because it was their favourite dish. Attention to trifles flatters self-love much more than attention to greater things, as it makes people think themselves almost the only objects of one's care and thoughts.

Chesterfield wished that he had known these 'arcana' so necessary for initiation in the great society of the world at his son's age. He had paid the price of three and fifty years for them ; but this price, heavy though it was, he would not grudge if the boy reaped the advantage. He returns again and again to these 'arcana.' When he was at court he was to speak advantageously of the people highest in fashion behind their backs, in companies who, he had reason to believe, would repeat what he said. At Turin let him express his admiration of the many great men that the House of Savoy has produced, and let him point out that nature instead of being exhausted by those efforts seems to have redoubled them in the persons of the present King and the Duke ; let him wonder at this rate where it will end. Let him stick to capitals, where the best company is always to be found. He had himself stuck to them all his lifetime.

But even at courts not a moment of time must be wasted. 'What would I not give,' he writes to his son when he has reached the age of seventeen, ' to have you read Demosthenes critically in the morning, and understand him better than anybody ; at noon behave yourself better than any person at court ; and in the evening trifle more agreeably than anybody in mixed companies.' If he only made a right use of the company he kept, his very pleasures would make him a successful negotiator, for company is in truth a constant state of negotiation. By the same means that a man makes a friend, guards against an enemy, or gains a mistress, he will make an advantageous treaty, baffle those who counteract him, and gain the court to which he is sent.

He must conform to the world, and such was the

present turn of the world that some valuable qualities
were even ridiculous if not accompanied by the genteeler
accomplishments. Plainness, simplicity and Quakerism
either in dress or manners would by no means do. He
must frequent those good houses where he had already a
footing, and wriggle himself somehow or other into every
other. He must flatter humours, he must study the
mollia tempora ; he must acquire confidence by seeming
frankness and profit of it by silent skill. Above all he
must gain and engage the heart to betray the understanding. *Hæ tibi erunt artes.*

The anger that Chesterfield from time to time rouses
in the hearts of his readers is far more roused by this vile
use of Virgil's noble lines, than by all the recommendations he gives his son to improve his manners at the
expense of his morals :—

> Tu regere imperio populos, Romane, memento ;
> Hæ tibi erunt artes ; pacisque imponere morem,
> Parcere subjectis, et debellare superbos.

This young man, too, was to aim at being a ruler.
He was the only one, his father said, whose education
was from the beginning calculated for foreign affairs.
He could, if he pleased, make himself absolutely necessary to the Government. He would first receive orders
as a minister abroad, and then in his turn send orders to

others as Secretary of State at home.   But he must begin
by wriggling.   *Hæ tibi erunt artes.*

Chesterfield had unhappily forgotten his own advice.
The lad was never to quote Greek or Latin, and never to
bring precedents from the virtuous Spartans, the polite
Athenians, and the brave Romans.   His father had himself, he owned, fallen into this folly.   At the time that he
left Cambridge, when he talked his best he quoted
Horace ; when he aimed at being facetious he quoted
Martial ; and when he had a mind to be a fine gentleman
he quoted Ovid.   Unhappily in his riper years when he
aimed at being base he quoted Virgil.

Yet Chesterfield had no suspicion of his own base-
ness.   He aimed, as he often reminds his son, at nothing
short of perfection in the education he was giving him.
He longed to make him that most perfect of all beings,
a man of parts and knowledge who has acquired the easy
and noble manners of a court.   He wished him to grow
up a virtuous man, a man who acted wisely, upon solid
principles, and from true motives, though he must keep
his motives to himself and never talk sententiously.   He
warns him that there is nothing so delicate as moral
character, and nothing which it is so much his interest to
preserve pure.

'For God's sake,' he writes, 'be scrupulously jealous

of the merit of your moral character ; keep it immaculate, unblemished, unsullied.' When the young man is first going into the great world he warns him that he will be tried and judged there not as a boy, but as a man, and he bids him remember that from that moment his character is fixed, and that for character there is no appeal.

He warns him again and again that if he has not the knowledge, the honour, and the probity which he expects of him, he will visit him with his severest displeasure. If once they quarrel, let him not count upon any weakness in his nature for a reconciliation. He has no such weakness about him. He will never forgive. But it was, he hoped, impossible that they should quarrel, for the lad was no stranger to the principles of virtue, and whoever knows virtue must love it.

In all this there is not the slightest insincerity nor the slightest hypocrisy. Horace Walpole admitted that to his great surprise the letters seemed really written from the heart. Chesterfield after all was only adapting to his times the lessons which the poet Horace had taught, and taught with applause, ages before.

The foundation of learning had been laid, but as the building was slowly rising Chesterfield was distressed by one dread. Knowledge and virtue were all, he felt, in vain, unless to them were added manners.

Take, he says, one man, with a very moderate degree of knowledge, but with a pleasing figure and prepossessing address, who is graceful in all that he says and does, who is in short adorned with all the lesser talents, and take another man with sound sense and profound knowledge, but without these advantages ; the former will not only get the better of the latter in every pursuit, of every kind, but in truth there will be no sort of competition.

Marlborough's success, he asserted, was chiefly due to his admirable manners. To the Graces quite as much as to Mars he owed the triumph of Blenheim. See what the Duke of Richelieu had done, and to what a station he had raised himself. He had not the parts of a porter, but he had a graceful figure, polite manners, and an engaging address.

The lad had had, he feared, but a bad start, for 'Westminster School was undoubtedly the seat of illiberal manners, and brutal behaviour.'[1] Nor was Leipzig the

---

[1] Cumberland, the dramatist, who was at Westminster School about the same time as young Stanhope, gives a very different account of the school. He says, 'Doctor Nichols (the Headmaster) had the art of making his scholars gentlemen ; for there was a court of honour in that school, to whose unwritten laws every member of our community was amenable, and which to transgress by any act of meanness, that exposed the offender to public contempt, was a degree of punishment, compared to which the being sentenced to the rod would have been considered as an acquittal or reprieve.

seat of refined and elegant manners. But eloquence and manners, that is to say, the graces of speech and the graces of behaviour, were to be had. They were as much in a young man's power as powdering his hair.

He was now to see better society. He was to visit Venice, Rome, and Paris. But everything must depend on himself. The Graces never came till after they had been long and eagerly wooed.

The young man was, it would seem, awkward by nature. Walpole says that Chesterfield 'was sensible what a cub he had to work on, and whom two quartos of licking could not mould, for cub he remained to his death.' Had young Stanhope been naturally graceful, I have no doubt that the tone of the Letters would have been not a little higher. He was intelligent, sensible, and well stocked with knowledge. There was little need therefore for the father in his later letters to dwell on

While I am making this remark, an instance occurs to me of a certain boy from the fifth, who was summoned before the seniors in the seventh, and convicted of an offence, which in the high spirit of that school argued an abasement of principle and honour. Dr. Nichols having stated the case, demanded their opinion of the crime, and what degree of punishment they conceived it to deserve ; their answer was unanimously—"The severest that could be inflicted." "I can inflict none more severe than you have given him," said the master, and dismissed him without any other chastisement.'—*Memoirs of Richard Cumberland*, vol. i. p. 71.

these points.   The whole strength of his exhortations he must turn, he felt, on that first of all qualities in which his son was so wanting.   He was timid and diffident of himself.   The father repeats again and again La Bruyère's maxim, *Qu'on ne vaut dans ce monde que ce qu'on veut valoir.*   He knew that in this faint-heartedness there was a great danger, for nothing sinks a young man into low company, both of women and men, so surely as timidity and diffidence of himself.

He had himself suffered from it in his youth.   He remembered the day when he had been intrepid enough to go up to a fine woman and tell her that he thought it was very warm.   She had pitied his embarrassment, and had even offered to take him in hand and to give him polish. She had called up three or four people to her and had said, 'Savez-vous que j'ai entrepris ce jeune homme, et qu'il le faut rassurer. . . . Il lui faut nécessairement une passion, et s'il ne m'en juge pas digne, nous lui en chercherons quelque autre.   Au reste, mon Novice, n'allez pas vous encanailler avec des filles d'Opéra. . . . si vous vous encanaillez, vous êtes perdu.   Ces malheureuses ruineront et votre fortune, et votre santé, corrompront vos mœurs, et vous n'aurez jamais le ton de la bonne compagnie.'

His son must follow his course.   He must shun bad

company with its ill examples, and, what is worse, with its infamous exhortations and invitations. He must listen to the advice given by a lady at Venice, a friend of Chesterfield's, who had at his request drawn his picture in a letter : 'Un arrangement avec quelque femme de condition et qui a du monde, est précisément ce qu'il lui faut.' He returns shortly to the same subject, and tells him that 'the gallantry of high life, though not strictly justifiable, carries, at least, no external marks of infamy about it. Neither the heart nor the constitution is corrupted by it ; character is not lost, and manners are, possibly, improved.'

When the young man arrives at Paris he is told that pleasure is now the principal remaining part of his education, for pleasure will soften and polish his manners ; it will make him pursue and at last overtake the Graces. But his pleasures must be the pleasures of a gentleman. He must no longer give much time to books, for living books are much better than dead ones. He must study mankind and the world. Iago did not more urge Roderigo to put money in his purse, than Chesterfield urged his son to cultivate the Graces. 'I would much rather,' he writes, 'that you were passionately in love with some determined coquette of condition, who would lead you a dance, fashion, supple, and polish you, than that you knew all Plato and Aristotle by heart.' A week or two later he writes : 'I hope you frequent La Foire St. Laurent. You will improve more by going there with your mistress, than by staying at home and reading Euclid with your geometry master.'

There was nothing immoral, Chesterfield would have maintained, in all this. He was the fondest of fathers, and he wished to make his son not only a good man, but a perfect man. He had been unwearying in the efforts he had made to have him well taught and well brought-up. He had laid, to use his own metaphor, a foundation of the Tuscan order, the strongest and most solid of all orders. On it must now rise the Doric, the Ionic, and the Corinthian orders, with all their beauty, proportions, and ornaments. This beauty, these proportions and ornaments, could be added only by the help of women, and of women who both were given to gallantry and lived in the best society. Without a fashionable air, address, and manner, a man might be esteemed and respected, but he could never please, much less could he shine. It was his duty to please, it was his duty to shine. If he did not, the foresight, the anxious care, the ardent hopes, the toil of many years would have been thrown away.

A young man was sure, he said, to lead a life of pleasures ; and it was right he should, for pleasures are as necessary as they are useful. They fashion and form a man for the world. They teach him character, and show him the human heart in its unguarded minutes. He had no regret for the time that he had passed in pleasures. They were seasonable, and he had enjoyed them while young. If he had not, he would probably have over-valued them in his old age, as men are apt to overvalue what they do not know. But his son's pleasures must be the pleasures of a man of fashion, and not the vices of a scoundrel. The pleasures he ought to pursue would give him that experience and that polish which, added to his good qualities and his learning, would make him both *respectable et aimable*, the perfection of a human character. If he once reached that perfection, nothing should be wanting on his father's part. The son should solidly experience all the extent and tenderness of his affection; but if he fell far short, let him dread the reverse.

Does his son ask for a man after whom he can fashion himself? Let him try to be a second Lord Bolingbroke, the 'all-accomplished St. John'; not as he was in his stormy youth, when unbounded ambitions and impetuous faults led him astray, but as he is now. Let him strive to join, as this great man joins, to the deepest erudition, the most elegant politeness and good breeding that ever adorned a courtier and man of the world. But let him take warning by his faults and by his failures. In the tumult and storm of pleasures which distinguished his youth he had disdained all decorum, and, as a necessary consequence, both his constitution and his character had suffered. His ambition had been under no guidance, and so had destroyed both his fortune and his reputation.

But what limits were set to the young man's ambition if he would but take the trouble to perfect his manners? He might in time rise to the highest rank. But he must make a beginning. The Duke of Newcastle loves to have a favourite, and to open himself to that favourite. He has now no such person with him : the place is vacant, and if he had dexterity he might fill it. But in one thing he must not humour him. He had never been drunk in his life, and if he tried to humour his Grace by drinking, he might say or do a little too much, and so kick down all that he had done before.

Chesterfield in some ways showed great political foresight. He foretold the French Revolution nearly forty years before it took place. He foresaw the growth of the House of Savoy, and the overthrow of the Papacy. But could he have been gifted with the prophet's vision, he would have seen in this our time a man run that course for which he had in vain so carefully trained his son, and gain that prize which he looked upon as the highest of all rewards. His disappointment in his own failure would have been, we may well believe, greatly lessened could he have foreseen the triumph of his system in the career of the Earl of Beaconsfield.

In the last chapter I attempted to prove that Lord Chesterfield and Johnson never were on terms of intimacy. Did the arguments that I have brought forward need strengthening, such strength would surely be given by the general tone of these Letters. Whoever carefully considers the character that Chesterfield here draws of himself, must feel that there was nothing in common between the two men. Chesterfield was, no doubt, a man of the world, and could, if he thought it worth the while, adapt himself to his company. Johnson also had seen so much of mankind that he felt at ease with men of almost every variety of character. But Chesterfield, when he had once learnt Johnson's power, and had once recognised the perfect simplicity of his nature, could never have felt at ease in his company ; while Johnson, when he had seen through the hollowness of his patron's character, would not have cared long to hide the contempt which he felt. There could never have been any intimacy, still less could there have been any affection between the author of the 'Vanity of Human Wishes' and the writer of these 'Letters to a Son.'

CHAPTER VIII.

BENNET LANGTON.[1]

IT is not the portrait of Johnson only that Boswell has drawn for us. To most men - Garrick and Burke, Sir Joshua Reynolds, and even Goldsmith, are known only so far as they appear in the pages of the Life. Great though these men were, no one of them was so fortunate as to find an artist so skilled in painting him that his likeness, though made the very centre of the picture, stands out to us half so clear as it shows when given in the very background of Boswell's wide canvas. By the side of their great figures are sketched in, with no weaker hand, a host of lesser men. Had he not written, their very names would long ago have passed away, but now the men themselves live for us. The thought arises, not what they, but what we should have lost if they had missed their *vates sacer*. It is the living, not the dead who are to be pitied, when the good of a bygone age

---

[1] Reprinted (with additions) from the *Cornhill Magazine.*

are left overwhelmed and unknown in the long night of which the Latin poet sings. What reader of Boswell does not almost feel that he would have had one friend less in the world had he never had his delightful pages to teach him the worth of the gentle Bennet Langton? Dear to us as are so many of the men who loved Johnson and whom Johnson loved, dear to us as is Goldsmith, dear to us as is the 'dear Knight of Plympton' himself, certainly not less dear is the tall Lincolnshire squire who, as a mere lad, came to London chiefly in the hope of getting introduced to the author of the 'Rambler,' and who, more than thirty years later, came up once more to tend his friend when the grand old man knew at last that that death which he had so long dreaded from afar was now close upon him and must be faced. Their long friendship had been but once broken. Happily, ten years or so before it was broken for ever it had been made whole again.

Boswell himself does not describe Bennet Langton's person, nor could he well have done so, as Langton was living when the Life was published. Miss Hawkins, however, in her 'Memoirs' has happily supplied the deficiency. She says, 'Oh! that we could sketch him with his mild countenance, his elegant features, and his sweet smile, sitting with one leg twisted round the other,

as if fearing to occupy more space than was equitable;
his person inclining forward, as if wanting strength to
support his height, and his arms crossed over his bosom,
or his hands locked together on his knee; his oblong
gold-mounted snuff-box, taken from the waistcoat pocket
opposite his hand, and either remaining between his
fingers or set by him on the table, but which was never
used but when his mind was occupied in conversation;
so soon as conversation began the box was produced.'

We find another description of him given by Mr.
Best, in his 'Personal and Literary Memorials.' 'He
was a very tall, meagre, long-visaged man, much resembling a stork standing on one leg near the shore, in
Raphael's cartoon of the Miraculous Draught of Fishes.
His manners were, in the highest degree, polished;
his conversation mild, equable, and always pleasing.'
Johnson, in a letter to Langton's tutor at Trinity College,
Oxford, thus pleasantly alludes to his great height: 'I
see your pupil sometimes; his mind is as exalted as his
stature. I am half afraid of him; but he is no less
amiable than formidable.' The nickname of Lanky that
he gave him was, no doubt, not merely, like Sherry or
Goldy, an abbreviation of a name; it was also a hit at
his friend's person. Topham Beauclerk's wife also had
her fling at his height.

In ' Boswelliana ' we read, ' Lady Di Beauclerk told me that Langton had never been to see her since she came to Richmond, his head was so full of the militia and Greek. "Why," said I, "madam, he is of such a length; he is awkward, and not easily moved." "But," said she, "if he had laid himself at his length, his feet had been in London and his head might have been here *eodem die*."' His sons were not unworthy of their father, and ' used,' as we read in Miss Hawkins' ' Memoirs,' ' to amuse the good people of Paris by raising their arms to let them pass.'

' Johnson,' as Boswell tells us, ' was not the less ready to love Mr. Langton for his being of a very ancient family; for I have heard him say with pleasure, "Langton, Sir, has a grant of free-warren from Henry II., and Cardinal Stephen Langton in King John's reign was of this family."' His grandfather had known Lord Chief Justice Hale, and had kept a note of a conversation in which ' that great man told him that for two years after he came to the Inn of Court he studied sixteen hours a day; however, by this intense application he almost brought himself to his grave, though he were of a very strong constitution, and after reduced himself to eight hours.' His father, ' old Mr. Langton, was a high and steady Tory, yet attached to the present Royal family.

Johnson said of him, Sir, you will seldom see such a gentleman, such are his stores of literature, such his knowledge in divinity, and such his exemplary life; and, Sir, he has no grimace, no gesticulation, no bursts of admiration on trivial occasions; he never embraces you with an overacted cordiality.' Yet at another time he said of him, ' He never clarified his notions by filtrating them through other minds. He had a canal upon his estate, where at one place the bank was too low. "I dug the canal deeper," said he.' The word canal, in Johnson's time, I may remark, was generally applied to an ornamental sheet of water.

Miss Hawkins in her ' Memoirs' gives a rather fuller account than Boswell of this curious piece of engineering. She, like him, had the anecdote from Johnson. ' Mr. Langton had bestowed considerable pains on enlarging a piece of water on his estate and was showing to some friends what he had achieved, when it was remarked to him, that the bank which confined the water was in one place so low as not to be a security against its overflowing. He admitted that *to the eye* it might appear dangerous; but he said he had provided against such an accident by having had the ground in that spot dug deeper to allow for it.' She had also from Johnson another amusing anecdote about the same worthy old gentleman.

'A legacy of £1,000 had been equally divided between himself and a person to whom he was indebted £100. He consented that this dèbt should be deducted from his moiety ; but when the deduction was made, and he saw the person to whom he was indebted with £200 more than he had, he could not admit it just, that when the other legatee was to have only £100 from him he should yet be £200 the richer. And when an attempt was made to demonstrate it by figures, he could acquiesce no further than to say it might be true *on paper*, but it could not be so in practice.'

Old Mr. and Mrs. Langton had both opposed sitting for their pictures. When Johnson, who thought it right that each generation of a family should have its portraits taken, heard of this, he exclaimed, 'Sir, among the anfractuosities of the human mind, I know not if it may not be one, that there is a superstitious reluctance to sit for a picture.' The old gentleman, though later on he suspected that Johnson was at heart a Papist, had offered him a living of considerable value in Lincolnshire if he were inclined to take orders. Happily for the world, perhaps not unhappily for the parish, Johnson declined. Of Peregrine Langton, Bennet's uncle, who Johnson says ' was one of those whom I loved at once by instinct and by reason,' and of his admirable economy, we have an interesting account from the pen of the nephew himself. 'He had an annuity for life of £200 per annum. His family consisted of a sister, who paid him £18 annually for her board, and a niece. The servants were two maids, and two men in livery. His common way of living at his table was three or four dishes; the appurtenances to his table were neat and handsome; he frequently entertained company at dinner, and then his table was well served with as many dishes as were usual at the tables of the other gentlemen in the neighbourhood. His own appearance as to clothes was genteelly neat and plain. He had always a post-chaise, and kept three horses. Some money he put into the stocks; at his death the sum he had there amounted to £150.' 'His art of life certainly deserves to be known and studied' as much now as when Johnson wrote.

Such was the family of the tall Lincolnshire lad who, at the age of seventeen or thereabouts, full of admiration for the 'Rambler,' which had just been brought to an end, eagerly sought an introduction to its author. He by good luck made the acquaintance of Robert Levett, 'the practiser in physic,' the man 'obscurely wise and coarsely kind,' who introduced him to Johnson. 'Mr. Langton was exceedingly surprised when the sage first appeared. He had not received the smallest intimation of his figure, dress, or manner. From perusing his writings, he fancied he should see a decent, well-dressed, in short, a remarkably decorous philosopher. Instead of which, down from his bed-chamber about noon, came, as newly risen, a huge uncouth figure, with a little dark wig which scarcely covered his head, and his clothes hanging loose about him. But his conversation was so rich, so animated, and so forcible, and his religious and political notions so congenial with those in which Mr. Langton had been educated, that he conceived for him that veneration and attachment which he ever preserved.' Johnson took no less pleasure in Langton's company. He described him as one of those men ' to whom Nature does not spread her volumes or utter her voices in vain,' ' as a friend at once cheerful and serious,' while rising yet higher, 'with a warm vehemence of affectionate regard, he exclaimed, " The earth does not bear a worthier man than Bennet Langton."' On another occasion he said, ' I know not who will go to Heaven if Langton does not. Sir, I could almost say, *Sit anima mea cum Langtono.*'

Miss Reynolds, in her ' Anecdotes,' tells us, ' I shall never forget the exalted character he drew of his friend Mr. Langton, nor with what energy, what fond delight, he expatiated in his praise, giving him every excellence that nature could bestow, and every perfection that humanity could acquire.' Boswell, too, describes 'our worthy friend'—for that is Langton's Homeric epithet in the modern Odyssey—as 'a gentleman eminent not only for worth and learning, but for an inexhaustible fund of entertaining conversation.'

In a note to the Life he quotes one of his stories. 'An honest carpenter,' we read, 'after giving some anecdote in Langton's presence of the ill-treatment which he had received from a clergyman's wife, who was a noted termagant, and whom he accused of unjust dealing in some transaction with him, added, " I took care to let her know what I thought of her;" and being asked, " What did you say?" answered, "I told her she was a scoundrel."' In 'Boswelliana' I find recorded two or three anecdotes that Langton told of Johnson that Boswell has not, I believe, worked up into the Life. 'A certain young clergyman,' we read, 'used to come about Dr. Johnson. The Doctor said it vexed him to be in his company—his ignorance was so hopeless. " Sir," said Mr. Langton, " his coming about you shows he wishes to help his ignorance." "Sir," said the Doctor, "his ignorance is so great I am afraid to show him the bottom of it."' Langton also told Boswell how 'Mr. Johnson used to laugh at a passage in "Carte's Life of the Duke of Ormond,"' where he gravely observes, 'that he was always in full dress when he went to court; too many being in the practice of going thither with double lapells.' Johnson, when insisting one day ' that the value of every story depends on its being true,' said, ' Langton used to think a story a story, till I showed him that truth was essential to it.'

He was endeared to Johnson by his Greek scarcely less than by his ancient lineage, his piety, his entertaining conversation, and his worth. He was the man who had read Clenardus's ' Greek Grammar.' ' Why, Sir,' said Johnson, ' who is there in this town who knows anything of Clenardus but you and I ?' He had learnt by heart the Epistle of St. Basil. ' Sir,' said Johnson, ' I never made such an effort to attain Greek.' It was at his house that Johnson spent an evening with the Rev. Dr. Parr, when ' he was much pleased with the conversation of that learned gentleman.' ' He has invited,' so Johnson writes to Boswell, ' Nicolaida, the learned Greek, to visit him at his house in Lincolnshire.' When he gets somewhat embarrassed in his circumstances, Johnson, though close on the end of his life, and nigh worn out with illness, writes to him, ' I am a little angry at you for not keeping minutes of your own *acceptum et expensum*, and think a little time might be spared from Aristophanes for the *res familiares*.' To him Johnson, now on his death-bed, gave the translations into Latin verse that he had made of Greek epigrams during the sleepless nights of his last illness. His name is not to be found to the celebrated Round Robin which Burke drew up, and that the company gathered round Sir Joshua Reynolds's table signed. 'Joe Warton, a scholar by profession, might be such a fool' as to put his hand to a petition that Goldsmith's epitaph should be not in Latin, but in English; but 'Mr. Langton, like a sturdy scholar, refused to sign it.'

In Miss Hawkins' 'Memoirs' we read how 'he would get into the most fluent recitation of half a page of Greek, breaking off for fear of wearying, by saying, as I well remember was his phrase, "and so it goes on;" accompanying his words with a gentle wave of his hand, indicating that you might better suppose the rest than bear his proceeding.' He could nevertheless enjoy a liberty taken with his beloved Greek, and one evening as Boswell writes, 'made us laugh heartily at some lines by Joshua Barnes in which are to be found such comical Anglo-Hellenisms as κλύββοισιν ἔβανχθεν, they were banged with clubs.'

Mr. Best has given an account of an evening that he once spent in his company. 'In the course of conversation he took out a small pocket-album, containing *bon-mots*, or heads and notices of *bon-mots*, which he filled out and commented upon in a most amusing manner. Among other witticisms was a short copy of macaronic Greek verses, of which I remember " five-poundon elendeto, ah! mala simplos."' He was no unfit successor to his great friend in the Professorship of Ancient Literature in the Royal Academy.

Johnson had taken him in the early days of their friendship to see Richardson, who had little conversation except about his own works. 'Johnson,' says Langton, ' professed that he could bring him out into conversation, and used this allusive expression, "Sir, I can make him *rear*." But he failed; for in that interview Richardson said little else than that there lay in the room a translation of his "Clarissa" into German.' Langton had also visited Young, who told him when they were walking in the garden, 'Here I had put a handsome sun-dial, with this inscription, *Eheu fugaces!* which (speaking with a smile) was sadly verified, for by the next morning my dial had been carried off.' 'Young,' he remarked, 'showed a degree of eager curiosity concerning the common occurrences that were then passing, which appeared somewhat remarkable in a man of such intellectual stores, of such an advanced age, and who had retired from life with declared disappointment in his expectations.' He was intimate indeed with most of the men of letters of his time, but it was in Johnson's house 'at his levee of morning visitors when he was declaiming over his tea, which he drank very plentifully,' that he was mostly to be found. Langton, early in their acquaintance, had invited Johnson to visit his father's house at Spilsby, but he wrote in reply that much as he would have liked to have gone, nevertheless he must forbear the pleasure. 'I will give the true reason,' he writes, 'which I know you will approve: —I have a mother more than eighty years old, who has counted the days to the publication of my book (his Dictionary) in hopes of seeing me; and to her, if I can disengage myself here, I resolve to go.'

A year or two later on he again writes to him, 'I go on, as I formerly did, designing to be some time or other both rich and wise; and yet cultivate neither mind nor fortune. Do you take notice of my example, and learn the danger of delay. When I was as you are now, towering in confidence of twenty-one, little did I suspect that I should be at forty-nine what I now am. But you do not seem to need my admonition. You are busy in acquiring and in communicating knowledge, and while you are studying, enjoy the end of study, by making others wiser and happier. I was much pleased with the tale that you told me of being tutor to your sisters. I, who have no sisters nor brothers, look with some degree of innocent envy on those who may be said to be born friends, and cannot see, without wonder, how rarely that native union is afterwards regarded.' He goes on to say, ' we tell the ladies that good wives make good husbands; I believe it is a more certain position that good brothers make good sisters.' He acknowledges in the same letter a present of game from Langton. He had left off house-keeping—his wife was by this time dead—and therefore gave the birds away. 'The pheasant I gave to Mr. Richardson' (the author of 'Clarissa').

He writes to him when he is at Trinity College, Oxford, and says, 'You who are very capable of anti-cipating futurity and raising phantoms before your own eyes, must often have imagined to yourself an academical life, and have conceived what would be the manners, the views, and the conversation of men devoted to letters; how they would choose their companions; how they would direct their studies, and how they would regulate their lives. Let me know what you expected and what you have found.' He thus ends his letter to the young student, 'I love, dear Sir, to think on you, and therefore should willingly write more to you but that the post,' &c. Two years later in again writing to him he says, 'While you have been riding and running, and seeing the tombs of the learned, and the camps of the valiant, I have only staid at home and intended to do great things, which I have not done ;' and he goes on to say, 'Let me hear from you again wherever you are, or whatever you are doing ; whether you wander or sit still, plant trees or make Rusticks, play with your sisters, or muse alone.' The Rusticks, Boswell tells us, were some essays, with that title, written about this time by Mr. Langton, but not published. We should be curious to know whether they are still preserved in the family house at Langton.

He wrote pleasantly enough, as we can see from the paper that he contributed to 'The Idler' (No. 67). He describes 'a man of vast designs and of vast performances, though he sometimes designed one thing and performed another.' He ends by enforcing a position which he had no doubt often heard Johnson maintain—for it was a familiar one with him—that 'he who finds himself strongly attracted to any particular study, though it may happen to be out of his proposed scheme, if it is not trifling or vicious, had better continue his application to it, since it is likely that he will, with much more ease and expedition, attain that which a warm inclination stimulates him to pursue, than that at which a prescribed law compels him to toil.'

He was an admirable reader aloud, but though his

readings surpassed, as was thought, the actor's recitations, yet he did not overcome Johnson's 'extreme impatience to be read to.' Boswell tells us how, 'when a very young man, he read to him Dodsley's "Cleone, a tragedy." As it went on Johnson turned his face to the back of his chair, and put himself into various attitudes, which marked his uneasiness. At the end of an act, however, he said, "Come, let's have some more, let's go into the slaughter-house again, Lanky. But I am afraid there is more blood than brains."'

If we may trust Miss Burney, however well Langton may have read, he had but little of the actor's power. In her Diary, after giving an account of Boswell's imitation of Johnson's manner, she says, 'Mr. Langton told some stories himself in imitation of Johnson ; but they became him less than Mr. Boswell, and only reminded me of what Dr. Johnson himself once said to me : "Every man has, some time in his life, an ambition to be a wag." If Mr. Langton had repeated everything from his truly great friend quietly, it would far better have accorded with his own serious and respectable character.'

'If I were called on,' writes Miss Hawkins, 'to name the person with whom Johnson might have been seen to the fairest advantage, I should certainly name Mr. Langton. His good breeding and the pleasing tone of his voice would have given the pitch to Johnson's replies; his classic acquirements would have brought out those of the other speaker; while the thorough respect Johnson entertained for him would have prevented that harshness which sometimes alarmed a third person.' He had, however, one failing—a failing that leaned to virtue's side. ' I mentioned,' says Boswell, 'a worthy friend of ours' (no doubt Langton) 'whom we valued much, but observed that he was too ready to introduce religious discourse upon all occasions. *Johnson*: "Why yes, Sir, he will introduce religious discourse without seeing whether it will end in instruction and improvement, or produce some profane jest. He would introduce it in the company of Wilkes and twenty more such."'

It was to what Johnson considered an indiscretion of this sort that the breach in their friendship was due. At a dinner at the Messieurs Dilly's, the booksellers in the Poultry, there had been a hot discussion on toleration. Johnson had just quarrelled with Goldsmith, when a gentleman present (who, there is little doubt, was Langton) 'ventured to ask him if there was not a material difference as to toleration of opinions which lead to action, and opinions merely speculative; for instance, would it be wrong in the magistrate to tolerate those who preach against the doctrine of the Trinity? Johnson was highly offended, and said, " I wonder, Sir, how a gentleman of your piety can introduce this subject in a mixed company." '

In spite of this sharp rebuke, on leaving the house Langton went with Johnson and Boswell to the club, and the following day Johnson, in fulfilment no doubt of an old engagement, dined at his house. At the club that evening occurred that fine scene when Johnson begged Goldsmith's pardon for what had passed at dinner, and Goldsmith answered placidly, 'It must be much from you, Sir, that I take ill.' I am inclined to think that Langton's resentment was increased by the contrast. Both had been harshly treated, but it was only Goldsmith to whom amends were made. On the following day Langton made his will, 'devising his estate to his three sisters in preference to a remote heir male. Johnson called them (Langton, of course, was not present) three *dowdies*, and said, with as high a spirit as the boldest baron in the most perfect days of the feudal system, " an ancient estate should always go to males." ' Boswell goes on to add, ' He now laughed immoderately, without any reason that we could perceive, at our friend's making his will, called him the *testator*, and added, " I dare say he thinks he has done a mighty thing. He won't stay till he gets home to his seat in the country to produce this wonderful deed—he'll call up the landlord of the first inn on the road ; and after a suitable preface upon mortality and the uncertainty of life, will tell him that he should not delay in making his will ; and here, Sir, will he say, is my will, which I have just made, with the assistance of one of the ablest lawyers in the kingdom ; and he will read it to him (laughing all the time). He believes he has made this will ; but he did not make it. You, Chambers, made it for him. I trust you have had more conscience than to make him say 'being of sound understanding ;' ha, ha, ha ! I hope he has left me a legacy. I'd have his will turned into verse like a ballad." It was in continuation of this merry strain that Johnson "burst into such a fit of laughter that he appeared to be almost in a convulsion ; and, in order to support himself, laid hold of one of the posts at the side of the foot-pavement, and sent forth peals so loud that in the silence of the night his voice seemed to resound from Temple Bar to Fleet Ditch." Johnson writes to Boswell two months later, "——" (no doubt Langton) "left the town without taking leave of me, and is gone in deep dudgeon to ——. Is not this very childish ? Where is now my legacy ?" '

It was in the autumn of this year that Johnson went to Scotland, but neither in going nor returning did he stop at Langton. In his journal of the tour Boswell says, 'we

talked of one of our friends taking ill for a length of time
a hasty expression of Dr. Johnson's to him,' on his in-
troducing, in a mixed company, a religious subject so
unseasonably as to provoke a rebuke. *'Johnson*: "What
is to become of society, if a friendship of twenty years is
to be broken off for such a cause? As Bacon says—

> ' Who then to frail mortality shall trust
> But limns the water, or but writes in dust.'"'

By the following summer much had been done to
bind up the friendship again, and Johnson writes to
Langton, telling him of poor Goldsmith's death. He
ends his letter by saying, 'Do not be sullen now, but let
me find a letter when I come back.' And in the next
winter, writing to Boswell, he says, 'Langton is here ! we
are all that ever we were. He is a worthy fellow, without
malice, though not without resentment.'

Langton had married, two or three years earlier than
the date of this quarrel, 'one of those three Countess
Dowagers of Rothes, who had all of them the fortune to
get second husbands at about the same time.' He had
invited Goldsmith and Reynolds, together with Johnson
as it would seem, to visit him at his seat in Lincolnshire.
Goldsmith in a pleasant letter, that Mr. Forster gives in
full, declines. He was so much employed 'in the coun-

try, at a farmer's house, quite alone, trying to write a comedy' ('She Stoops to Conquer'), that he has to put off his intended visit to Lincolnshire for this season, and, as it proved, alas! for all seasons. 'Everybody,' says he, 'is a visiting about and merry but myself. And that is hard, too, as I have been trying these three months to do something to make people laugh.' He goes on to say, 'I have published, or Davies has published for me, an "Abridgment of the History of England," for which I have been a good deal abused in the newspapers for betraying the liberties of the people. God knows I had no thought for or against liberty in my head; my whole aim being to make up a book of a decent size that, as 'Squire Richard says, would do no harm to nobody. However, they set me down as an arrant Tory, and consequently an honest man. When you come to look at any part of it, you'll say that I am a sour Whig.'

Johnson did make a visit to Lincolnshire, the remembrance of which was long preserved. For when, many many years later, Mr. Best visited Langton, 'after breakfast,' he writes, 'we walked to the top of a very steep hill behind the house. When we arrived at the summit, Mr. Langton said, 'Poor, dear Dr. Johnson, when he came to this spot, turned back to look down the hill, and said he was determined "to take a roll down." When we understood what he meant to do, we endeavoured to dissuade him ; but he was resolute, saying, "he had not had a roll for a long time;" and taking out of his lesser pockets whatever might be in them—keys, pencil, purse, or pen-knife—and laying himself parallel with the edge of the hill, he actually descended, turning himself over and over till he came to the bottom."' Mr. Best goes on to say : 'The story was told with such gravity, and with an air of such affectionate remembrance of a departed friend, that it was impossible to suppose this extraordinary freak of the great lexicographer to have been a fiction or invention of Mr. Langton.'

It was on this visit that Johnson 'was so socially ac-commodating that, once when Mr. Langton and he were driving together in a coach, and Mr. Langton complained of being sick, he insisted that they should go and sit on the back of it in the open air, which they did; and being sensible how strange the appearance must be, observed, that a countryman whom they saw in a field would probably be thinking, "If those two madmen should come down, what would become of me?"'

Langton, for some years of his married life, lived at an expense almost beyond his means. He could not, I suppose, spare time from his Aristophanes for his minutes of *acceptum et expensum*. Johnson, in a letter to Boswell, says, ' I do not like his scheme of life, but as I am not permitted to understand it, I cannot set anything right that is wrong.'

When Mrs. Thrale, in Miss Burney's hearing, 'asked Johnson whether Mr. Langton took any better care of his affairs than formerly, "No, Madam," cried the Doctor; "and never will. He complains of the ill effects of habit, and rests contentedly upon a confessed indolence. He told his father himself that he had "no turn to economy," but a thief might as well plead that he had "no turn to honesty."'

When Boswell was next up in London, 'we talked,' says he, 'of a gentleman' (Langton we may feel almost sure) 'who was running out his fortune in London; and I said, "We must get him out of it. All his friends must quarrel with him, and that will soon drive him away." *Johnson* : "Nay, sir, we'll send *you* to him. If your company does not drive a man out of his house, nothing will."' A few days later on they were again talking of 'a gentleman who, we apprehended, was gradually involving his circumstances by bad management.' Langton again, no doubt, is meant. Johnson said, 'Wasting a fortune is evaporation by a thousand imperceptible means. If it were a stream, they'd stop it. You must speak to him. It is really miserable. Were he a gamester, it could be said he had hopes of winning. Were he a bankrupt in trade, he might have grown rich; but he has neither spirit to spend nor resolution to spare. He does not spend fast enough to have pleasure from it. He has the crime of prodigality and the wretchedness of parsimony.' Another time he said, 'He is ruining himself without pleasure. A man who loses at play, or who runs out his fortune at court, makes his estate less, in hopes of making it bigger; but it is a sad thing to pass through the quagmire of parsimony to the gulf of ruin. To pass over the flowery path of extravagance is very well.' Later on he writes to Boswell, that ' —— has laid down his coach, and talks of making more contractions of his expense : how he will succeed, I know not. It is difficult to reform a household gradually; it may be better done by a system totally new.' He goes on to add : 'What I told him of the increasing expense of a growing family seems to have struck him. He certainly had gone on with very confused views, and we have, I think, shown him that he is wrong; though, with the common deficience of advisers, we have not shown him how to do right.'

Though Langton showed indolence in money matters, yet Johnson praised him for his vigour as a captain of militia. 'Langton,' he writes, 'has been encamped with his company of militia on Warley Common; I spent five days amongst them; he signalized himself as a diligent officer, and has very high respect in the regiment. He presided when I was there at a court-martial.' Boswell also pats him on the back, and writes to express to Johnson the pleasure with which he had found 'that our worthy friend Langton was highly esteemed in his own county town.'

If Langton was a tender brother, he was no less tender a father. Johnson indeed at one time complained in writing about the table he kept, that 'he has his children too much about him.' In one of his letters, however, he seems to hint that Boswell might, with advantage, see a little more of his. 'Langton has been down with the militia,' he says, 'and is again quiet at home, talking to his little people, as, I suppose, you do sometimes.' In writing to Langton, he begs him to keep him 'in the memory of all the little dear family, particularly pretty Mrs. Jane' (his god-child); and in another letter he says, after describing his own mournful state, 'You, dear Sir, have, I hope, a more cheerful scene; you see George fond of his book, and the pretty misses airy and lively, with my own little Jenny equal to the best; and in whatever can contribute to your quiet or pleasure, you have Lady Rothes ready to concur.' In the last year of his life he writes, 'How does my own Jenny? I think I owe

Jenny a letter, which I will take care to pay. In the meantime tell her that I acknowledge the debt.' A month later he pays the debt. · 'He took the trouble to write the letter in a large, round hand, nearly resembling printed characters, that she might have the satisfaction of reading it herself.' 'The original,' says Boswell, 'now lies before me, but shall be faithfully restored to her; and I dare say will be preserved by her as a jewel as long as she lives.' She did preserve it, and nearly sixty years later showed it to Mr. Croker. The letter begins, 'My dearest Miss Jenny,' and ends, 'I am, my dear, your most humble servant, Sam. Johnson.'

'Of the children of the family,' says Miss Hawkins, 'Dr. Johnson was very fond. They were, in their full number, ten, with not a plain face nor a faulty person. They were taught to behave to Johnson as they would have done to a grandfather, and he felt it.' In a letter to Mrs. Thrale he says 'You find, now you have seen the *progenies Langtoniana* that I did not praise them without reason. Yet the second girl is my favourite.'

'It was Langton's intention,' Miss Hawkins states, 'to educate his children at home, and under only parental tutelage. He therefore settled in Westminster, determined to live very quietly, and devote himself to this grand duty, in which the children of both sexes were to be

T

equally considered. He told my father he should not only give his sons but his daughters a knowledge of the learned languages, and that he meant to familiarise the latter to the Greek language to such perfection, that while five of his girls employed themselves in feminine works, the sixth should read a Greek author for the general amusement.'

Miss Burney records how Dr. Johnson gave a very droll account of the children of Mr. Langton, 'who,' he said, ' might be very good children if they were let alone; but the father is never easy when he is not making them do something which they cannot do; they must repeat a fable, or a speech, or the Hebrew alphabet; and they might as well count twenty for what they know of the matter; however, the father says half, for he prompts every other word. But he could not have chosen a man who would have been less entertained by such means.'

In one of Johnson's letters to Mrs. Thrale a passage occurs which there is little doubt refers to Langton and his eldest boy, though the names are suppressed. 'I dined,' he writes, ' yesterday with ———. His children are very lovely. . . . He begins to reproach himself with neg-lect of ———'s education, and censures that idleness or that deviation, by the indulgence of which he has left uncultivated such a fertile mind. I advised him to let the child alone; and told him that the matter was not great whether he could read at the end of four years, or of five, and that I thought it not proper to harass a tender mind with the violence of painful attention. I may perhaps procure both father and son a year of quiet; and surely I may rate myself among their benefactors.'

The home education would not seem to have succeeded. 'Mr. Langton knew not how much the possession of extensive learning sometimes overshoots the power of communicating first elements; he was bewildered in his own labyrinth of ideas, and, I believe, was a little sickened of his plan by the late King's frequently repeated inquiry, "How does education go on?"' George Langton, the eldest son, at all events, had, as Mr. Best tells us, 'profited by the conversation and instruction of his father, so as to become a man of almost universal, though perhaps superficial, literary knowledge.' A tutor, named Lusignan, had been engaged to teach him modern Greek, of whom he used to tell the following anecdote: 'It had been imposed on him by his director as a penance to recite a certain number of times, before breakfast, the words Κύριε ἐλεείσον. He paced his chamber impatiently, repeating with what seemed practised rapidity the words prescribed, ever and anon, however, opening his door, and calling downstairs to the maid, "Is my breakfast ready?"'

On one occasion, when Johnson was at Langton's house, 'before dinner,' says Boswell, 'he said nothing but "Pretty baby!" to one of the children. Langton said very well to me afterwards, that he could repeat Johnson's conversation before dinner, as Johnson had said that he could repeat a complete chapter of the "Natural History of Iceland," from the Danish of Horrebow, the whole of which was exactly thus:—

'"CHAP. LXXII.—CONCERNING SNAKES.—There are no snakes to be met with throughout the whole island."'

When, on Beauclerk's death, Langton received by his will Reynolds' portrait of Johnson, with the inscription on the frame—

> Ingenium ingens
> Inculto latet hoc sub corpore,

he had the lines effaced. Johnson said, complacently, ' It was kind in you to take it off;' and then, after a short pause, added, ' and not unkind in him to put it on.' We must not forget that the great painter and the great lexicographer, as men then delighted to call him, had thought so highly of the two friends, that when they were still quite young men, they had invited them, with Goldsmith and Burke, to join them in founding The Club.

Nothing is more pleasant in Langton's life than that scene for a comedy, as Sir Joshua described it, when the penitent got into a panic and belaboured his confessor. 'When I was ill,' said Johnson, 'I desired Langton would tell me sincerely in what he thought my life was faulty. Sir, he brought me a sheet of paper, on which he had written down several texts of Scripture, recommending Christian charity. And when I questioned him what occasion I had given for such animadversion, all that he could say amounted to this—that I sometimes contradicted people in conversation. Now what harm does it do to any man to be contradicted?' Boswell, in describing the scene, says that 'Johnson, at the time when the paper was presented to him, though at first pleased with the attention of his friend, whom he thanked in an earnest manner, soon exclaimed, in a loud and angry tone, "What is your drift, Sir?"' What an admirable subject for Hogarth, if he had lived to paint it!

When Johnson's last illness was upon him, Langton, as we have said, came up from Lincolnshire to be with his dying friend. He took lodgings in Fleet Street, so that he might be near at hand. 'Nobody,' says Boswell, 'was more attentive to him than Mr. Langton, to whom he tenderly said, "*Te teneam moriens deficiente manu.*"'

His failing hand did not, indeed, at the very moment of death hold his friend's. Stupor had set in, and even the gentle Bennet Langton, the friend of thirty years, would have been as a stranger to him. A letter has been preserved, in Langton's handwriting, a letter which was never finished and never sent, but was meant likely enough for Boswell, in which we read, 'I am now writing in the room where his venerable remains exhibit a spectacle, the interesting solemnity of which, difficult as it would be in any sort to find terms to express, so to you, my dear Sir, whose own sensations will paint it so strongly, it would be of all men the most superfluous to attempt to——.' Here grief, it would seem, got the better of the writer, and the letter was left, with all the eloquence of a broken utterance.

Langton survived Johnson many years. Mrs. Piozzi, in a passage which shows all the spite of a small mind, writes, 'The Dean of Winchester's account of Bennet Langton coming to town some few years after the death of Dr. Johnson, and finding no house where he was even asked to dinner, was exceedingly comical. Mr. Wilberforce dismissed him with a cold " Adieu, dear Sir; I hope we shall meet in heaven." How capricious is the public taste! I remember when to have Langton at a man's house stamped him at once a literary character.'

Public taste is capricious, but yet as long as Boswell's ' Life of Johnson ' is read, so long will there be men to love the memory of the gentle Bennet Langton, the worthy friend who was serious and yet cheerful, who did not keep his minutes of *acceptum et expensum*, but had read Clenardus.

CHAPTER IX.

TOPHAM BEAUCLERK.[1]

'GOLDSMITH,' says Lord Macaulay, 'lived in what was intellectually far the best society of the kingdom, in a society in which no talent or accomplishment was wanting, and in which the art of conversation was cultivated with splendid success. There probably were never four talkers more admirable in four different ways than Johnson, Burke, Beauclerk,[2] and Garrick; and Goldsmith was on terms of intimacy with all the four.' Many a reader, as he has come upon this passage, must have paused to reflect who this Beauclerk was, who is thus matched with Johnson, Burke, and Garrick, and whose society was an honour to Goldsmith. He may at length have called to mind the lively, the learned, the witty, the

[1] Reprinted (with additions) from the *Cornhill Magazine.*

[2] 'There is a poignancy without effort in all that he (Talleyrand) says, which reminds me a little of the character which the wits of Johnson's circle give of Beauclerk.'—*Life of Macaulay*, by Trevelyan, vol. i. p. 231.

fashionable Topham Beauclerk, as he is shown to us in the pages of Boswell. In the last chapter I have given a sketch of Bennet Langton. I shall do my best to present a companion portrait of the friend of his college days and of his mature life—Topham Beauclerk.

I have, I feel, a far harder task before me, for Langton's life lay in a much narrower circle. The books that tell of Johnson tell also of him, but Beauclerk knew a world that was known to neither Langton nor Johnson. He was a man of fashion, as well as an accomplished scholar and an eager student, and had mixed with men whom neither Johnson nor Langton would have cared to have known. Though I have not failed in diligence in consulting the memoirs of last century, yet I have not succeeded so well as I had hoped in gathering information about many periods of his life. Especially had I wished to illustrate his marvellous conversational powers, to which so many of his contemporaries bear witness, but the good sayings of his that I have come upon are but few indeed.

Topham Beauclerk's wildness and wit may well have come from one and the same source, for he was the great-grandson of Charles II. and Nell Gwyn. Boswell says that ‘Mr. Beauclerk's being of the St. Albans’ family, and having, in some particulars, a resemblance to Charles II., contributed, in Johnson's imagination, to throw a lustre upon his other qualities.' In another passage we learn that Johnson had an extraordinary partiality for that prince, and took fire at any attack upon him. Beauclerk's father, Lord Sidney Beauclerk, the third son of the first Duke of St. Albans, was not unworthy of his illustrious grandparents. 'Sir C. H. Williams calls him "Worthless Sidney." He was notorious for hunting after the fortunes of the old and childless. Being very handsome, he had almost persuaded Lady Betty Germaine (Swift's correspondent) in her old age to marry him. He failed also in obtaining the fortune of Sir Thomas Reeve, Chief Justice of the Common Pleas, whom he used to attend on the circuit with a view of ingratiating himself with him. At length he induced Mr. Topham, of Windsor, to leave his estate to him.'

If Mr. Topham together with his fortune left him also his famous collection of pictures and drawings,[1] it is likely enough that from them his godson derived much of his accurate taste and judgment in painting and sculpture. It was certainly not to his mother that Beauclerk owed the powers of his mind. In the course of his tour to the Hebrides, Johnson one day told Boswell the following anecdote of this lady: 'Beauclerk and I, and

---

[1] 'He buys for Topham, drawings and designs.'—Pope's *Moral Essays*, Epistle iv.

Langton, and Lady Sidney Beauclerk, mother to our friend, were one day driving in a coach by Cuper's Gardens (an inferior place of popular amusement), which were then unoccupied. I, in sport, proposed that Beauclerk and Langton and myself should take them ; and we amused ourselves with scheming how we should all do our parts. Lady Sidney grew angry, and said, "An old man should not put such things in young people's heads." She had no notion of a joke, Sir ; had come late into life, and had a mighty unpliable understanding.'

It was at Trinity College, Oxford, that Beauclerk formed an acquaintance with his fellow-collegian Bennet Langton. Boswell says that 'though their opinions and modes of life were so different, that it seemed utterly improbable that they should at all agree, yet Mr. Beauclerk had so ardent a love of literature, so acute an understanding, such elegance of manners, and so well discerned the excellent qualities of Mr. Langton, that they became intimate friends.' They entered college within a few months of each other in 1757, when Beauclerk was eighteen years old. 'Johnson, soon after this acquaintance began, passed a considerable time at Oxford. He at first thought it strange that Langton should associate so much with one who had the character of being loose, both in his principles and practice ; but by degrees he himself was fascinated.' The resemblance to Charles II. was too much for him. 'And in a short time the moral, pious Johnson and the gay, dissipated Beauclerk were companions. "What a coalition!" (said Garrick, when he heard of this) ; "I shall have my old friend to bail out of the round-house."'

Boswell goes on to say that 'it was a very agreeable association. Beauclerk was too polite, and valued learning and wit too much, to offend Johnson by sallies of infidelity or licentiousness ; and Johnson delighted in the good qualities of Beauclerk, and hoped to correct the evil. Innumerable were the scenes in which Johnson was amused by these young men. Beauclerk could take more liberty with him than anybody with whom I ever saw him ; but, on the other hand, Beauclerk was not spared by his respectable companion when reproof was proper. Beauclerk had such a propensity to satire, that at one time Johnson said to him, "You never open your mouth but with intention to give pain ; and you have often given me pain, not from the power of what you said, but from seeing your intention." At another time, applying to him, with a slight alteration, a line of Pope, he said, " Thy love of folly and thy scorn of fools—everything thou dost shows the one, and everything thou say'st the other." At another time he said to him, "Thy body is all vice, and thy mind all virtue." Beauclerk not seeming to relish the compliment, Johnson said, "Nay, Sir, Alexander the Great, marching in triumph into Babylon, could not have desired to have had more said to him."'

The pious Johnson at times so far forgot to correct the evil that he saw in his friend, that he even allowed himself to be led astray. When he was staying at Beauclerk's house at Windsor, 'one Sunday when the weather was very fine, Beauclerk enticed him insensibly to saunter about all the morning. They went into a churchyard, in the time of Divine service, and Johnson laid himself down at his ease upon one of the tomb-stones. "Now, Sir" (said Beauclerk), "you are like Hogarth's idle apprentice."' On another occasion, as Boswell tells us, 'when Beauclerk and Langton had supped at a tavern in London, and sat till about three in the morning, it came into their heads to go and knock up Johnson, and see if they could prevail on him to join them in a ramble. They rapped violently at the door of his chambers in the Temple, till at last he appeared in his shirt, with his little black wig on the top of his head, instead of a night-cap, and a poker in his hand, imagining, probably, that some ruffians were coming to attack him. When he discovered who they were, and was told their errand, he smiled, and with great good humour agreed to their proposal: "What, is it you, you dogs! I'll have a frisk with you." He was soon dressed, and they sallied forth together into Covent Garden, where the greengrocers and fruiterers were beginning to arrange their hampers, just come in from the country. Johnson made some attempts to help them, but the honest gardeners stared so at his figure and manner, and odd interference, that he soon saw his services were not relished. They then repaired to one of the neighbouring taverns, and made a bowl of that liquor called Bishop, which Johnson had always liked, while in joyous contempt of sleep, from which he had been roused, he repeated the festive lines—

> Short, O short then be thy reign
> And give us to the world again!

They did not stay long, but walked down to the Thames, took a boat, and rowed to Billingsgate. Beauclerk and Johnson were so well pleased with their amusement that they resolved to persevere in dissipation for the rest of the day; but Langton deserted them, being engaged to breakfast with some young ladies. Johnson scolded him for "leaving his social friends to go and sit with a set of wretched *un-idea'd* girls."'

Shortly after Beauclerk must have left college, we

learn by a letter of Mrs. Montague's that this lively young gentleman came within a very little of being married. 'Mr. Beauclerk,' she writes, 'was to have been married to Miss Draycott, but by a certain coldness in his manner she fancied her lead mines were rather the objects of his love than herself, and so after the licence was taken out she gave him his *congé*. Rosamond's pond was never thought of by the forsaken swain. His prudent parents thought of the transmutation of metals, and to how much gold the lead might have been changed, and rather regret the loss.'

A few months later in the same year Beauclerk, let us hope to drive away his grief for the loss of his bride, went the grand tour. Langton accompanied him, at all events part of the way. Johnson wrote to Mr. Baretti at Milan, 'I beg that you will show Mr. Beauclerk all the civilities which you have in your power, for he has always been kind to me.' Five months later he writes to the same gentleman, 'I gave a letter to Mr. Beauclerk, who, in my opinion, and in his own, was hastening to Naples for the recovery of his health; but he has stopped at Paris, and I know not when he will proceed.' In George Selwyn's Letters we read, 'Topham Beauclerk is arrived. I hear he lost £10,000 to a thief at Venice, which thief, in the course of the year, will be at Cashiobury.' Johnson, with Beauclerk's example before him, had certainly some reason for saying that 'Time may be employed to more advantage from nineteen to twenty-four almost in any way than in travelling.'[1]

Beauclerk, a few years after his return, had an opportunity of repaying the civilities he had received from Mr. Baretti. That gentleman was put on his trial for murder. He had been assailed in the grossest manner possible by a woman of the town, and, driving her off with a blow, was set upon by three bullies. He thereupon ran away in great fear, for he was a timid man, and being pursued had stabbed two of the men with a small knife he carried in his pocket. One of them died within a few hours of the wound. In his defence he had said, ' I hope it will be seen that my knife was neither a weapon of offence nor defence. I wear it to carve fruit and sweetmeats, and not to kill my fellow-creatures.' It was important to prove that abroad everyone carried a knife as a matter of course, not for offensive or defensive purposes, but simply for convenience in eating. The Hon. T. Beauclerk gave evidence as follows :—

' In France they never lay anything upon the table but a fork, not only in the inns, but in public-houses. It is usual for gentlemen and ladies to carry knives with

---

[1] See page 108.

them without silver blades. I have seen those kind of knives in toy-shops.' (Baretti's knife had a 'silver case over the blade, and was kept in a green shagreen case.') Garrick testified to the same custom. He was asked, 'When you travel abroad do you carry such knives as this?' He answered, 'Yes, or we should have no victuals.' Had Johnson by this time been to the Hebrides, his evidence also might have helped to confirm the statement of his friends. In a letter he wrote from Skye to Mrs. Thrale he states, 'Table-knives are not of long subsistence in the Highlands; every man, while arms were a regular part of dress, had his knife and fork appendant to his dirk.'

Beauclerk also bore evidence to the position Baretti held in his own country. He was asked, 'How long have you known Mr. Baretti?' He answered, 'I have known him ten years. I was acquainted with him before I went abroad. Some time after that I went to Italy, and he gave me letters of recommendation to some of the first people there, and to men of learning. I went to Italy the time the Duke of York did. Unless Mr. Baretti had been a man of consequence he could never have recommended me to such people as he did. He is a gentleman of letters, and a studious man.'

In 1768 Beauclerk married the eldest daughter of the

second Duke of Marlborough, two days after her divorce from her first husband, Frederick Viscount Bolingbroke, the nephew and heir of the great Lord Bolingbroke.

Boswell reports a conversation with Johnson, which sets forth the history of this unhappy affair. 'While we were alone,' he writes, 'I endeavoured as well as I could to apologise for a lady who had been divorced from her husband by Act of Parliament. I said that he had used her very ill, had behaved brutally to her, and that she could not continue to live with him without having her delicacy contaminated; that all affection for him was thus destroyed; that the essence of conjugal union being gone, there remained only a cold form, a mere civil obligation; that she was in the prime of life, with qualities to produce happiness; that these ought not to be lost; and that the gentleman on whose account she was divorced had gained her heart while thus unhappily situated. Seduced, perhaps, by the charms of the lady in question, I thus attempted to palliate what I was sensible could not be justified; for when I had finished my harangue, my venerable friend gave me a proper check. "My dear Sir, never accustom your mind to mingle virtue and vice. The woman's a ——, and there's an end on't."' As Lady Diana Beauclerk did not die till the year 1808, she lived to see this story, so slightly veiled as it was by the omission of names, submitted to the world. A short time before the divorce Horace Walpole writes : 'Lady Bolingbroke has declared she will come into waiting on Sunday se'nnight; but as the Queen is likely to be brought to bed before that time, this may be only a bravado.' It may be interesting to mention, with a view to help us towards forming a kind of link with the past, that the child that was soon after born to the Queen was the Duke of Kent, the father of Queen Victoria.

In a letter written to Selwyn by Gilly Williams we read, 'Lady D. Spencer was married at St. George's on Saturday morning. They are in town at Topham's house, and give dinners. Lord Ancram dined there yesterday, and called her nothing but Lady Bolingbroke the whole time.' In another letter he says, 'Topham goes on with his dinners. Report says neither of them will live a twelvemonth, and if it is so, their life ought to be a merry one.'

Johnson on one occasion gave, as regards this marriage, an instance of that real delicacy of mind that beneath all his outside roughness belonged to him in so high a degree. He was talking of Blenheim, and said 'he should be very glad to see it, if properly invited, which in all probability would never be the case, as it was not worth his while to seek for it. I observed' (says

Boswell) 'that he might be easily introduced there by a common friend of ours, nearly related to the Duke. He answered, with an uncommon attention to delicacy of feeling, "I doubt whether our friend be on such a footing with the Duke as to carry anybody there; and I would not give him the uneasiness of seeing that I knew he was not, or even of being himself reminded of it."'

Lady Di Beauclerk in her second marriage seems to have been a faithful and devoted wife, though her faithfulness and her devotion met with but a poor return. Miss Burney in the following passage in her Diary gives a sad account of her married life.

'From the window of the dining-parlour, Sir Joshua directed us to look at a pretty white house which belonged to Lady Di Beauclerk.

'"I am extremely glad," said Mr. Burke, "to see her at last so well housed; poor woman! the bowl has long rolled in misery; I rejoice that it has now found its balance. I never, myself, so much enjoyed the sight of happiness in another, as in that woman, when I first saw her after the death of her husband. It was really enlivening to behold her placed in that sweet house, released from all her cares, a thousand pounds a year at her disposal, and—her husband was dead! Oh, it was pleasant, it was delightful to see her enjoyment of her situation!"

' " But, without considering the circumstances," said Mr. Gibbon, " this may appear very strange, though, when they are fairly stated, it is perfectly rational and unavoidable."

' "Very true," said Mr. Burke, " if the circumstances are not considered, Lady Di may seem highly reprehensible."

'He then, addressing himself particularly to me, as the person least likely to be acquainted with the character of Mr. Beauclerk, drew it himself in strong and marked expressions, describing the misery he gave his wife, his singular illtreatment of her, and the necessary relief the death of such a man must give.'

I cannot but hope that there may have been some exaggeration either in Burke's statements or in Miss Burney's record of what he said. If, however, Lady Di Beauclerk suffered such unkindness from her husband, she showed no resentment. She tended him to the last with the utmost faithfulness and affection.

Johnson writes to Boswell some years after the marriage, 'Poor Beauclerk is so ill that his life is thought to be in danger. Lady Di nurses him with very great assiduity.' When he died he left his children to her care; and, if she died, to the care of Mr. Langton. David Hume describes her as being 'handsome, agreeable, and ingenious beyond the ordinary rate.' Horace Walpole often speaks in very high terms of her powers as an artist.

In writing of a portrait she had drawn of the Duchess of Devonshire he says, 'The likeness is perfectly preserved, except that the paintress has lent her own expression to the Duchess, which you will allow is very agreeable flattery. What should I go to the Royal Academy for? I shall see no such *chefs-d'œuvre* there.' In writing of another of her pictures he says, 'Miss Pope, the actress, dined here yesterday, and literally shed tears, though she did not know the story. I think this is more to Lady Di's credit than a tom-tit pecking at painted fruit.' Mr. Hardy, in his 'Life of the Earl of Charlemont,' says, 'Lord Charlemont has often mentioned to me that Sir Joshua Reynolds frequently declared to him that many of her ladyship's drawings might be studied as models.'

A lively letter of hers to George Selwyn is given in his 'Memoirs.' She is staying in Bath and she writes: 'The fog has been choking me all the morning, and now the sun is blinding me. A thousand children are running by the windows. I should like to whip them for not being mine.' Boswell bears witness to her pleasant conversations.[1] It was from her he won a small bett

---

[1] See page 162.

(*sic*) by asking Johnson as to one of his peculiarities, 'which her Ladyship laid I durst not do.' Both Beauclerk and Garrick had wondered at his pocketing at the club the Seville oranges after he had squeezed out the juice, and 'seemed to think that he had a strange unwillingness to be discovered.' Boswell, though he won his 'bett,' did not succeed in learning what he did with them.

To Beauclerk's great natural powers, and to his fine scholarly mind, testimony is borne, as I have already said, by many competent witnesses. Boswell, in describing a dinner at his house, says : 'Mr. Beauclerk was very entertaining this day, and told us a number of short stories in a lively, elegant manner, and with that air of the world which has I know not what impressive effect, as if there were something more than is expressed, or than perhaps we could perfectly understand. As Johnson and I accompanied Sir Joshua Reynolds in his coach, Johnson said : " There is in Beauclerk a predominance over his company that one does not like. But he is a man who has lived so much in the world that he has a short story on every occasion ; he is always ready to talk, and is never exhausted." ' Langton, in a letter to Boswell, gives further proof of the way in which his extraordinary powers were regarded by Johnson :—

' The melancholy information you have received concerning Mr. Beauclerk's death is true. Had his talents been directed in any sufficient degree, as they ought, I have always been strongly of opinion that they were calculated to make an illustrious figure; and that opinion, as it had been in part formed upon Dr. Johnson's judgment, receives more and more confirmation by hearing what, since his death, Dr. Johnson has said concerning them. A few evenings ago he was at Mr. Vesey's, where Lord Althorpe, who was one of a numerous company there, addressed Dr. Johnson on the subject of Mr. Beauclerk's death, saying, "Our club has had a great loss since we met last." He replied, " A loss that perhaps the whole nation could not repair." The Doctor then went on to speak of his endowments, and particularly extolled the wonderful ease with which he uttered what was highly excellent. He said that no man ever was so free when he was going to say a good thing from a *look* that expressed that it was coming; or, when he had said it, from a look that expressed that it *had* come. At Mr. Thrale's, some days before, when we were talking on the same subject, he said, referring to the same idea of his wonderful facility, "that Beauclerk's talents were those which he had felt himself more disposed to envy than those of any whom he had known." ' And yet what

great men he had known ! On an earlier occasion,
when Boswell had remarked to Johnson that 'Beauclerk
has a keenness of mind which is very uncommon ;' Johnson replied, 'Yes, Sir ! and everything comes from him
so easily.   It appears to me that I labour when I say a
good thing.'   Boswell replied, 'You are loud, Sir ; but it
is not an effort of mind.'   Dean Barnard, in those admirable verses with which he so wittily rebuked Johnson's
rudeness, shows the opinion held by no mean judge of
conversation of Beauclerk's powers :

> If I have thoughts and can't express 'em,
> Gibbon shall teach me how to dress 'em
>   In terms select and terse ;
> Jones teach me modesty and Greek ;
> Smith, how to think ; Burke, how to speak ;
>   And Beauclerk to converse.

Hawkins writes, 'His conversation was of the most
excellent kind ; learned, witty, polite, and where the subject required it serious ; and over all his behaviour there
beamed such a sunshine of cheerfulness and good
humour as communicated itself to all around him.'
Lord Charlemont, who was a member of the Literary
Club and knew him well, said that 'he possessed an
exquisite taste, various accomplishments, and the most perfect good breeding.   He was eccentric, often querulous,

entertaining a contempt for the generality of the world, which the politeness of his manners could not always conceal; but to those whom he liked, most generous and friendly. Devoted at one time to pleasure, at another to literature, sometimes absorbed in play, sometimes in books, he was altogether one of the most accomplished and, when in good humour and surrounded by those who suited his fancy, one of the most agreeable men that could possibly exist.' Wilkes, in a marginal note in his copy of Boswell's 'Johnson,' describes Beauclerk as being ' shy, sly, and dry.'

Miss Burney speaks of him as 'that celebrated wit and libertine.' It is a pity that so admirable a talker had not his Boswell, though, perhaps, much of what he said depended to a very great extent on the manner in which he said it. Lord Pembroke said, with perhaps more wit than truth, that 'Dr. Johnson's sayings would not appear so extraordinary were it not for his *bow-wow way.*' There are, however, very few talkers whose conversation if written down would still strike us with wonder. I have gathered together the few good sayings of Beauclerk that I have been able to find. When Johnson got his pension, Beauclerk said to him in the humourous phrase of Falstaff, 'I hope you'll now purge and live cleanly like a gentleman.' Boswell gives the following account which he received from Beauclerk of a curious affair between Dr. Johnson and Mr. Hervey. 'Tom Hervey had a great liking for Johnson, and in his will had left him a legacy of fifty pounds. One day he said to me, "Johnson may want this money now more than afterwards. I have a mind to give it him directly. Will you be so good as to carry a fifty-pound note from me to him?" This I positively refused to do, as he might, perhaps, have knocked me down for insulting him, and have afterwards put the note in his pocket.' Boswell repeated this story, with certain other circumstances into which it is not necessary to enter here, to Johnson. Afterwards he wrote to tell Johnson that he had become very uneasy lest his having done so 'might be interpreted as a breach of confidence, and offend one whose society he valued.' Johnson wrote back, 'I have seen Mr. ——, and as to him, have set all right without any inconvenience, as far as I know, to you. Mrs. Thrale had forgot the story. You may now be at ease.'

Mr. Croker says that there is reason to fear that this mention of Beauclerk's name by Boswell impaired the cordiality between Beauclerk and Johnson.

It was Beauclerk who, when he heard that Tom Davies clapped Moody the player on his back, when in an argument that was going on 'he once tried to say something upon our side,' exclaimed 'he could not conceive a more humiliating situation than to be clapped on the back by Tom Davies.' A few days after this, a discussion was going on as to the belief in immortality. Boswell writes : 'I said it appeared to me that some people had not the least notion of immortality, and I mentioned a distinguished gentleman of our acquaintance. *Johnson*: "Sir, if it were not for the notion of immortality, he would cut a throat to fill his pockets." When I quoted this to Beauclerk,' Boswell goes on to add, 'who knew much more of the gentleman than we did, he said, in his acid manner, "He would cut a throat to fill his pockets, if it were not for fear of being hanged." ' Johnson, as we read on another occasion, 'thought Mr. Beauclerk made a shrewd and judicious remark to Mr. Langton, who after having been for the first time in company with a well-known wit about town, was warmly admiring and praising him,—"See him again," said Beauclerk.' 'In the only instance remembered of Goldsmith's practice as a physician,' as we read in Mr. Forster's interesting Life, 'it one day happened that, his opinion differing somewhat from the apothecary's in attendance, the lady thought her apothecary the safer counsellor, and Goldsmith quitted the house in high indignation. He would leave off prescribing for his friends, he said. "Do so, my dear Doctor," observed Beauclerk. "Whenever you undertake to kill, let it only be your enemies."'

A hot discussion, not the only one of its kind, one day arose between Beauclerk and Johnson, which Beauclerk closed by an admirable saying. 'It was mentioned that Dr. Dodd had once wished to be a member of the Literary Club.

' *Johnson*: "I should be sorry if any of our club were hanged. I will not say but some of them deserve it."

'Beauclerk (supposing this to be aimed at persons for whom he had at that time a wonderful fancy, which, however, did not last long) was irritated, and eagerly said, "You, Sir, have a friend (naming him) who deserves to be hanged, for he speaks behind their backs against those with whom he lives on the best terms, and attacks them in the newspapers. *He* certainly ought to be *kicked.*"

' *Johnson*: "Sir, we all do this in some degree, *veniam petimus damusque vicissim.* To be sure it may be done so much that a man may deserve to be kicked."

' *Beauclerk*: " He is very malignant."

' *Johnson*: " No, Sir, he is not malignant. He is mischievous, if you will. He would do no man an essential injury; he may, indeed, love to make sport of people by vexing their vanity. I, however, once knew an old gentleman who was absolutely malignant. He really wished evil to others, and rejoiced at it."

'*Boswell*: "The gentleman, Mr. Beauclerk, against whom you are so violent, is, I know, a man of good principles."

'*Beauclerk*: "Then he does not wear them out in practice."'

Boswell in one instance tries to give his readers a conception of Beauclerk's manner of telling a story. He writes: 'Here let me not forget a curious anecdote, as related to me by Mr. Beauclerk, which I shall endeavour to exhibit as well as I can in that gentleman's lively manner; and in justice to him it is proper to add that Dr. Johnson told me that I might rely both on the correctness of his memory and the fidelity of his narrative. "When Madame de Boufflers was first in England (said Beauclerk) she was desirous to see Johnson. I accordingly went with her to his chambers in the Temple, where she was entertained with his conversation for some time. When our visit was over, she and I left him and were got into Inner Temple Lane, when all at once I heard a voice like thunder. This was occasioned by Johnson, who, it seems, upon a little reflection, had taken it into his head that he ought to have done the honours of his literary residence to a foreign lady of quality, and eager to show himself a man of gallantry, was hurrying down the staircase in violent agitation. He overtook us before we reached the Temple Gate, and brushing in between me and Madame de Boufflers, seized her hand and conducted her to her coach. His dress was a rusty-brown morning suit, a pair of old shoes by way of slippers, a little shrivelled wig sticking on the top of his head, and the sleeves of his shirt and the knees of his breeches hanging loose. A considerable crowd of people gathered round, and were not a little struck by this singular appearance." '

Boswell records 'a violent altercation that arose between Johnson and Beauclerk, which,' he writes, ' having made much noise at the time, I think it proper, in order to prevent any future misrepresentation, to give a minute account of it. In talking of Hackman (the Rev. Mr. Hackman, who in a fit of frantic jealous love had shot Miss Ray), Johnson argued, as Judge Blackstone had done, that his being furnished with two pistols was a proof that he meant to shoot two persons. Mr. Beauclerk said, " No : for that every wise man who intended to shoot himself took two pistols, that he might be sure of doing it at once. Lord ——'s cook shot himself with one pistol, and lived ten days in great agony. Mr. ——, who loved buttered muffins, but durst not eat them because they disagreed with his stomach, resolved to shoot himself; *he* had two charged pistols: one was found lying charged upon the table by him, after he had shot himself with the other." "Well" (said Johnson, with an air of triumph), "you see here one pistol was sufficient." Beauclerk replied smartly, "Because it happened to kill him." And either then, or a very little afterwards, being piqued at Johnson's triumphant remark, added, "This is what you don't know, and I do."

'There was then a cessation of the dispute; some minutes intervened, during which dinner and the glass went on cheerfully; when Johnson suddenly and abruptly exclaimed, "Mr. Beauclerk, how came you to talk so petulantly to me, as 'This is what you don't know, but what I know'? One thing *I* know which *you* don't seem to know, that you are very uncivil."

'*Beauclerk*: "Because *you* began by being uncivil (which you always are)."

'The words in parenthesis were, I believe, not heard by Dr. Johnson. Here again there was a cessation of arms. Johnson told me that the reason why he waited at first some time without taking any notice of what Mr. Beauclerk said, was because he was thinking whether he should resent it. But when he considered that there were present a young lord and an eminent traveller, two men of the world with whom he had never dined before,

he was apprehensive that they might think they had a
right to take such liberties with him as Beauclerk did,
and therefore resolved he would not let it pass; adding
that "he would not appear a coward." A little while
after this, the conversation turned on the violence of
Hackman's temper. Johnson then said, "It was his
business to *command* his temper, as my friend Mr.
Beauclerk should have done some time ago."

'*Beauclerk* : "I should learn of *you*, Sir."

'*Johnson* : "Sir, you have given *me* opportunities
enough of learning, when I have been in *your* company.
No man loves to be treated with contempt."

'*Beauclerk* (with a polite inclination towards Johnson):
"Sir, you have known me twenty years, and however I
may have treated others, you may be sure I could never
treat you with contempt."

'*Johnson* : "Sir, you have said more than was necessary."

'Thus it ended; and Beauclerk's coach not having
come for him till very late, Dr. Johnson and another
gentleman sat with him a long time after the rest of the
company were gone; and he and I dined at Beauclerk's
on the Saturday se'nnight following.'

Johnson on another occasion showed a certain irrita-
bility towards Beauclerk. Boswell, in speaking of the

projected journey to Italy with the Thrales, writes: 'I mentioned that Mr Beauclerk had said that Baretti, whom they were to carry with them, would keep them so long in the little towns of his own district, that they would not have time to see Rome. I mentioned this to put them on their guard. *Johnson* : " Sir, we do not thank Mr. Beauclerk for supposing that we are to be directed by Mr. Baretti."'

In the chapter on 'Bennet Langton' I have quoted the happily chosen quotation that Beauclerk had put on Johnson's portrait. No less happy was he in the inscription from *Love's Labour's Lost*, which he placed under the portrait of Garrick. 'Mr. Beauclerk,' as Boswell writes, 'with happy propriety, inscribed under that fine portrait of him, which by Lady Diana's kindness is now the property of my friend Mr. Langton, the following passage from his beloved Shakspeare—

> —a merrier man
> Within the limit of becoming mirth
> I never spent an hour's talk withal, &c.'

In the Life of Lord Charlemont are given a few letters by Beauclerk written in a very lively manner. Langton, it will be remembered, had said that if his friend's talents had been directed as they ought, they were calculated to make an illustrious figure. Beauclerk in these letters shows that he himself is fully aware of his own indolence. He apologises for his neglect in 'keeping up an intercourse with one for whom I shall always retain the greatest and tenderest regard,' and lays the blame on 'that insuperable idleness, which accompanies me through life, which not only prevents me from doing what I ought, but likewise from enjoying my greatest pleasure, where anything is to be done.' Later on he writes, saying he has been very ill, but he goes on to add, 'in spite of my doctor, or nature itself, I will very soon pay you a visit. Business, it is true, I have none to keep me here; but you forget that I have business in Lancashire, and that I must go there when I come to you.' (Lord Charlemont was in Ireland.) 'Now, you will please to recollect that there is nothing in this world I so entirely hate as business of any kind, and that I pay you the greatest compliment I can do when I risque the meeting with my own confounded affairs in order to have the pleasure of seeing you ; but this I am resolved to do.'

He owns his detestation of politics and politicians. He writes, in a letter dated Muswell Hill, Summer Quarters, July 18, 1774: 'Why should you be vexed to find that mankind are fools and knaves ? I have known it so long that every fresh instance of it amuses me, provided it does not immediately affect my friends or myself. Politicians do not seem to me to be much greater rogues than other people; and as their actions affect in general private persons less than other kinds of villainy do, I cannot find that I am so angry with them. It is true that the leading men in both countries at present are, I believe, the most corrupt, abandoned people in the nation; but, now that I am upon this worthy subject of human nature, I will inform you of a few particulars relating to the discovery of Otaheite, which Dr. Hawkesworth said placed the King above all the conquerors in the world; and if the glory is to be estimated by the mischief, I do not know whether he is not right. When Wallis first anchored off the island, two natives came alongside of the ship, without fear or distrust, to barter their goods with our people. A man, called the boat-keeper, who was in a boat that was tied to the ship, attempted to get the things from them without payment. The savages resisted, and he struck one of them with the boat-hook, upon which they immediately paddled away. In the morning great numbers came in canoes of all sizes about the ship. They behaved, however, in the most peaceable manner, still offering to exchange their commodities for anything that they could obtain from us.

The same trick was played by attempting to take away
their things by force. This enraged them, and they had
come prepared to defend themselves with such weapons
as they had; they immediately began to fling stones, one
of which went into the cabin window. Wallis on this
ordered that the guns, loaded with grape-shot, should be
fired. This, you may imagine, immediately dispersed
them. Some were drowned, many killed, and some few
got on shore, where numbers of the natives were assembled. Wallis then ordered the great guns to be played,
according to his phrase, upon them. This drove them
off, when he still ordered the same pastime to be continued in order to convince them, as he says, that our
arms could reach them at such a distance. If you add
to this that the inhabitants of all these islands are eat up
with vile disorders, you will find that men may be much
worse employed than by doing the dirtiest job that ever
was undertaken by the lowest of our clerk-ministers.'

Beauclerk might write that 'every year, every hour,
adds to my misanthropy, and I have had a pretty considerable share of it for some years past ;' but the generous
indignation that blazes forth in this letter of his belongs
to any one rather than a misanthrope. It was in such
feelings as these, as well as in their literary pursuits, that
he and Johnson had so much in common. My readers

will remember Johnson's hatred of every kind of oppression of the less civilized races, and how, 'upon one occasion, when in company with some very grave men at Oxford, his toast was, " Here's to the next insurrection of the negroes in the West Indies." ' Another time he said, with 'great emotion and with generous warmth, " I love the University of Salamanca; for when the Spaniards were in doubt as to the lawfulness of their conquering America, the University of Salamanca gave it as their opinion that it was not lawful." ' In a letter written a year earlier than Beauclerk's, he says, " I do not much wish well to discoveries, for I am always afraid they will end in conquest and robbery.'

Beauclerk's letters are very interesting from the frequent mention made in them of the other members of the club. He writes : ' Why should fortune have placed our paltry concerns in two different islands? If we could keep them, they are not worth one hour's conversation at Elmsly's (the bookseller). If life is good for anything, it is only made so by the society of those whom we love. At all events I will try to come to Ireland, and shall take no excuse from you for not coming early in the winter to London. The club exists but by your presence; the flourishing of learned men is the glory of the State. Mr. Vesey will tell you that our club consists of the greatest men in the world, consequently you see there is a good and patriotic reason for you to return to England in the winter. Pray make my best respects to Lady Charlemont and Miss Hickman, and tell them I wish they were at this moment sitting at the door of our ale-house in Gerrard Street.' (The Turk's Head Tavern, where the Literary Club met, was in that street.) Later on he writes : ' Our poor club is in a miserable decay; unless you come and relieve it, it will certainly expire. Would you imagine that Sir Joshua Reynolds is extremely anxious to be a member of Almack's? You see what noble ambition will make a man attempt. That den is not yet opened, consequently I have not been there ; so, for the present, I am clear upon that score.' He ends his letter by saying, ' We cannot do without you. If you do not come here, I will bring all the club over to Ireland to live with you, and that will drive you here in your own defence. Johnson shall spoil your books, Goldsmith pull your flowers, and Boswell talk to you : stay then if you can.'

At a later date he writes : ' Our club has dwindled away to nothing. Nobody attends but Mr. Chambers, and he is going to the East Indies. Sir Joshua and Goldsmith have got into such a round of pleasures that they have no time.' Poor Goldsmith's round ended in less than two months after this letter was written. In an earlier letter we read, 'I have been but once at the club since you left England; we were entertained as usual by Dr. Goldsmith's absurdity.' 'Goldsmith,' he writes in another letter, 'the other day put a paragraph into the newspapers in praise of Lord Mayor Townshend. The same night we happened to sit next to Lord Shelburne at Drury Lane; I mentioned the circumstance of the paragraph to him; he said to Goldsmith that he hoped that he had mentioned nothing about Malagrida in it. "Do you know," answered Goldsmith, "that I never could conceive the reason why they call you Malagrida, *for* Malagrida was a very good sort of man." You see plainly what he meant to say, but that happy turn of expression is peculiar to himself. Mr. Walpole says, that this story is a picture of Goldsmith's whole life. Johnson has been confined for some weeks in the Isle of Sky; we hear that he was obliged to swim over to the mainland taking hold of a cow's tail. Be that as it may, Lady Di has promised to make a drawing of it.' A few weeks later he writes: 'I hope your Parliament has finished all its absurdities, and that you will be at leisure to come over here to attend your club, where you will do much more good than all the patriots in the world ever did to anybody, viz., you will make very many of your friends extremely happy, and you know Goldsmith[1] has informed us that no form of government ever contributed either to the happiness or misery of anyone. I saw a letter from Foote, with an account of an Irish tragedy; the subject is Manlius, and the last speech which he makes, when he is pushed off from the Tarpeian Rock, is "Sweet Jesus, where am I going?" Pray send me word if this is true. We have a new comedy here' ('The School for Wives'), 'which is good for nothing; bad as it is, however, it succeeds very well, and has almost killed Goldsmith with envy. I have no news either literary or political, to send you. Everybody, except myself, and about a million of vulgars, are in the country.' He gives an amusing account of a naval review. 'I have been at the review at Portsmouth. If you had seen it you would have owned that it is a very pleasant thing to be a king. It is true, —— made a job of the claret to ——, who furnished the first tables with vinegar under that denomination. Charles Fox said, that Lord S—wich should have been impeached ; what an abominable world do we live in, that there should not be above half-a-dozen honest men *in* the world, and that

[1] How small of all that human hearts endure
That part which laws or kings can cause or cure.
The Traveller.

These lines were really written by Johnson, not by Goldsmith.

one of those should live in Ireland. You will, perhaps, be shocked at the small portion of honesty that I allot to your country; but a sixth part is as much as comes to its share; and, for anything I know to the contrary, the other five may be in Ireland too, for I am sure I do not know where else to find them.'

I will give but one more extract from these interesting letters. He writes, ' I can now give you a better reason for not writing sooner to you than for any other thing that I ever did in my life. When Sir Charles Bingham came from Ireland, I, as you may easily imagine, immediately enquired after you ; he told me that you were very well, but in great affliction, having just lost your child. You cannot conceive how I was shocked with this news ; not only by considering what you suffered on this occasion, but I recollected that a foolish letter of mine, laughing at your Irish politics, would arrive just at that point of time. A bad joke at any time is a bad thing; but when any attempt at pleasantry happens at a moment that a person is in great affliction, it certainly is the most odious thing in the world. I could not write to you to comfort you ; you will not wonder, therefore, that I did not write at all.'

The great width of Beauclerk's reading is shown by the size and variety of his library, which was sold after his death. A copy of the catalogue is to be seen in the British Museum. The title-page is as follows : ' Biblio- theca selectissima et elegantissima Pernobilis Angli, T. Beauclerk, S.R.S. Price three shillings. Comprehending an excellent choice of Books, to the number of upwards of thirty thousand volumes, in most languages, and upon almost every branch of science and polite literature, which will be sold on Monday April 9, 1781, and the forty-nine following days (Good Friday excepted).' Two days' sale were given to the works on divinity, including ' Heterodoxi et Increduli. Angl. Freethinkers and their opponents ;' six days to ' Itineraria. Angl. Voyages and Travels ;' and twelve days to historical works.

Boswell records that ' Mr. Wilkes said he wondered to find in Mr. Beauclerk's library such a numerous collection of sermons, seeming to think it strange that a gentleman of Mr. Beauclerk's character in the gay world should have chosen to have many compositions of that kind. *Johnson* : " Why, Sir, you are to consider that sermons make a considerable branch of English literature, so that a library must be very imperfect if it has not a numerous collection of sermons ; and in all collections, Sir, the desire of augmenting them grows stronger in proportion to the advance in acquisition, as motion is accelerated by the continuance of the impetus. Besides,

Sir (looking at Mr. Wilkes with a placid but significant smile), a man may collect sermons with intention of making himself better by them.   I hope Mr. Beauclerk intended that some time or other that should be the case with him.'"'

Beauclerk was especially eager in scientific researches. In the University which Johnson and Boswell amused themselves with founding in the air, Beauclerk was to have the Chair of Natural Philosophy. Goldsmith writes, ' I see Mr. Beauclerk very often both in town and country. He is now going directly forward to become a second Boyle : deep in chymistry and physics.' Boswell, in a letter to his friend Temple, says, ' He has one of the most numerous and splendid private libraries that I ever saw ; greenhouses, hothouses, observatory, laboratory for chymical experiments, in short, everything princely.'

To all this eagerness after knowledge, and this delight in one of the most uncourtly of men, Beauclerk 'added the character of a man of fashion, of which his dress and equipage showed him to be emulous. In the early period of his life he was the exemplar of all who wished, without incurring the censure of foppery, to become conspicuous in the gay world.' In 'Selwyn's Letters,' we read that ' Madame Pitt (sister to Lord Chatham) met with an accident (a sprained leg) leaning on Topham as she was stepping out of her chaise, and swears she will trust to the shoulders of no Macaroni for the future.' Johnson's name for him of Beau fitted him very well.

Beauclerk's health seems never to have been vigorous, and he suffered a great deal at times. His temperament, however, was a very happy one. Johnson one day talking of melancholy said, 'Some men, and very thinking men too, have not those vexing thoughts. Sir Joshua Reynolds is the same all the year round. Beauclerk, except when ill and in pain, is the same.' In spite of occasional altercations the affection between the men was very strong. 'As Beauclerk and I walked up Johnson's Court,' writes Boswell, 'I said, " I have a veneration for this court ; " and was glad to find that Beauclerk had the same reverential enthusiasm.' Johnson in his turn often showed his high regard for Beauclerk. 'One evening,' says Boswell, 'when we were in the street together, and I told him I was going to sup at Mr. Beauclerk's, he said, " I'll go with you." After having walked part of the way, seeming to recollect something, he suddenly stopped and said, " I cannot go, but *I do not love Beauclerk the less.*" '

'Johnson's affection for Topham Beauclerk,' Boswell says in another passage, 'was so great, that when Beauclerk was labouring under that severe illness which at last occasioned his death, Johnson said (with a voice faultering with emotion), "Sir, I would walk to the extent of the diameter of the earth to save Beauclerk."' We are reminded how, when he heard that Mr. Thrale had lost his only son, he said, 'I would have gone to the extremity of the earth to have preserved this boy.' On Beauclerk's death he wrote to Boswell, 'Poor, dear, Beauclerk—*nec, ut soles, dabis joca.* His wit and his folly, his acuteness and maliciousness, his merriment and his reasoning are now over. Such another will not often be found among mankind. He directed himself to be buried by the side of his mother, an instance of tenderness which I hardly expected.' When a year later Boswell was walking home with Johnson from the first party that Mrs. Garrick had given after her husband's death, 'We stopped,' he says, 'a little while by the rails of the Adelphi, looking on the Thames, and I said to him with some emotion that I was now thinking of two friends we had lost, who once lived in the buildings behind us, Beauclerk and Garrick. "Ay, Sir," (said he tenderly), "and two such friends as cannot be supplied."'

CHAPTER X.

OLIVER GOLDSMITH.[1]

'ONE day,' writes the younger Colman, 'I met the poet Harding at Oxford—a half-crazy creature, as poets generally are, with a huge broken brick and some bits of thatch upon the crown of his hat. On my asking him for a solution of this prosopopœia, " Sir," said he, " today is the anniversary of the celebrated Dr. Goldsmith's death, and I am now in the character of his ' Deserted Village.'"' When anyone sets about celebrating the anniversary of a great writer's death, even if he does not go to the lengths of poor Harding, he is likely enough to make himself foolish. He is weighed down with the feeling that to celebrate it properly, he must celebrate it in character ; and yet he is by no means certain what is the character that he should assume. It is the anniversary of a death, and so a certain degree of gloom would not be unsuitable ; but, on the other hand, it may be the

[1] Reprinted from the *Times*, April 4, 1874.

anniversary of the death of a humourist, and so a certain
degree of mirth would be most becoming. Like Hamlet's
uncle, he is

> With an auspicious and a dropping eye,
> In equal scale, weighing delight and dole.

And like Hamlet's uncle, as the play goes on, he does not
feel altogether at his ease in his part. The difficulties,
then, of keeping anniversaries are so great that no sensible person troubles himself to keep them at all.

There are, however, those who think that just as the
aloe makes an effort once every hundred years to put out
flowers, so, though we are more than justified in disregarding anniversaries, we ought nevertheless to make
an effort to celebrate centenaries. Such people as these,
then, would have felt a kindly sympathy with poor poet
Harding if it had been the centenary, and not the anniversary, of Goldsmith's death. They would not, perhaps, have
shown their enthusiasm by carrying about a huge broken
brick and some bits of thatch ; but likely enough they
would have held a kind of jubilee at the Crystal Palace.

While, however, we do not love the ostentatious cele-
bration of anniversaries and centenaries, yet it is by no
means unbecoming when some day memorable in a great
man's life comes round to have his name freshly remem-

bered among us. Thus, it is natural enough on this 4th of April to dwell on the memory of that writer whose death just one hundred years ago to-day made sharers in one common and almost overwhelming grief Johnson, Burke, and Reynolds, and many an outcast of this great city. It may be well to reflect on all that we, too, even in these days when each season counts its new books by thousands, have lost by the death of an author who, when he had written in the last thirteen years of his life 'The Citizen of the World,' 'The Vicar of Wakefield,' 'The Traveller,' 'The Good Natured Man,' 'The Deserted Village,' 'She Stoops to Conquer,' and 'Retaliation,' 'yielding to the united pressure of labour, penury, and sorrow,' sank into his grave when he was but forty-five years old.

'He died of a fever,' wrote Johnson, 'made, I am afraid, more violent by uneasiness of mind. His debts began to be heavy, and all his resources were exhausted. Sir Joshua is of opinion that he owed not less than two thousand pounds. Was ever poet so trusted before?' One, certainly, of his resources had not been exhausted. His last illness attacked him as he was painting Reynolds with his pen no less gracefully than Reynolds had painted him with his pencil.

Two thousand pounds was a heavy debt for a writer to

owe. Yet if an author who so largely increased 'the public stock of harmless pleasure' could have 'reached a hand through time to catch the far-off interest' that was due to him, and that would have been so cheerfully paid, how trifling would the debt have appeared! It is not too much to say that if Goldsmith had been rewarded by the Crown, like Johnson, we might now have another 'Vicar of Wakefield,' another 'Traveller,' another 'Good Na-tured Man.' He was improvident, no doubt, and the little that he did receive he did not manage wisely. Like the Man in Black, he was 'perfectly instructed in the art of giving away thousands before he was taught the more necessary qualifications of getting a farthing.' But his improvidence, doubtless, was due not only to the training of his childhood and to his own natural tempera-ment, but also to the uncertainty with which, when he had once learnt how to earn money, money came in. Had he had either the fixed income of a pension on which to count, or, far better, the certainty of fair pay which attends a man of any literary powers at the present day, his mind would not have lost its balance every time he had ten guineas in his pocket. Had there only been some Thrale to have taken him, as the great brewer took Johnson when in his state of utter despondency, some one who would have provided for him prudence, as the Thrales provided cheerfulness for Johnson, how lengthened might have been his life, how different its decline and end! 'Is your mind at ease?' asked his physician a day or two before his death. 'No, it is not,' was Goldsmith's answer. He never spoke again. What a different end in this chamber in Brick Court from that to which he had four or five years earlier looked forward in his 'Sweet Auburn'!

> And as a hare whom hounds and horns pursue
> Pants to the place from whence at first he flew,
> I still had hopes, my long vexations past,
> Here to return—and die at home at last.

Sad though was Goldsmith's end, sad, too, many a scene in his life, yet we must not forget the light that such a mind as his, while the world is still young and hopes still fresh and high, ever casts before itself. In a letter which Mr. Forster quotes in his 'Life of Goldsmith,' we read, 'His debts rendered him, at times, so very melancholy and dejected that I am sure he felt himself, at least the last years of his life, a very unhappy man.'

We doubt, however, if till his health began to fail he had not, we cannot say his fair share of happiness—for who could venture to fix the share which the author of 'The Vicar of Wakefield' might have fairly claimed?—

but, at all events, such a share as would make life desirable enough. No unhappy man could have written the books that Goldsmith wrote. Is he a philosopher and enlarging with all seriousness on the vanity and misery of this world? then, as Johnson's old college friend complained, 'cheerfulness is always breaking in on his philosophy.' Have 'eight years of disappointment, and anguish, and study worn him down?' he is still ready to enjoy 'a Shoemaker's Holiday' with any one; still ready, when no fool is near, to cry out to his friends, 'Come, now, let us play the fool a little.' Children delighted in him, and children do not delight in an unhappy man.

Walter Scott in writing of him says, 'We bless the memory of an author who contrives so well to reconcile us to human nature.' Can it be the case that an author can reconcile his readers to human nature who has not first reconciled himself to it? Goldsmith was of all men the most artless. He could no more hide his failings than his merits, his sorrows than his joys. In every book he is the hero of his own story, and his heroes are far from being unhappy men. He suffers, indeed, from what he calls 'an exquisite sensibility of contempt;' but his sufferings are more than balanced by many an exquisite sensibility besides. He had an exquisite sensibility of admiration, of friendship, of kindliness, of love, of the beauties of nature and the beauties of great writers, of all simple and harmless pleasures.

In his own innocent vanity, which others mocked at, and through which he was often so grievously wounded, he had no small pleasure too. Was he slighted by the world? He was a far better judge than the world of greatness, and he knew that he was great. They are very ignorant of human nature who, while they delight in Goldsmith's writings, yet regret that he was so vain! If Goldsmith had been stripped of his vanity he might have been a great writer, but he would not have been Goldsmith. Both he and Swift delight in painting the weaknesses of the heart, but while one paints with all the savageness of a man who is caricaturing his bitter enemy, the other paints with all the tenderness that would be found in an artist who, sitting before a mirror, is amusing himself by drawing his own likeness. We cannot doubt that Goldsmith knew all his own weaknesses much better than did Johnson, Garrick, or Boswell, and that when alone he had many a smile over that queer fellow, himself. It was from this exact knowledge of his own mind that he derived that exquisite sensibility of contempt from which he suffered. He knew only too well that he had a hundred weaknesses which exposed him to the contempt of those who can fathom only the shallows of the human mind, and not the depths which lie so close alongside them. ^ He could laugh at his own weaknesses, for his weaknesses he knew were, like Samson's locks, closely connected with his strength. Deprived of them, where would he have made that study of the human heart in which his knowledge, so far as it went was so exact? The greater passions may be studied in others, but the little failings which form so large a part of our everyday life are best studied in ourselves.

Goldsmith, then, to a mind that was gifted with a wonderful power of analysing character united a heart that in a no less wonderful degree was worthy of analysis. There have been, no doubt, equally clever artists and equally good subjects. Scarcely ever have so clever an artist and so good a subject been joined in one. In a literary point of view we might apply to him his own line, and say of him, as he said of the parish priest in his 'Deserted Village'—

'Even his failings lean'd to Virtue's side.'

Though the names of the great writers of 'that past Georgian day' are still familiar in our mouths as household words, it is a pity that their works are not familiar in our hands as household things. 'The Vicar of Wakefield' is read by every one, of course, or, at least, like a municipal address to the Queen, must be taken as read. We should be curious to know, however, how many editions of 'The Citizen of the World' have been called for in the last thirty years. Out of every hundred people who can quote Mr. Pickwick, could we count on finding one who could quote the Man in Black? Nay, to go further, and to take, not Charles Dickens, but the second, or third, or tenth-rate authors of the present day, has 'The Citizen of the World' a twentieth of the readers that some among the popular novelists can boast of?

The literature of last century is divided from us as if by a great gulf, and though on the other side of the gulf there is a perfect paradise of intellectual delight, yet few care to face the trouble of crossing over. With the great stir in men's minds that set in on the Continent with the French Revolution, and in England with its fullest force on the close of the French war, began a literature which, even if it excites every man's interest, yet, to use Mr. Disraeli's expression, 'harasses' every man's mind. The age of optimism had passed away with the meeting of the States General—not for ever, but certainly for a long time. 'Whatever is, is not best,' was the text on which all preachers began to hold forth. The parish priest in whom Fielding and Goldsmith delighted, who was a Christian, and not a theologian, and who neither harassed himself nor yet his people, had passed away.

Yet there are persons who, weary of endless talk on reforms and improvements, like at times to drop out of the stream of this uneasy age to seek for quiet thought among men who never so much as heard that there was a social science. A time, indeed, comes to many a reader when, in the literature of the eighteenth century, the mind finds its best repose. And among the great writers of that great age of writing not the least dear, as not the least resting, must be held that 'child of the public,' to use his own words, Oliver Goldsmith. If any of our readers desire to keep fittingly the centenary of Oliver Goldsmith, let them take down from the book-shelf the old copy of the ' Deserted Village' or the 'Vicar of Wakefield,' and in the noble characters they find in those charming pages will be seen what manner of man he was whose death made Reynolds lay aside his brush and Burke seek relief in tears.

APPENDIX.

THE DURATION OF JOHNSON'S RESIDENCE AT OXFORD. [1]

MR. FITZGERALD in his edition of Boswell's 'Johnson' has reopened a question which, though perhaps of no very great importance in itself, is yet not without its interest. Johnson, as I have already shown, was forced, through want of means, to leave the University before he had completed his residence and taken his degree. Boswell had stated that Johnson had been a member of Pembroke College for little more than three years. No doubt was thrown, so far as I know, on this statement, till Mr. Croker, after an inspection of the College books with the help of Dr. Hall, the Master of Pembroke, maintained that Boswell was altogether wrong, as Johnson had only been an actual member fourteen months. But neither Mr. Croker nor Mr. Fitzgerald has brought together all the facts that bear on this question, though each, without first carefully summing up the case, has ventured to speak with all the authority of a judge from whose decision there was no appeal. I have little confidence in my own power of arriving at a decision one way or the

---

[1] Reprinted (with alterations) from the *Saturday Review,* September 12, 1874.

other, and I shall content myself with putting before my readers the statements made on each side, the difficulties which have to be overcome, and the facts which I have myself at some labour gathered together. Like Mr. Fitzgerald, I must express my obligations to Professor Chandler of Pembroke College, for the assistance he has so kindly rendered me by his searches into the musty old battel books.

Boswell's statement as to Johnson's residence is precise, and Boswell, as I need scarcely say, when he speaks of any matter positively, is very rarely proved to be wrong. He says, 'The *res angusta domi* prevented him from having the advantage of a complete academical education. The friend to whom he had trusted for support had deceived him. His debts in College, though not great were increasing, and his scanty remittances from Lichfield, which had all along been made with great difficulty, could be supplied no longer, his father having fallen into a state of insolvency. Compelled, therefore, by irresistible necessity, he left the College in autumn 1731, without a degree, having been a member of it little more than three years.'

Hawkins's statement, in his 'Life of Johnson,' agrees with Boswell's. He says : 'The time of his continuance at Oxford is divisible into two periods, the former whereof commenced on the 31st day of October, 1728, and determined in December 1729, when, as appears by a note in his diary in these words—"1729, Dec., S. J. Oxonio rediit"—he left that place, the reason whereof was a failure of pecuniary supplies from his father; but meeting with another source, the bounty, as it is supposed, of one or more of the members of the Cathedral, he returned, and made up the whole of his residence—about three years.' These two statements, though they differ in some points, are almost at one as to the time of Johnson's residence.

It might be objected that after all we have the evidence only of one writer, and not of two, as Boswell, whose work was the later of the two, might have merely followed Hawkins. But Boswell not only took a great deal of trouble to test the accuracy of all the statements he made on the authority of others, but in this case also he had independent authority of his own. He had lived in the house of Dr. Adams, the Master of Pembroke, who had been a Fellow when Johnson entered, and who was able, therefore, to speak with exact knowledge in 'that authentic information which he obligingly gave' Boswell. Nevertheless, as I shall presently consider, it is not impossible that Boswell may have been influenced by Hawkins's statement. According, then, both to Hawkins and Boswell, Johnson entered Pembroke in October 1728, and left it in the autumn of 1731. When, however, Dr. Hall consulted the College books, he found that they were very far from agreeing with this statement. On the information he furnished, Mr. Croker maintained that Boswell was altogether wrong both in his statement as to residence and in one or two anecdotes which depend on the duration of his residence. Dr. Hall says : 'He was not quite three years a member of the College, having been entered October 31, 1728, and his name having been finally removed October 8, 1731. It would appear by the temporary suspension of his name, and replacements of it, as if he had contemplated an earlier departure from College, and had been induced to continue on with the hope of returning ; this, however, he never did after his absence December 1729, having kept a continuous residence of sixty weeks.'

Mr. Croker remarks on this : 'It will be observed that Mr. Boswell slurs over the years 1729, '30, and '31, under the general inference that they were all spent at Oxford, but Dr. Hall's accurate statement of dates from the College books proves that Johnson *personally* left College on the 12th of December, 1729, though his *name* remained on the books till October 8, 1731.'   He goes on to add : 'That these two years were not pleasantly or profitably spent may be inferred from the silence of Johnson and all his friends about them.   It is due to Pembroke to note particularly this absence, because that institution possesses two scholarships, to one of which Johnson would have been eligible, and probably (considering his claims) elected in 1730, had he been a candidate.' I may say, in passing, that these scholarships a few years ago were worth only £10 each, and that there is no likelihood that they were ever of greater value.

Hereupon Mr. Fitzgerald comes on the scene. He, too, has had the College books investigated, and 'with the assistance of the Rev. Whitwell Elwin has arrived at the conclusion that Mr. Croker was wrong, and that Boswell, as indeed he always is in points of importance, is right. I found,' says Mr. Fitzgerald, 'to my surprise, that "the authority of the College books," which sounds impressively enough, resolved itself into no more than certain entries for commons, or "battles," in the buttery books ; while on the absence of " charges " against Johnson's name during particular years the whole argument is founded.' Mr. Fitzgerald is, I notice, a Master of Arts. If he belongs to either Oxford or Cambridge he ought surely to know that in all cases the proof of residence is established by these entries in the buttery books. The authority of the College books not only sounds impressively, but is impressive—impressive, that is to say, on any mind that is capable of understanding a fact, and receiving from it an impression. From December 12, 1729, till October 1, 1731, the charges against Johnson amount to only a few shillings in all. It is certainly worth noticing that these charges are somewhat scattered, and that his name disappears from the College books more than once, to reappear a few weeks further on.

Mr. Whitwell Elwin, whose authority on a matter connected with the early part of last century is deserving of respect, thus attempts to get over the difficulty. He agrees with Hawkins in his statement that in December 1729 Johnson would have had to leave College had he not obtained assistance from outside his family. He does not agree with him as to the source whence that assistance came. 'It must, I think, have been the gift of the College,' he says, 'or it would have been charged to Johnson, whatever might have been the quarter from which he derived the money to pay the bill. If we may guess the course of events from the materials we possess, I should say that Johnson, just before the Christmas vacation, informed the tutor of his inability to remain at College; that it was then settled that he should return home and consult with his father; and that in the two or three weeks which elapsed before he set out, his *ordinary* " battles " were supplied gratis. The result, we may presume, of his Lichfield visit was an announcement to the tutor that he could not raise funds to complete his residence, and the result of the announcement that the College, in consideration of his great learning and abilities, resolved that he should have his " battles " free.'

I have now put before my readers the original statement of Boswell and Hawkins, the facts brought forward by Mr. Croker to upset it, and the assumptions made by Mr. Elwin

to support it. Boswell and Hawkins are very positive ; but
no less positive with their silent record are the old College
books. Had there been no other facts to go by, I should
have been inclined to assume that Boswell had learnt from
Dr. Adams that Johnson had had his name three years on
the books, and perhaps, not aware how often it has happened
that residence has ceased long before a name is removed,
having Hawkins's statement moreover to follow, had jumped
at the not unnatural conclusion that he had resided as long
as he was a member of the College.

But there are other facts which I will set forth as briefly
as I can. Boswell states, ' I have from the information of
Dr. Taylor a very strong instance of that rigid honesty
which he (Johnson) ever inflexibly preserved. Taylor had
obtained his father's consent to be entered of Pembroke,
that he might be with his schoolfellow Johnson, with whom
he was very intimate. This would have been a great comfort
to Johnson. But he fairly told Taylor that he could not in
conscience suffer him to enter where he knew he could not
have an able tutor.' Taylor went to Christ Church, and, as
Boswell goes on to say, it was in going to get his friend's
notes at second-hand that Johnson saw that his poverty was
noticed by the Christ Church men. It is not quite clear
from Boswell whether this latter part of the story rests on
the authority of Taylor. If it does, then the question is
decided, for on Taylor's evidence we may rely, and Taylor
did not enter Christ Church till June 27, 1730. If Johnson
then was in residence at the same time with him, he clearly
did not leave in 1729. This seems indeed, at first sight, to
follow from that part of the story which, as we are expressly
told, rests on the information of Dr. Taylor. But we must
remember that Taylor might have had his name entered

some months before he came into residence, and that after his name was entered Johnson might have left. Nevertheless the whole story is very strong evidence that Johnson was in residence in the latter half of the year 1730. Mr. Croker remarks on it, 'Circumstantially as this story is told, there is good reason for disbelieving it. Taylor was admitted Commoner of Christ Church, June 27, 1730 : but it will be seen that Johnson left Oxford six months before.'

There is still stronger evidence to be found that Johnson and Taylor were fellow students at Oxford, which had apparently escaped Mr. Croker's notice. Mrs. Piozzi, in her anecdotes records that once when Johnson was considering who was likely to be his future biographer, he said, 'the history of my Oxford exploits lies all between Taylor and Adams.'

Next to Dr. Taylor's evidence comes that which Dr. Adams can be made to furnish. He, as Boswell says, 'has generally had the reputation of being Johnson's tutor. The fact however is, that in 1731, Mr. Jorden quitted the College, and his pupils were transferred to Dr. Adams ; so that, had Johnson returned, Dr. Adams would have been his tutor. Boswell goes on to say, ' Dr. Adams paid Johnson this high compliment. He said to me at Oxford in 1776, " I was his nominal tutor, but he was above my mark." When I repeated it to Johnson, his eyes flashed with grateful satisfaction, and he exclaimed, " That was liberal and noble." '

Mr. Croker has the following note on this passage : ' If Adams called himself his nominal tutor only because the pupil was above his mark, the expression would be liberal and noble ; but if he was his nominal tutor, only because he would have been his tutor if Johnson had returned, the case is different, and Boswell is, either way, guilty of an inaccuracy.'

Mr. Fitzgerald pays no attention to Mr. Croker, but broadly says, in speaking of Hawkins's statement about Johnson's three years' residence, 'Nothing can be more explicit, or more consistent with Boswell's narrative, and with the statement that Dr. Adams was his "nominal" tutor in 1731.'

I cannot admit, however, with Mr. Croker that Boswell is, either way, guilty of an inaccuracy. Suppose a brief pause between the two parts of Dr. Adams's statement, and all is explained. 'I was his nominal tutor; that is to say, his name was on my lecture lists; but even if he had attended I should still have been his nominal tutor, his tutor only in name, for he was above my mark.' Both Mr. Croker and Mr. Fitzgerald should have tried to find out when it was that Adams took Jorden's place. Jorden's fellowship was filled up, as I have ascertained, on December 23, 1730. His name appears for the last time on the list of Fellows in the College books on December 4, 1730. He does not appear to have been in residence during any part of the last term of 1730. It is very improbable that he continued to be tutor after he had vacated his fellowship, and I may fairly assume that his pupils were transferred to Adams in the beginning of 1731, if not, indeed, at the beginning of Michaelmas term, 1730. If so, what becomes of the statement that Johnson was resident till the October of 1731 ?[1]

I will next consider the evidence to be derived from the case of Mr. Edwards, Johnson's fellow-collegian. Johnson,

---

[1] I have lately ascertained that Jorden was elected to a living by the University on March 16, 1729. This renders it likely that his tutorship came o an end even earlier than his fellowship.

in his diary for 1778, says, 'In my return from church I was accosted by Edwards, an old fellow-collegian, who had not seen me since 1729.' Mr. Croker, first noting that Edwards entered Pembroke in June 1729, says, 'This deliberate assertion of Johnson, that he had not seen Edwards since 1729, is a confirmation of the opinion derived by Dr. Hall from the dates in the College books, that Johnson did not return to Pembroke after Christmas 1729—an important fact in his early history.' Mr. Fitzgerald finding, I suppose, no means of meeting Mr. Croker's argument, passes it over in silence. It did not occur to Mr. Croker that it might have been Edwards, and not Johnson, who left Pembroke early. I have ascertained that Edwards's name occurs for the last time on April 24, 1730, but, to judge from the amount of his battels, it would seem likely that he did not reside after April 10. To a man used to Old Style, as Johnson was, April 10, 1730, is so near to 1729 that at the distance of nearly fifty years Johnson may easily have been wrong by a week or two. Edwards's case, therefore, seems to me to prove nothing.

Boswell, in giving an account of Johnson's health, says that 'while he was at Lichfield in the College vacation of 1729, he felt himself overwhelmed with a terrible hypochondria.' Now the College books show—if battels can be trusted—that Johnson was absent only one week in the Long vacation of 1729. Boswell may have meant the Christmas vacation, which, according to the old Style, would have all fallen in 1729. It was in a vacation, however, that Johnson had this long illness, and he enjoyed, as it seemed, no vacation (except one of a week's duration) till the end of 1729 and the beginning of 1730 (N.S.). If Boswell then is correct in his statement that it was in a vacation that he was attacked, it would follow that Johnson returned to College in 1730.

As an argument on the other side we may set the statement, which Boswell mentions merely to refute, that Johnson had been 'assistant to the famous Anthony Blackwall.' Boswell says this cannot have been the case, 'for Mr. Blackwall died on the 8th of April 1730, more than a year before Johnson left the University.' The statement, however, may be taken in evidence for what it is worth, that Johnson did leave at the end of 1729. The entry, too, in Johnson's diary '1729, Dec. S. J. Oxonio rediit,' is of no small weight. He may simply have recorded his return home for the Christmas vacation. But it is certainly an important fact that the entry is made in the very month in which the College books seem to show that his residence came to an end.

In the Caution Book of Pembroke College occur the two following entries, which I am, I believe, the first to publish :—

'Oct. 31, 1728.
'Recd. then of Mr. Samuel Johnson Com̃r : of Pem : Coll : ye sũm of seven Pounds for his Caution, which is to Remaiñ in ye Hands of ye Bursars till ye said Mr. Johnson shall depart ye said College leaving ye same fully discharg'd.

'Recd. by me
'JOHN RATCLIFF, Bursar.

'March 26, 1740.—At a convention of the Master and Fellows to settle the account of the Caution it Appear'd that the Persons Accounts underwritten stood thus at their leaving the College.

'Caution not Repayd.	'Battells not Discharg'd.
'Mr. Johnson. 7 o o	'Mr. Johnson. 7 o o'

It scarcely seems probable that the College authorities, if they resolved, as Mr. Elwin guesses, to give Johnson his battels free, should have retained till the year 1740 his caution money in their hands. If they were generous enough to support him without payment, they would, I should think, have been generous enough to return him the money which they had received from him as security. For why should security for payment be required from those who are free from the payment itself?

I will now, as briefly as I can, enter upon one head of evidence which, so far as I know, has not been touched on. Johnson, Mr. Fitzgerald and Mr. Elwin say, was at Pembroke in 1730. Can they show that among his fellow-collegians there were any who entered so late as that year? I have somewhat carefully gathered together the names of all his fellow-collegians whom he mentions, and, with one remarkable exception, I have ascertained that all of them entered before 1730. It is possible, however, that some name has escaped my notice. Adams, as I have shown, was already a Fellow when Johnson entered. Meeke, whose superiority he could not bear, and from whom, to quote his own words, 'I tried to sit as far as I could, that I might not hear him construe,' matriculated in 1725; Edwards, as I have shown, in 1729. Phil. Jones and Fludyer, with whom he used to play at draughts—the one of whom loved beer and did not get very forward in the Church, while the other turned out a scoundrel and a Whig—were about of Johnson's standing. Jones, indeed, must have been his senior.

To this fact, for such I believe it to be, that Johnson mentions no Pembroke man who entered after 1729, there is the one exception of the celebrated preacher George Whitfield. He is twice mentioned in Boswell as having been Johnson's fellow-collegian. In Boswell's account of October 12, 1779, on the passage beginning 'Of his fellow-collegian the celebrated Mr. George Whitfield,' &c., Mr. Croker quotes this note of Dr. Hall's : 'George Whitfield did not enter at Pembroke College before November 1732, more than twelve months after Johnson's name was off the books ; so that, strictly speaking, they were not fellow-collegians, though they were both of the same College.' But in Boswell's 'Journal of a Tour to the Hebrides' we find the following passage, under the date of August 15 : 'We talked of Whitfield. He said he was at the same College with him, and knew him before he began to be better than other people (smiling).'

Now Johnson read this journal in manuscript, and, as Boswell on one occasion tells us, corrected any mistakes he had made. Yet it is quite certain that Johnson, even if he was at College in 1731, most certainly was not there in 1732. Not only have we Boswell's statement and the authority of the College books, but we have the evidence of a letter he wrote from Lichfield on October 30, 1731, and two entries in his diary for 1732. If he had known Whitfield he would have known Shenstone, for Shenstone entered Pembroke six months before Whitfield ; but, so far as I know, there is no evidence that they were ever acquainted. I cannot pretend to reconcile Boswell's statement—and for the matter of that Johnson's, seeing that he revised the manuscript—with the facts of the case. We are told, indeed, that a year or two after he left Oxford he borrowed a book from the library of Pembroke College. It would not have been impossible, or even improbable, that a man who, like Johnson, frequently walked from Lichfield to Birmingham and back, would have trudged all the way to Oxford to

fetch the book.   In that case he might have seen Whitfield.
But Boswell tells us that 'the first time of his being at
Oxford after quitting the University' was in 1754.

The evidence, then, as those who have had patience to
follow me will have seen, is strong on both sides, and in one
part at least full of perplexity.   It had at one time occurred
to me that, when his means failed, he might have occupied
the post of a servitor.   A servitor I thought, perhaps, had
no charge made against him in the books.   But by the kindness of Mr. Mowat, the Bursar of Pembroke College, I
have since inspected the College books, and I have satisfied
myself that at no time of his University course was Johnson
a servitor.   I have looked at Whitfield's battels, who was
a servitor, and I have found that though they were more
moderate in amount they were kept like a commoner's.   His
name, moreover, as a servitor, is entered on a different part
of the page from those of the commoners.   He comes after
the *Obsonator*, *Promus*, and *Coquus*, while Johnson's name
remains from first to last in the same division.

Mr. Elwin is bound to show in support of his hypothesis
at least one instance at the University of free commons.
Even if a man had free commons, nevertheless, as a matter of
account and as a proof of residence we should have expected
that his battels would have been kept in the usual way.

The more I consider the question, the more I incline to
the opinion that Johnson's residence at Oxford practically
came to an end in December 1729.   The books seem to
show that he was in residence one week in March 1730, and
one week in the following September.

As I have said above, the proof of residence is established, and alone established, by the entries in the buttery
books.   It is not by residing in college, but by eating in

college, that the required number of terms is kept. Had the college authorities wished to assist Johnson, they could have done so by subscribing together to pay his battels, but the account of his battels would have been kept just the same. With what Mr. Elwin calls free battels, he could never have taken his degree.

NOTE.

I HAD already received from the printer the revised proofs of this chapter, when, in the hope of throwing more light on this perplexing question, I examined, by the kind permission of the Treasurer of Christ Church, the battel-books of the College. I have been more than repaid for the trouble that I have taken by the discovery that I have made. I now feel no doubt whatever that Johnson's residence at Pembroke College came to an end, as the Pembroke battel-books show, in December, 1729. Mr. Croker therefore was right, I hold, in maintaining that, so far from being three years at Oxford, he was there barely fourteen months. I should before this have come with full certainty to this conclusion, had it not been for Mr. Croker's statement as to the date of Dr. Taylor's matriculation at Christ Church. Hawkins, indeed, and Boswell both say that Johnson was at college three years. His name certainly was not finally taken off the books till three years after his matriculation. But the only contemporary evidence (excluding the statement about Whitfield) that seemed to prove that Johnson was in residence after December 1729, was his own statement about Taylor. He had himself told Mrs. Thrale, as I have pointed out, that the history of his Oxford exploits lay all between Taylor and Adams. One of these ' exploits ' has been handed down in the story told about Johnson's visit to Taylor in the worn-out pair of shoes. 'Authoritatively,' says Mr. Croker, ' and circumstantially as this story is told, it seems impossible to reconcile it with some indisputable facts and dates.' Indisputable though Mr. Croker's facts and dates may be, I shall nevertheless venture to dispute them. As I was revising this chapter and balancing once more in my mind the evidence that seemed so strong and yet was so contradictory, it occurred to me that, perhaps, it was Mr. Croker himself who had blundered. He it was who first asserted that Johnson had left college in December 1729. He it was who first asserted that Taylor, Johnson's companion at the University, had matriculated on June 27th, 1730.

I obtained permission to examine the battel-books of Christ Church. As I turned over the pages covered with the dust of long years, I certainly found the entry of the matriculation of John Taylor on June 27, 1730 ; but I was not discouraged. Taylor is not an uncommon name, and there might be not only two Taylors but also two John Taylors at one College at the same time. On a different page I had noticed the name of another Taylor. His Christian name, however, was not given. With some anxiety but with more confidence I eagerly traced him backwards through two or three volumes, and at last came upon the entry of his matriculation. John Taylor matriculated on February 24, 1728–9. This, I felt sure, was the Dr. Taylor of Boswell. He came into residence therefore but four months after Johnson. My satisfaction was complete. At that moment, perhaps, one of the happiest men in Oxford was to be found in a garret in Christ Church into which the light of the sun never makes its way. The reader may smile, but I will exclaim with Goldsmith ' I do not love a man who is zealous for nothing.'

 Against all the evidence that can be brought forward on the other side there is nothing left of any weight but the statements of Boswell and Hawkins. I have already said that it is not unlikely that Boswell has merely followed the account given by Hawkins. He would have been the less likely to have discovered Hawkins' error from the fact that, as Johnson's name was for about three years on the College books, he was so long, in name at least, a member of the College.

 The following table that I have drawn up will assist the reader in arriving at a conclusion on this matter.

1723. Adams elected to a Fellowship at Pembroke.

1725. J. Meeke entered.

1727. Corbet   „

1728. Jones   „

 „ Oct.   31. Johnson entered.

 „ Nov.   Fludyer   „

 „ Dec.   16. Johnson matriculated.

1729 Feb.   24. Taylor   „

 „ March 16. Jorden elected to a University living.

 „ June   Edwards entered.

 „ Oct.   24. No charge for battels against Johnson this week.

'Johnson at Lichfield in the College vacation of 1729 overwhelmed with hypochondria.'

 „ Dec.   12. Johnson's period of regular battels came to an end.

 „   „   Entry in his diary, *S. J. Oxonio rediit.*

 „   „   26. Johnson charged 5*d.* in battel-books.

1730 Jan.	2.	Johnson charged 5*d*. in battel-books.		
„ „	30.	„	„	„
„ March	13.	„	4*s*. 7*d*.	„
„ „	27.	„	5*d*.	„

„ April　8. Blackwall died.

„ „　10. Edwards left college.

„ Sept.　18. Charges against Johnson in battel-books but the account not added up.

„ Nov.　27. Johnson's name disappears from the battel-books.

„ Dec.　23. Jorden's Fellowship filled up.

1731 Jan.　29. Johnson's name reappears for this week, with no charge added to it.

„ March 12. Johnson's name reappears and remains on the books till the following October, when it finally disappears.

„ Oct.　30. Johnson, in a letter written at Lichfield, says, 'as I am yet unemployed.'

„ Dec.　Michael Johnson died.

1732 May　25. Shenstone matriculated.

„ July　16. Entry in Johnson's diary : *Bosvortiam pedes petii*.

„ Nov.　7. Whitfield matriculated.

LONDON : PRINTED BY
SPOTTISWOODE AND CO., NEW-STREET SQUARE
AND PARLIAMENT STREET

AUTOBIOGRAPHY of HARRIET MARTINEAU. With Memorials by Maria Weston Chapman. With Portraits and Illustrations. Third Edition. 3 vols. 32s.

A HISTORY of ENGLISH THOUGHT in the EIGHTEENTH CENTURY. By Leslie Stephen. 2 vols. demy 8vo. 28s.

ETRUSCAN BOLOGNA : a Study. By Richard F. Burton, Author of 'Pilgrimage to El Medinah and Mecca,' 'City of the Saints and Rocky Mountains to California,' &c. Small 8vo. 10s. 6d.

The LIFE of MAHOMET. From Original Sources. By Sir William Muir, LL.D. New and Cheaper Edition. In 1 vol. with Maps. 8vo. 14s.

GEOLOGICAL OBSERVATIONS on the VOLCANIC ISLANDS and PARTS of SOUTH AMERICA, visited during the voyage of H.M.S. *Beagle.* By Charles Darwin, M.A., F.R.A.S. New Edition, with Maps and Illustrations. Crown 8vo. 12s. 6d.

The STRUCTURE and DISTRIBUTION of CORAL REEFS. By Charles Darwin, M.A., F.G.S., F.R.S. Second Edition, revised. With 3 Plates. Crown 8vo. 7s. 6d.

CAMILLE DESMOULINS and HIS WIFE : Passages from the History of the Dantonists. Founded upon New and hitherto Unpublished Documents. Translated from the French of Jules Claretie, by Mrs. Cashel Hoey. With a Portrait. Demy 8vo. 16s.

LORENZO DE' MEDICI the Magnificent. By Alfred von Reumont. Translated from the German by Robert Harrison. 2 vols. 30s.

REASONABLE SERVICE. By W. Page Roberts, M.A., Vicar of Eye, Suffolk, Author of 'Law and God.' Crown 8vo. 6s.

HARBOURS of ENGLAND. Engraved by Thomas Lupton from Original Drawings made expressly for the Work by J. M. W. Turner. With Illustrative Text by John Ruskin, Author of 'Modern Painters' &c. A New Edition. Imp. 4to. 25s.

FRENCH PICTURES in ENGLISH CHALK. By the Author of 'The Member for Paris' &c. Crown 8vo. 7s. 6d.
'Delightful stories of French life.........There are no short tales in contemporary literature which come at all near these in wit, observation, grace, and ease of style, and skill in construction.'—*Academy.*

The CHURCH and LIBERTIES of ENGLAND. The True Character and Public Danger of the present Extreme Movement in the National Church. By Nevison Loraine, Vicar of Grove Park, West London. With Introduction by the Very Rev. the Dean of Chester. Sixth Edition, crown 8vo. 1s. 6d.
'Lucid, pointed, and singularly readable.'—*English Churchman.*
'A very close and withal unprejudiced inquiry.'—*Public Opinion.*

The SHORES of LAKE ARAL. By Herbert Wood, Major Royal Engineers. With Maps. Crown 8vo. 14s.
'A very able and well-written book of travels in a country all but unknown.—*Standard.*
'A valuable contribution to physical and political geography.'—*Athenæum.*

LIFE with the HAMRAN ARABS : a Sporting Tour of some Officers of the Guards in the Soudan during the winter of 1874-5. By Arthur B. R. Myers, Surgeon, Coldstream Guards. With Photographic Illustrations, crown 8vo. 10s.
'A most graphic and fascinating account of daring adventure—very pleasant reading indeed.'—*Daily Telegraph.*
'Much to amuse and interest.........Those who wish to try conclusions with a lion, or see how quickly a rhinoceros can get over the ground when he means business, can scarcely follow a better guide than Mr. Myers.'—*Athenæum.*
'Always more or less exciting.........They tell us just what we want to know.'
Saturday Review.

London : SMITH, ELDER, & CO., 15 Waterloo Place.

SHAKESPEARE COMMENTARIES. By Dr. G. G. GERVINUS, Professor at Heidelburgh. Translated, under the Author's superintendence, by F. E. BUNNETT. A New and Cheaper Edition, thoroughly revised by the Translator. With a Preface by F. J. FURNIVALL, Esq. 8vo. 14s.

HOURS in a LIBRARY. First Series. Second Edition. By LESLIE STEPHEN. Crown 8vo. 9s.

HOURS in a LIBRARY. Second Series. By LESLIE STEPHEN. Crown 8vo. 9s.

MOHAMMED and MOHAMMEDANISM: Lectures delivered at the Royal Institution of Great Britain, in February and March 1874. By R. BOSWORTH SMITH, M.A. Second Edition. Crown 8vo. 8s. 6d.

SANITARY ARRANGEMENTS for DWELLINGS, intended for the Use of Officers of Health, Architects, Builders, and Householders. With 116 Illustrations. By WILLIAM EASSIE, C.E., F.L.S, F.G.S., &c., Author of 'Healthy Houses.' Crown 8vo. 5s. 6d.

LIBERTY, EQUALITY, FRATERNITY. By Sir JAMES FITZJAMES STEPHEN, Q.C. Second Edition, with a new Preface. 8vo. 14s.

The BORDERLAND of SCIENCE. By R. A. PROCTOR, B.A., Author of 'Light Science for Leisure Hours.' Large Crown 8vo. with Portrait, 10s. 6d.

SCIENCE BYWAYS. By R. A. Proctor, B.A. With Portrait. 10s. 6d.

ERASMUS: his Life and Character as shown in his Correspondence and Works. By ROBERT B. DRUMMOND. With Portrait. 2 vols. Crown 8vo. 21s.

DISTINGUISHED PERSONS in RUSSIAN SOCIETY. Translated from the German by F. E. BUNNETT. Crown 8vo. 7s. 6d.

RUSSIAN FOLK TALES. By W. R. S. RALSTON, M.A., Author of 'Krilof and his Fables,' 'Songs of the Russian People,' &c. Crown 8vo. 12s.

POEMS BY ROBERT BROWNING.

POETICAL WORKS of ROBERT BROWNING. New and Uniform Edition. 6 vols. Fcp. 8vo. 5s. each.

LA SAISIAZ: The Two Poets of Croisic. Fcp. 8vo. 7s.

The AGAMEMNON of ÆSCHYLUS. Transcribed by ROBERT BROWNING. Fcp. 8vo. 5s.

PACCHIAROTTO, and How He Worked in Distemper; with other Poems. Fcp. 8vo. 7s. 6d.

The INN ALBUM. Fcp. 8vo. 7s.

BALAUSTION'S ADVENTURE; including a Transcript from Euripides. By ROBERT BROWNING. Fcp. 8vo. 5s.

ARISTOPHANES' APOLOGY; including a Transcript from Euripides, being the Last Adventure of Balaustion.

FIFINE at the FAIR. Fcp. 8vo. 5s.

PRINCE HOHENSTIEL-SCHWANGAU, SAVIOUR of SOCIETY. Fcp. 8vo. 5s.

RED COTTON NIGHT-CAP COUNTRY; or, Turf and Towers. Fcp. 8vo. 9s.

The RING and the BOOK. 4 vols. Fcp. 8vo. 5s. each.

A SELECTION from the POETICAL WORKS of ROBERT BROWNING. New Edition, enlarged. Crown 8vo. 7s. 6d. Gilt edges, 8s. 6d.

POEMS BY ELIZABETH BARRETT BROWNING.

POEMS by ELIZABETH BARRETT BROWNING. 5 vols. Tenth Edition. With Portrait. Crown 8vo. 30s.

AURORA LEIGH. With Portrait. Eleventh Edition. Crown 8vo. 7s. 6d. Gilt edges, 8s. 6d.

A SELECTION from the **POETRY of ELIZABETH BARRETT BROWNING.** With Portrait and Vignette. Crown 8vo. 7s. 6d. Gilt edges, 8s. 6d.

STORIES BY LADY VERNEY.

LLANALY REEFS. Crown 8vo. 7s. 6d.

STONE EDGE. With 4 Illustrations. Crown 8vo. 6s.

LETTICE LISLE. With 3 Illustrations. Crown 8vo. 6s.

The **HOME LIFE** in the **LIGHT** of its **DIVINE IDEA.** By JAMES BALDWIN BROWN, M.A. Fifth Edition. Small crown 8vo. 4s. 6d.

HOUSEHOLD MEDICINE: Containing a Familiar Description of Diseases, their Nature, Causes, and Symptoms, the most approved Methods of Treatment, the Properties and Uses of Remedies, &c., and Rules for the Management of the Sick Room. Expressly adapted for Family Use. By JOHN GARDNER, M.D. Ninth Edition, revised and enlarged. With numerous Illustrations. Demy 8vo. 12s. 6d.

The **DOMESTIC MANAGEMENT of CHILDREN.** By P. M. BRAIDWOOD, M.D., Surgeon to the Wirral Hospital for Sick Children. 2s. 6d.

On **EXERCISE and TRAINING,** and their Effect upon Health. By R. J. LEE, M.A., M.D. (Cantab.), Lecturer on Pathology at Westminster Hospital, &c. 1s.

The **LIFE of GOETHE.** By GEORGE HENRY LEWES. Third Edition, revised according to the latest Documents. Demy 8vo. with Portrait, 16s.

ARISTOTLE: a Chapter from the History of Science. With Analyses of ARISTOTLE's Scientific Writings. By GEORGE HENRY LEWES. Demy 8vo. 15s.

The **STORY of GOETHE'S LIFE.** By GEORGE HENRY LEWES. Crown 8vo. 7s. 6d. Tree calf, 12s. 6d.

CANOE TRAVELLING. Log of a Cruise on the Baltic; and Practical Hints on Building and Fitting Canoes. By WARRINGTON BADEN-POWELL 24 Illustrations and a Map. Crown 8vo. 6s.

A HISTORY of CRIME, and of its Relations to Civilised Life in England. By LUKE OWEN PIKE, M.A., Author of 'The English and their Origin.'
Vol. I.—From the Roman Invasion to the Accession of Henry VII. Demy 8vo. 18s.
Vol. II.—From the Accession of Henry VII. to the Present Time. Demy 8vo. 18s.

HISTORY of ART. By Dr. WILHELM LÜBKE. Translated by F. E. BUNNETT. With 415 Illustrations. Second Edition. 2 vols. imp. 8vo. 42s.

HISTORY of SCULPTURE, from the Earliest Period to the Present Time. By Dr. WILHELM LÜBKE. Translated by F. E. BUNNETT. 377 Illustrations. 2 vols. imp. 8vo. 42s.

The **LADY of LATHAM**: being the Life and Original Letters of CHARLOTTE DE LA TRÉMOILLE, Countess of Derby. By Madame GUIZOT DE WITT. With a Portrait of CHARLOTTE DE LA TRÉMOILLE, Countess of Derby, from a Picture in the possession of the Earl of Derby. Demy 8vo. 14s.

London : SMITH, ELDER, & CO., 15 Waterloo Place.

ILLUSTRATED EDITIONS

OF

POPULAR WORKS

Handsomely bound in cloth gilt, each volume containing
Four Illustrations.   Crown 8vo. 3s. 6d.

THE SMALL HOUSE AT ALLINGTON.
By ANTHONY TROLLOPE.

FRAMLEY PARSONAGE.
By ANTHONY TROLLOPE.

THE CLAVERINGS.
By ANTHONY TROLLOPE.

THE LAST CHRONICLE OF BARSET.
By ANTHONY TROLLOPE.   2 vols.

TRANSFORMATION: a Romance.
By NATHANIEL HAWTHORNE.

ROMANTIC TALES.
By the Author of 'John Halifax, Gentleman.'

DOMESTIC STORIES.
By the Author of 'John Halifax, Gentleman.'

NO NAME.
By WILKIE COLLINS.

ARMADALE.
By WILKIE COLLINS.

AFTER DARK.
By WILKIE COLLINS.

MAUD TALBOT.
By HOLME LEE.

THE MOORS AND THE FENS.
By Mrs. J. H. RIDDELL.

PUT YOURSELF IN HIS PLACE.
By CHARLES READE.

London : SMITH, ELDER, & CO., 15 Waterloo Place.